Butto

MW01129554

Penelope Sky

Hartwick Publishing
Buttons and Pain
Editing Services provided by Final-Edits.com
Copyright © 2017 by Penelope Sky
All Rights Reserved

Buttons and Pain

Chapter One

Pearl

"Oh, baby. Did you miss me?" I cocked my head to the side and pursed my lips. My voice came out high-pitched and affectionate, and my disdain added a nice ring to it.

Jacob's jaw dropped when he saw me on his doorstep. Shirtless and with messy hair, he looked like he'd been hitting the sheets with some poor girl who had no idea her boyfriend was the biggest piece of shit on the planet. "Pearl...oh my god. You're okay." Once the shock subsided, he pretended to give a damn. "I'm so glad you're okay. I was so worried—"

I kneed him right in the balls. "Save it."

He cupped his balls and leaned forward, moaning under his breath. He gripped the doorframe for balance and breathed hard through the pain.

"I'm sorry. Did that hurt?"

He closed his eyes and gripped the frame harder. His knuckles began to turn white.

"Try getting fucked in the ass." I pushed past him and walked into the apartment I used to live in. All I had was the purse I stole from that woman. I had a driver's license, a passport, and some Euros. But that

1

was it. I opened the fridge and took out an old box of pizza. Since I was starving, I ate a slice cold.

A woman appeared from the hallway wearing nothing but one of his t-shirts. "Who the hell are you?"

I gave her a quick wave and finished my pizza. "I'm Pearl, Jacob's ex-girlfriend."

"He never told me about anyone named Pearl."

"Probably because he sold me into sex trafficking to pay off his gambling debts."

Her eyes dilated, but her reaction didn't change. She glanced at Jacob, who was still hunched over by the door, and then turned back to me. She couldn't decide if she believed me or not. I couldn't blame her. The story was so ridiculous I couldn't believe it actually happened.

Jacob finally recovered from the hit to his balls and stood upright. His cheeks were flooded with blood, and when he took a step, he winced. I got him hard with my knee, and he wouldn't be able to get an erection for at least a week.

I finished the pizza and left the box on the counter. It was the most delicious thing I'd ever eaten. But then again, I'd just gotten off a twelve-hour plane ride with nothing to eat but peanuts. "Damn, this is pretty good."

His girlfriend crossed her arms over her chest and stared at Jacob. She didn't feel comfortable talking in front of me, so she just glared at him. Like that would somehow get rid of me quicker.

Jacob finally spoke to her. "Danielle, can I have a moment alone?"

"Why?" I asked. "Don't you think she should know you're a cold motherfucker?" I leaned against the counter and stared him down. Now that I was face-to-face with him, I wanted to beat him bloody. There was no trace of feelings or compassion for this man. All I felt was hate.

Strong, furious hate.

Jacob kept his mouth shut. He knew there was nothing he could say to make himself look good. It was best not to say anything at all.

"Is that true?" Danielle asked.

Now Jacob was being attacked on both fronts. "Baby, could you please give us a moment?"

"No, not a moment," I said. "Get the hell out. I'm about to castrate your boyfriend, and I'm not sure if you want to see it."

3

"That's it." She headed to the bedroom. "I'm calling the police."

"Whoa, wait." Jacob turned her way immediately, his body moving faster than the pain would allow. He cringed after each movement, feeling it deep in his groin. "Don't call the police."

I smiled in victory. That was as good as a confession.

"Then what the hell, Jacob?" she screamed. "Is she really your ex?"

"Yes," he said quietly.

"Did you really sell her into trafficking?" she pressed.

I grinned from ear to ear and watched him struggle. If he lied and said no, I'd put him in his place. And if he said yes, he would lose the sexy blonde he was sleeping with. "Jacob, she asked you a question."

He turned his face toward me, and his expression was ice-cold.

"Wow. You have a lot of nerve to look at me like I'm the bad guy." Maybe when she was gone, he would try to kill me himself. That would be the perfect ending. I'd end his life with a knife through his heart and take off. Could you try a missing person in a court of law? I didn't think so.

Jacob's voice came out firmer. "Danielle, can we talk tomorrow?"

"Oh my god." She covered her mouth with her hand. "You did it…" She ran into the bedroom and grabbed her clothes and purse. Without even changing, she darted out in just his t-shirt. Not once did she look at him as she left.

"Ouch," I said. "Looks like you just got dumped."

He turned on me, the fury in his eyes.

I smiled because I loved that look. "What are you going to do, Jacob?"

He gripped the edge of the counter. His shoulders tensed with rage. The bloodlust was in his eyes. He hated me for coming back into his life and ruining his relationship with the boobalicious blonde.

"Do your worst." I'd learned a lot over the past year of my life. I was ruthless and resilient. Even though Jacob was bigger and stronger than I was, I could still kick his ass. And I would do more than that.

Jacob seemed to realize it was a fight he couldn't win. His hold on the counter loosened, and his shoulders relaxed. "What do you want?"

5

He wasn't going to apologize or make excuses for what he did. He was just as cold as I made him out to be. That made the conversation easier—because there wasn't any bullshit. "I want a hundred thousand dollars by noon tomorrow."

His expression didn't change for the first heartbeat. Then his eyes narrowed to slits. "What?"

I spoke slower, being as much of a smartass as possible. "One. Hundred. Thousand. Dollars. Do you need me to write it out for you?"

"What the fuck? You think I have that kind of money lying around?"

"I don't care if you do or don't. That's what you owe me."

"*Owe you?*" Now that he wasn't lying anymore, I saw exactly who he really was. He was an emotionless fiend of the underworld. I'd seen a lot of different shades of evil, and he was, by far, the blackest. The villains who didn't consider themselves to be villains were the most dangerous kind.

"You were paid a hundred thousand dollars for me to be a slave. I'm the one who did the time, so that money is mine. Give it to me by noon tomorrow, or I'm going to the police and telling them exactly what you did."

"Pearl—"

"Don't say my name ever again." I didn't like hearing it—especially from his lips. It was a name I hadn't heard in a lifetime. The only name I was familiar with was one I'd never hear again. "You have twelve hours to figure it out."

"Look, I don't have that kind of money."

"Not my problem, Jacob."

He threw his arms down. "I used that money to pay off my debts. You know that."

"Again, I don't care. That money is mine. Give it to me, or you'll spend the rest of your life in jail. Choice is yours. I'm cool with either one."

He clenched his jaw tightly, and his hands formed tight fists. He wanted to punch me in the face, but that wouldn't fix the mess he'd made.

"And I'm staying here tonight. Leave your keys before you go."

"You're taking my apartment too?" he asked incredulously.

"Yep. I think it's the least you can do after turning me into a sex slave. Would you like to hear about it?"

He looked away, finally ashamed. "I need to ask around for the money, alright?"

"I don't give a shit what you need to do. Just do it." I grabbed his wallet and keys off the counter and pulled out two twenties from his wallet. "You can knock this off the total—and the pizza if you're really a dick."

He stepped away, his shoulders tense. "How did you get away?"

"Like you care. Get your shit and go."

He walked into the bedroom and packed a bag full of clothes. He came back out and grabbed his wallet then shoved it into his pocket.

"I need the spare key."

"You already have one."

"And I need the other." I snapped my fingers for him to hurry up. I wasn't sleeping there if he could walk in at any moment without me knowing about it.

He glared at me before he opened a drawer and fished it out. He tossed it onto the counter with a loud clank.

"You can go now. If that money isn't here by noon, I'm going straight to the police."

He shouldered his bag and walked out. When he opened the front door, I hit the last nail into the coffin.

"Just don't sell your girlfriend into trafficking. You know how that worked out last time..."

***

When I was face-to-face with Jacob, I utilized all my strength and didn't show an ounce of fear. I never told him how much his betrayal hurt me. I never confessed all the gruesome things that happened to me while I was in captivity. I kept up the fight the entire way until I got what I needed.

But after he was gone, I broke down.

When I returned to the city, I had nowhere to go. My friend Stacy didn't live at her old apartment anymore, and McKenzie had moved back to California. I didn't know their cell phone numbers by heart, and I had no idea what happened to my old phone.

Jacob was my only choice.

I stole his apartment because I had nowhere to sleep. I could have gone to the police and turned Jacob in. I would have probably gotten a free motel stay and maybe cash for food. But that wouldn't get me far.

9

With that hundred thousand dollars, I could start over. I could get an apartment and take my time finding a new job. I didn't feel pathetic demanding that money.

If you asked me, it was mine.

I was the one who paid that debt. I was sold to a madman, and I worked for every penny of the fortune people collected. It was only fair I got a cut after I gave up my body to the devil. I didn't care how Jacob got that money.

It was mine.

Despite the fact that I was back in America, I felt alone. That Tuscan estate made me feel safe. It felt like home. I went to sleep every night knowing I belonged somewhere. Crow made me feel like a person rather than an object. He showed me the greatest generosity anyone had ever given me. He was in a situation where he could have done whatever he wanted without any repercussions, but he never did. He always gave me a voice and a choice.

But now, that was gone.

New York didn't feel the same. It was more foreign than the country I'd just left. It didn't smell of fresh bread and grape leaves. It was full of pollution and smog. Instead of stunning hillsides, all I saw were billboards with half-naked people on them. People walked on the streets every single day without knowing how good they had it.

It was despicable.

I couldn't sleep in Jacob's bed, so I lay on the couch with a thin blanket. I'd lived in that apartment for a year, but now, it felt like a new place. All my clothes and possessions were gone because Jacob probably sold everything at a garage sale. All my pictures, my yearbooks, and everything else that ever meant anything to me.

It was all gone.

The second I closed my eyes, I saw Crow's face. I never told him what happened to me or that I'd escaped. The tracker was still in my ankle where he inserted it, so he'd probably figured it out on his own. He never came for me, so I assumed he was letting me go. He didn't expect me to pay off the debt.

I was finally free.

I should've hated him for everything he did to me, but I didn't. When I thought of him, respect and longing were still in my heart. I confessed that I'd somehow fallen in love with him during our time together.

And that was the stupidest thing I'd ever done.

He rejected me—coldly. I locked up my heart and threw away the key. All I was experiencing was Stockholm syndrome. He gave me a home and took care of me. He made me feel safe and valued. Afraid and alone, I latched on to him. But I'd forgotten he was the one who'd kidnapped me. I'd forgotten he made me sleep with him in exchange for freedom. I'd forgotten all of that because he made me feel loved.

I was so stupid.

I wanted to keep sobbing because it somehow made me feel better, but I knew it'd gone on long enough. An hour was all I would allow myself before I shut everything down and got my head in the game. A lot of bullshit had happened to me in the past year, but that didn't mean I couldn't get my life together. I could find a good job, a nice apartment, and start over.

I could start over.

***

After I got the cash from Jacob, I went to the police department to take myself off the missing persons list. If they were still looking for me, they were wasting their time—because I was right here.

Buttons and Pain

They questioned me about everything I could remember in the hope of getting a lead on the men who ran the operation. Sex trafficking was still a huge problem in our nation, and the police were determined to put an end to it. I told them everything that I knew—except that Jacob was the one who sold me.

I didn't care about turning him in. He only did it to pay off his gambling debts, and I knew he wouldn't do it to another woman. The damage had already been done, and I needed the cash more than the satisfaction of making him sit behind bars. Besides, I could always ask him for help and threaten to turn him in if he didn't cooperate. For the rest of his life, he would look over his shoulder and dread seeing my face.

That was punishment enough.

When I was at Crow's estate, the police came looking for me. At the time, I thought it was Cane who'd tipped them off, but that didn't make any sense. If someone had been looking for me, I wanted to know who it was. Maybe it was one of my friends, and the police could get me in touch with them. "Who reported I was missing?"

The detective flipped through his notes. "Your boyfriend, Jacob, called us from the Caribbean and told us you'd been taken. A few months went by, and the trail went cold. But then, the trail picked up again when one of your friends found evidence to suggest this specific organization carried their prisoners to Italy."

One of my friends?

"He insisted we continue the search there, but we didn't find anything. He was adamant about finding you. When I call him and tell him you're safe and sound, he's going to be so relieved. That guy looked sicker and sicker with every month."

It was a he? I didn't have a clue who it could be. "What's his name?"

"Jason." He answered immediately, like the name rested on the tip of his tongue. "He said you two used to date in college."

Blood pounded in my ears, and I stopped breathing for nearly thirty seconds. Jason and I ended on good terms, but I never expected him to work tirelessly to find me. If I'd known that, I would have turned myself over when the police came to the house. I was touched in ways I couldn't explain. "Jason…"

"He's a nice guy. If you don't mind me saying so, he seemed to care a lot more than your boyfriend did."

No surprise there. "Do you have his number, so I can call him?"

"Sure." He wrote it down on a piece of paper. "I need to call him anyway to tell him you've been found. You want to wait here, so he can see you? I know it would really mean a lot to him."

"He's in the city?" Last time I checked, he was living in California.

"He moved here shortly after you were abducted. When he saw your face on the news, he got involved."

I still couldn't believe Jason had done so much for me. He was a great guy, and it was a shame we broke up to begin with. Long-distance relationships never worked, and we thought it would be best if we stayed friends instead of going through a painful breakup.

"So, you'll stay?"

I turned my gaze away from the note in my hand. "Sorry…lost my train of thought."

"Will you stay while I give him a call?"

"Yeah, of course." Right now, Jason was the only person on the planet who gave a shit about me. Jacob never cared.

And neither did Crow.

***

When Jason saw me, his eyes immediately watered. The relief was mixed with gratitude. He stared at me for several heartbeats before he closed the gap between us and stood just inches away from me. He examined my face to make sure it was really me.

I stared at my savior and felt emotion catch in my throat. When I returned to the city, I felt completely alone. I had to get money from the man who originally sold me, and I had to sleep in his apartment. I didn't have parents to care about me, and I didn't have any family. The fact that there was someone, even a single person, made me believe I really could start over.

"Pearl, I'm so glad you're alright." He didn't hug me even though it was clear he wanted to. "I was scared we would never see you again."

"I'm glad I'm alright too. It's nice to be back."

He extended his arms but still didn't touch me. "Can I hug you?"

"Of course." He didn't even need to ask.

He wrapped his arms around me and held me tightly. The embrace was full of the tenderness I desperately needed. Feeling a pair of strong arms around me was exactly what I needed to get back on my feet. It gave me hope. It gave my joy.

"I have a million questions to ask, but I'll get to them later." He pulled away and looked into my face with his blue eyes. He was exactly the same as he was years ago. He had a strong jaw with prominent cheekbones. His body was tight with muscle and lean from a slender build. Nothing had changed. "Do you have somewhere to stay?"

"I was going to check in to a hotel—"

"You're staying with me. I have a nice place over by Park Avenue."

I couldn't refuse his offer. I would much rather be in someone's home than a lonely hotel room. "Thanks. I appreciate it."

"Great. Let's go." He wrapped his arm around my waist and guided me out of the police station. Despite the fact that he hadn't touched me in years, the affection felt right. Like no time had passed and that connection was there. He still cared about me and never gave up on me. And I was grateful I had at least one person in my life who cared.

Buttons and Pain

Chapter Two

Crow

I stared at the ceiling for hours.

The shadows shifted across the walls as the night deepened. Sometimes they formed patterns. One looked like a harmless cloud drifting over the clear sky. Another one looked like a butterfly.

And another looked like a button.

I stared at that one the longest, trying to figure out if it was real or if I was just pretending it was real. Four little holes marked the ceiling, and the round curvature of the surface made it look exactly like a button.

It was painful to look at.

Within the blink of an eye, the sun started to emerge over the horizon and fill my bedroom with the gentle pastels of the morning. I slept on one side of the bed because I was used to sharing it with someone.

Button.

I got out of bed when I realized there was no point in lying there any longer. I showered and got ready for work. My brain was dead from exhaustion, and I struggled to think clearly. Sleep was a foreign luxury.

I hadn't gotten any since she left.

I went into my study and started the fire in the hearth. I didn't go downstairs for breakfast like I usually did. My appetite wasn't the same. A few buttons sat on the table next to the armchair, so I grabbed one and felt it between my fingers. It was one of the few I had left. The rest were sitting in her jar in her old bedroom.

I hadn't touched them.

I stared at the special button in my hand. It had gold trimming along the outside, and a pearl in the center. The irony wasn't lost on me. It symbolized her in every way imaginable. It was as if the button was made just for her.

"Your Grace?" Lars stepped into the study with his hand behind his back. "Will you be having breakfast in here today?"

"Just coffee."

"Of course." Lars walked out. He hadn't asked me about Button since she left. He knew she was gone, and she wasn't coming back. That was all the information he needed to know. Now this house was empty once again.

Except for the shadows.

Buttons and Pain

I pulled out my phone and checked the signal still in her ankle. I checked it every single day to see where she was. It was only a matter of time before she hired a surgeon to remove it for her.

Then I would lose her forever.

I opened the app on my phone and saw the red dot emerge on the map. She was inside a building on Park Avenue in Manhattan. Central Park was nearby. The dot wasn't moving, so she was probably sleeping. It was the middle of the night in her time zone.

What was she doing on Park Avenue?

I wasn't worried about her safety. Button was resourceful and smart. She could take care of herself without any problems. She didn't need me or anyone else to get through the night.

But I knew she didn't have the money to stay on Park Avenue.

And that meant she was staying with someone.

It wasn't a friend because she didn't have any of those. It wasn't a family member because those didn't exist either. It had to be an old boyfriend.

Bile flooded my mouth.

The idea of her fucking someone else repulsed me. Large hands caressing her soft skin and firm lips kissing that gentle mouth. Her legs spreading and a man taking her roughly on the edge of the bed. The images haunted me. I felt so sick I didn't even want my coffee anymore.

But I had no right to feel that way.

She wasn't mine anymore. And I was never hers.

Buttons and Pain

Chapter Three

Pearl

Jason had a beautiful apartment. It was spacious and clean. It had two bedrooms on opposite sides of the apartment, and I didn't feel like a burden since there was plenty of room. The kitchen was big, and so was the living room.

"How did you sleep?" He was sitting at the kitchen table eating cereal when I walked in.

I wore the pajamas he let me borrow. The sweatpants were too big, so I rolled them several times. His cotton t-shirt was soft and clean. It smelled like a man, and I think that helped me sleep.

Because my body subconsciously pretended I was beside Crow.

"Good. You?" I sat across from him and poured myself a bowl of Fruity Pebbles.

"Great." He had the newspaper beside him, but he didn't pick it up and read it. His eyes were on me, examining me with critical detail. When he brought me to his apartment last night, he didn't ask me anything. All he did was make dinner for both of us and showed me where I was sleeping.

I appreciated that. "Do you work today?"

23

"Yeah. I would take the day off, but I just started this job."

"No, don't feel bad," I said quickly. "I'll be fine. As long as I've got some Fruity Pebbles, I'll be fine."

When he smiled, it reached his eyes. "I'm glad you have the same sense of humor."

"I think it's ingrained in my personality at this point."

"I just meant—"

"I know what you meant." After being a sex slave, I should've been so fucked up that I couldn't find any reason to laugh. Maybe that's how I would have turned out if I'd stayed any longer with Bones. Being with Crow put me back together. He showed me that I could still enjoy sex—love it—even after being raped. "When bad things happen, you can let them defeat you, or you can rise above them. I've chosen the latter."

He continued to watch me with mesmerized eyes. "I think that's a good attitude."

I poured the milk into my bowl and took a bite. "Thanks for letting me stay here."

"Of course. Stay as long as you like."

"So...when did you move here?"

Buttons and Pain

"Less than a year ago. When I got here, I tried calling you to see if we could get together, but I couldn't get a hold of you. After some digging, I figured out what happened. I was a total wreck." He stirred his cereal with his spoon, his eyes downcast. "I was so worried about you. That's just terrible. I can't even..." He shook his head and sighed. "You don't need to hear this. I'm sorry. I need to be positive."

"It's okay. It's traumatic for people who care about me too."

He took a few bites of his cereal. "Does Jacob know you're okay?"

The police must have told him about my former boyfriend. "Yeah." I didn't want to talk about Jacob, and I certainly didn't want to tell Jason what really happened. He would demand I turn Jacob over to the police. Financially, I wasn't ready to do that at the moment. I'd rather use him for whatever I needed than throw him behind bars. "He and I broke up shortly before it happened. We don't talk anymore."

Jason didn't ask any further questions. He must have sensed I didn't want to talk about Jacob.

"So, why did you relocate here?" Keeping the conversation light was good for both of us.

25

"I was offered a job in the city. The pay was too good for me to turn down."

"That's great. Good for you."

"Thanks," he said. "Honestly...I was kinda hoping that when I moved here, you and I could...you know." He rested both elbows on the table and looked at me. "I've had a few girlfriends over the years, but none of them was ever the right fit. I guess I kept comparing them to what we had. I didn't appreciate it until it was over."

I stilled at the confession, unsure how I felt about it.

He noticed my unease. "I don't expect anything to ever happen between us. After everything you've been through, I'm sure it's the last thing on your mind. I wasn't making a move. I just wanted to be honest about my intentions when I moved here. That's why I was so upset that you'd been taken. Broke my heart."

"I'm not looking for romance right now." I had to put that out there so there was no misunderstanding. Jason was just as handsome as he used to be, and our relationship had been great. If we hadn't moved apart for work, we probably still would have been together.

Buttons and Pain

We'd probably be married by now. But I wasn't in any place to feel anything for anyone.

Jason didn't seem to take offense to that. "I completely understand, Pearl. It's off the table."

I breathed a sigh of relief when he took my request so well. He seemed genuine about it, that he was helping me because he really cared and didn't just want to hook up. Jason had always been a sweet guy. "Thanks…"

"Of course." He finished his cereal before he left it in the sink. "I get off around five. I'll cook dinner when I get home."

"It's okay. I'll take care of that. I'll pick up some groceries." I noticed he didn't have many options in the fridge.

He opened his wallet and set cash on the counter. "Alright. Here's some cash."

"I got it. But, thanks."

"Come on, Pearl. Please, I insist." He pushed the money toward me. "Let me take care of you for a while. You just concentrate on getting better."

***

I lost all my possessions after I was abducted, so I had to start over. I went shopping and bought new clothes and toiletries. Thankfully, I had the cash from Jacob because buying a new wardrobe was pricey.

I'd need to get a job as soon as possible.

By the time Jason came home from work, I had dinner on the table, and I was wearing clothes that actually fit.

"Something smells good."

"Oh, that's just my perfume," I teased.

He chuckled and set his satchel on the counter. "Food-flavored perfume—I like it." He wore a suit and tie that highlighted his muscled shoulders and chest. He must work out every day to keep up that kind of form.

"How was work?"

"It was alright. But you know, it's work." He stood beside me in front of the stove and looked down into the pot. "Italian food. Awesome."

It was the diet I was used to eating. "It's almost ready."

"Alright. I'm going to change." He walked into his bedroom and shut the door.

I served the dishes and set them on the table. I didn't buy any wine because I didn't know what was good. And I also thought that would be too romantic. Water would work.

He walked out in his jeans and a t-shirt and sat across from me. "Thanks."

"Sure."

He dug into his food and ate quietly, his eyes always looking at something other than me.

I suspected he did that on purpose, so I wouldn't feel uncomfortable. He rarely touched me, and when he came close to me, he still put several feet between us. And he never hugged me unless he had my explicit permission. "I applied for a few jobs today."

He swallowed his food quickly, and it went down the wrong way. He coughed into his napkin until his throat was clear. "Already? There's really no rush to get back to work. This apartment is big enough for two people."

"Actually, I'd like to go back to work. I liked my job."

"Don't you think they would give it back to you? Under the circumstances?"

"I already tried. They hired a new person a year ago. They can't just let her go. That wouldn't be fair."

"That's too bad. But I'm sure there will be something else."

"I know there will be."

"But there's really no pressure to get a job and find a new place. I'm not just saying that to be nice. There's no reason to stress out."

"I know, Jason. But the quicker I return to normal, the more I'll feel normal."

He averted his gaze again, his eyes on his food. "You went shopping today."

"Yeah." I glanced down at my blouse. "Desperately needed new clothes."

"You look nice. I like that color on you."

"Thanks."

He finished his dinner and wiped his mouth with a napkin. "Well, that was great. Thanks for cooking."

"Of course." I hadn't cooked anything in a year. I was surprised I remembered how.

"Want to watch TV? Or would you like to go out and do something?"

I didn't want to be around people. When I lived with Crow, I never saw other humans. Ironically, I actually liked it that way. I used to love the interesting people of the city, but now, I just wanted to be alone. "TV sounds nice."

"Okay."

***

Two weeks came and went. Jason and I developed a routine together. I always had dinner on the table when he came home from work, and he always did the dishes before he went to bed. We spent our evenings watching TV or playing board games. He always kept his distance from me, usually sitting on the opposite couch.

I went on a few interviews but hadn't gotten a call back. Hopefully, something good would pop up. I was eager to get back to work, so I would have some normalcy in my life. Right now, I didn't have a purpose.

By the beginning of the third week, the withdrawals kicked in. I went from having amazing sex on a daily basis to quitting cold turkey. I didn't think it would affect me at all because Crow hurt me so deeply.

But it did.

The area between my legs burned with pent-up aggression, and my lips ached for his kiss. My mind always drifted to fantasies of him pounding into me from above. His hand would fist my hair, and he'd crush my mouth with his.

I missed it.

While Jason was at work, I borrowed his laptop and watched porn. I tried touching myself to the videos I watched, but nothing worked for me. All I kept thinking about was how artificial it felt.

I gave up on the idea altogether and didn't know what to do. I could sleep with Jason, but I didn't want to cross that line. Right now, we were companionable friends and roommates. I didn't want to tamper with that. Maybe one day, we could start dating again, but right now wasn't the time. As much as I hated to admit it, Crow was still on my mind.

In time, I would stop thinking about him. Eventually, it would be hard for me to picture his face. And one day, he would be out of my mind, and I wouldn't even realize I'd stopped remembering him. Then I could move on with my life. Maybe I could settle down with a husband and have kids someday.

Maybe.

I tried touching myself while using my own imagination. I pictured a random hot guy with a perfect body. I tried to keep it purely physical just so I could get off. But by sheer force, Crow broke into my mind and stole the show. He pleased me just the way he used to, and I rubbed my clit harder as I came, whispering his name.

It felt so good that I didn't feel guilty. I really needed that.

***

Jason sat on the other couch while the TV played. A Yankees game was on because he was a baseball fan. But he didn't seem interested in the game. "Pearl, can I ask you something?"

"Yeah, sure." He steered clear of uncomfortable topics, so I didn't see the harm. I had a blanket on top of my legs while I rocked my pajamas and a messy bun. Jason had seen me without makeup before. I used to sleep at his place all weekend.

"I found a few good therapists in the city. I looked into their experience and qualifications, and they work with victims just like yourself. Maybe you could talk to them about everything. You know...just so you have someone who understands how you feel."

It was a sweet thing to do. Jason was just trying to help and wanted me to be happy. "That's very nice of you, but I think I'm okay." No amount of therapy would erase what happened to me. I had to stay strong and move on. Talking about my feelings and the past would just make things worse. And if I confessed I'd developed strong feelings for one of my captors, they would know just how crazy I was. "These things just take time."

"I'm always here to talk if you need me. I can't begin to understand what you went through, but I'm always here to listen."

"I know that too, Jason."

When he understood I wasn't going to budge, he looked at the TV again.

And we spent the night in silence.

***

"You really don't need to leave." Jason helped me carry one of the two boxes I possessed into my new apartment. I got a job working for a construction company, and I knew I'd be able to pay my bills for the long term. It was nice having somewhere to be in the morning. "I feel like you're rushing it. I told you I don't mind sharing my apartment with you."

"I know, but I need to get out on my own."

"But you don't even have a bed."

"It's next on the list," I said with a chuckle.

"And where will you sleep tonight? On the floor?"

I hadn't anticipated that problem. "Yeah...my back is gonna kill me tomorrow."

"Stay at my place until you get some furniture. You aren't overstaying your welcome. Truly."

"You've done so much for me, Jason. I feel bad taking advantage of your hospitality any longer."

"Nonsense. We've known each other for nearly ten years. We're like family."

My eyes softened. "Jason..."

"Come on. I'm not letting you stay here until there's some decent furniture in here. If you sleep on the floor, your back will go out. And last time I checked, you needed that thing."

"Alright. You convinced me. But I suspect you just want a cook around the apartment."

He shrugged. "Yeah...maybe."

"Well, I'll take one of these boxes back. I don't need the other one."

"Pretty soon, this apartment is going to be full of stuff. And then it'll feel like a home."

Penelope Sky

Chapter Four

Crow

I leaned back in my chair and looked out the window. I was inside my office at the winery, but instead of working, I chose to look out the window and to the vineyards beyond. I had invoices, payroll, and insurance papers to work on.

But I couldn't concentrate.

Every time I opened a new bottle of wine, the smell didn't make me think of pressed grapes from a good harvest. It didn't make me think of the beautiful vineyards right outside my house. It only reminded me of one thing.

The taste of her lips.

They always possessed the sweetness of wine. Slightly bitter but mostly sweet. We always shared a bottle over dinner, so our sex reeked of it. When she panted and moaned in my face, I could smell it on her breath. I could taste it from her pores.

She'd been gone for a month, but it felt like only a day. I still found strands of her hair inside my home. Buttons were scattered everywhere. Some even made it into my drawer. I hadn't gone into her old bedroom yet because I wasn't ready. Her clothes were still in there, along with the few other possessions she had. And her jar of buttons was still there as well.

How long would this go on?

I never missed my previous partners. When we went our separate ways, that was the end. I didn't usually think about them anymore. I moved on to my next conquest and got lost in the throes of passion. Sex wasn't about the person—only the act.

But I couldn't stop thinking about Button. I continued to sleep on one side of the bed. When I had dreams, they were always about her. I still checked her tracker constantly and waited for the signal to go out.

I noticed she moved positions during the day. From the morning to late afternoon, she was across town in a building. I suspected that meant she'd gotten a job. She also wasn't on Park Avenue anymore. She'd moved a few blocks over into a different neighborhood. I could only assume that meant she'd gotten her own apartment.

Hopefully, she was living alone.

Maybe the person she was with before was a girlfriend. Maybe she'd steered clear of men altogether after everything she'd been through. She told me she didn't trust men and never would again.

I hope she meant it.

It was none of my business what she did now that she wasn't mine anymore. She could sleep with whomever she wanted. She could get married if she wanted. She could pop out a couple of kids. It didn't make a difference to me.

But every time she went back to the Park Avenue apartment, I got nervous. If she were sleeping with someone, it would kill me. I tried to fool myself with a lie, but it didn't work. Maybe it was jealousy, or maybe I still felt possessive. All I knew was, I would die if she let anyone touch her.

My office door opened. "Crow?"

I recognized her voice immediately. "Hello, Jasmine." I locked the screen of my phone and hid the GPS signal still going strong in New York. Button must've wanted me to know where she was. Otherwise, she would have removed the tracker. Unless she just forgot about it. Maybe she didn't give a damn about me at all.

I wouldn't blame her if she didn't.

Jasmine approached my desk. She wore a skintight dress with sky-high heels. Her hair was thick and curly, and she wore so much makeup she almost looked like a prostitute. "How are you?"

"Good." Horrible. "You?"

"Great," she said. "International business is really booming."

"That's great." I don't care.

"So...I heard through the grapevine your visitor left a few weeks ago."

I should have known she was there for a reason besides business. "Who told you this?"

She shrugged. "I can't remember."

It wasn't Lars. He would never tell anyone. The only other person who knew was Cane. He had a big mouth, so he was probably the culprit.

"So, that means she's really gone?"

"Yeah. She went home." I needed some scotch. My throat was closing up, and I suddenly felt warm.

"I see." She pursed her lips together to hide her smile. "How about you and I get dinner after work? I would love to catch up."

Desperation was not attractive. This woman tried so hard to be with me, but I didn't understand why. I wasn't particularly nice to her, and our relationship didn't last long. It was my fault for dating a member of the staff. I should have known better. "I don't do back-to-backs." That was a rule I made up on the spot. It was true enough. Very rarely did I hook up with an old lover unless it was spontaneous. What Jasmine was doing was the direct opposite of spontaneous. It was forceful—and annoying.

She sat at the edge of the desk and flipped her hair over one shoulder. She was trying to be sexy, but once a woman had to try, she missed the mark. "Oh, come on. I'm available, and so are you, master."

She was trying to hit my trigger with that keyword.

It didn't work.

Button never called me that. She never called herself my slave either. She only gave part of herself willingly, the part outside the playroom. I should have known then we were headed to destruction. "Jasmine, you're a beautiful woman, but it's not going to happen. Don't make me say it again."

She stiffened on my desk, the rejection stinging like salt in an open wound. She tried to shake it off by standing and smoothing out her dress. "This ship is leaving the port, Crow. You're going to miss your chance."

I didn't want a chance. "I understand. You deserve someone better than me anyway." She wanted someone to buy her chocolates and flowers for an anniversary. She wanted a man to marry her and vow to love her forever. She wanted so many things I was incapable of giving. So many things I didn't want to give.

"Crow." She leaned over the desk, her eyes level with mine. "There is no one better."

***

I sat in my study and stared at the fire. That was how I spent all my free time. I looked into the flames and lived in the past. That dark brown hair swept across my fingertips, and those slender legs wrapped tightly around my waist. The flames in the hearth only reminded me of the fire deep in her soul.

She wouldn't leave.

A knock sounded on the door before it opened. "Your Grace, Cane is here to see you."

I hadn't seen him since Button left. He called a few times, but I didn't answer. Once she was gone, I lost motivation to do anything. Even when I went to work, I didn't get anything done. I just sat there and looked out the window, daydreaming about the afternoon I spent with her at the beach. "Send him in."

"Yes, Your Grace." Lars shut the door.

I poured two glasses of scotch and waited for my brother to arrive.

Cane walked in a moment later, wearing dark jeans and a leather jacket. He dropped into the armchair beside me and snatched the drink off the table. He leaned back in the chair, his knees falling open and his back slouching.

I'd stopped trying to teach him manners a long time ago.

"What the hell have you been doing for the past month?" He blurted out his thoughts like a child.

"You know, the usual."

"No, I don't know. You're the most mysterious guy I've ever known—and I'm your brother."

I rested the scotch on my leg, my fingertips feeling the cool glass.

"Do you have a new woman in your life?"

"No."

"Still hung up on the last one, huh?"

"No." I was never hung up on anyone.

"Are you sure about that? You seem pretty down."

"I'm always down." That was my innate personality. Life passed by without any meaning. I took comfort in wine and solitude.

Cane chuckled in a sarcastic way. "You got it bad. Just admit it."

"Did you come here for a reason?" Other than to annoy me.

"Why don't you just talk to her?"

"About what?" I took a drink. "There's nothing to say."

"Crow, I don't understand why you're being such a cunt about this. If you love the girl, go tell her."

"I don't."

"Bullshit."

"I don't." I would say it as many times as necessary.

"Then why have you been moping around the house for a month?"

"Again, I always mope around."

"You wouldn't let me touch her. But you've let me touch your other girls before."

"That doesn't mean anything."

"Fuck yeah, it does. I'm just trying to help you."

"Well, don't." It was going to be a bad night, so I poured myself another glass. "Can we talk about business now?"

Crow leaned back in the chair and sighed. "Whatever. I did my best to pull your head out of your ass."

I changed the subject. "When are the shipments going out?"

"Monday." He moved with the change, finally giving up on his ridiculous theory about my feelings toward Button.

Now we could all move on.

***

Unable to sleep, I left my bedroom and went down into the kitchen. I hardly ever walked inside there because the staff prepared all my meals throughout the day. But it was easy to find a glass of water. I stood over the sink while I drank it and looked out the window. It was pitch black outside.

Buttons and Pain

"Your Grace."

I didn't hear Lars approach. I was focused on the blackness outside my house. I set the glass down and turned around. "Do you ever sleep, Lars?"

"Not when someone is in my kitchen." He wore pajamas and slippers. I only saw him wear suits around the house. It was strange to see him so casual. "Is there anything I can get you, Your Grace?"

"No. I'm sorry I woke you." I turned back to the sink and grabbed the glass.

Lars didn't move. He stood there with his hands behind his back, watching everything I did.

"Did you need something?" I finished the glass and left it in the sink.

"May I say something, Your Grace?"

I turned around, provoked by the strange request. "I suppose."

"If you're lucky enough to find someone who makes you happy, hold on to them as long as you can. One day, you'll lose them, but keeping them at a distance won't make it any easier in the end."

I leaned against the counter with my arms over my chest. I stared him down with a stoic expression, not giving away any of the thoughts circling in my mind. I knew Lars had lost his wife and daughter a long time ago. He'd never been the same since, and he stayed busy so the sorrow wouldn't swallow him whole.

"Good night, Your Grace." He made a quick bow before he walked out.

I stared at the spot where he'd been standing, thinking about everything he just said. He wasn't explicit in his words, but he made his point very clear. "Good night, Lars."

Buttons and Pain

Chapter Five

Pearl

Two months had come and gone.

And I was starting to go crazy.

I missed sex so much. I missed the way Crow would grip me tightly and thrust into me. I missed the way his powerful fingers dug into my hair and claimed me as his own. I missed being suspended from the ceiling while he took me from underneath. I missed his kisses.

I missed everything.

I needed to get laid.

Masturbation wasn't cutting it anymore. It didn't feel nearly as good, and after a while, it just felt pathetic. Porn didn't work for me either because I just fantasized about Crow. And that wasn't helping me move on.

I never allowed myself to think about him. When I was at work, his face would come into my mind, but I would quickly brush it off. When I was home, I wondered what he was doing, but then I halted those thoughts immediately. The only time I couldn't stop myself from thinking about him was when I touched myself.

Penelope Sky

He was the only thing I could get off to.

I'd convinced myself it was just about the sex. I'd never had good sex like that before, so I didn't have anything else to compare it to. It had nothing to do with the man, just the package that was included.

Jason stopped by my apartment that night with a pizza box in his hands. "I come with gifts."

"Ooh...really good gifts."

He came inside and set the box on the counter. "Did you have plans tonight?"

"Just a hot date with my TV."

"Then it's cool if I'm the third wheel tonight?"

"If you don't mind being left out sometimes."

He chuckled. "Not at all."

We grabbed our beer and pizza and watched TV on the couch. Like always, he stayed far away from me. He purposely put unnecessary space between us. He continued to look at me as a rape victim, not as a friend or a woman he was attracted to.

I didn't want that label. I didn't want to be viewed that way. While those months in captivity were the worst of my life, they didn't define who I was. I was still the same woman as when I left New York.

48

I just wished Jason would see me that way.

***

After a few beers and demolishing the pizza, I was loose and so was he. He wore his college alumni t-shirt, and it was tight against his muscular chest and shoulders. His dirty-blond hair was styled meticulously, and his handsome face was framed by a chiseled jaw and nice cheekbones.

I was attracted to Jason.

When we were together, I loved him. The breakup was hard for the first few months. I cried a lot. And when I found out he was seeing someone new, I felt dead inside. But as time went on, it got easier. Then I finally got over him.

The sex was decent. Sometimes I would come. He was gentle with me, always making love to me and never taking me harshly.

I knew he was still attracted to me.

I was ready to get back on the horse and move on with my life. I needed a good lay and some affection. My body yearned to be touched. My skin craved kisses and mild bites. My thighs desperately wanted to squeeze a man's hips. I wanted to get hot and sweaty and roll across my sheets. Crow

49

undoubtedly had replaced me with some exotic, beautiful woman, and he probably didn't think about me anymore.

And I shouldn't have thought about him.

I left my couch and took the seat beside Jason.

He immediately looked at me, surprised by the proximity. His hands stayed in his lap, but his eyes glanced at the curve of my tits in my dress. He quickly looked away like he was ashamed for looking at all.

He would never make a move, so I did. I cupped his face then pressed my mouth to his. It immediately felt foreign. His lips were nothing like Crow's. They were thicker, and the scruff didn't rub against my delicate skin. There wasn't power in his touch. I didn't feel the dominance course through him in powerful waves.

Once the initial shock wore off, Jason pulled me farther into him and deepened the kiss. His strong arms wrapped around me and made me feel safe. It was so nice to feel the heat from a man's body. It was a relief to feel needed and attractive.

I straddled his hips and pressed my tits against his chest as I sucked his bottom lip. My arms wrapped around his neck, and I slowly grinded against his erection through his jeans. The definition was noticeable, but not thick like Crow's. I already knew how Jason felt because I'd been with him hundreds of times. But I couldn't stop myself from comparing him to Crow.

I unbuttoned his jeans and pulled down the zipper. His boxers were in the way. I yanked them down, so his cock could be free. My lips still moved against his, and our tongues danced together. Then I pulled up my dress and moved my panties to the side.

Jason gripped my hips and pulled me back slightly. "Pearl, wait." He was out of breath, his eyes dark with arousal. His face was flushed with heat, and his cheeks were tinted. "I don't think we should do this." His fingertips kneaded into my ass. His hips grinded slightly, wanting to rub his shaft against my clit. His movements contradicted everything he said. "Maybe we should take things slow because...you've been through a lot."

I was tired of him looking at me that way. I was a victim once in my life, but that was in the past. I'd dealt with my problems and moved on. "Jason, I'm fine. Stop worrying about me. Now, do you want to fuck me or not?"

He closed his eyes and took a deep breath before he rolled on a condom and pointed his cock at my entrance. He gripped my hips and lowered me onto his length slowly, moaning from deep in his throat as he felt me.

It felt good to feel a man inside me again. It wasn't nearly as amazing as when Crow was inside me, but I had to stop thinking about those months I spent with him in Italy. I had to move on and find new ways of pleasure.

Hopefully, Jason was a solution.

***

My alarm went off, and I moaned as I hit the snooze button. My life had had a semblance of normalcy again, and I hated waking up early in the morning just the way I used to. But I had a job to get to and bills to pay.

Jason moaned from beside me, not wanting to wake up either. "Let's quit our jobs and live on welfare."

"That's the best idea I've ever heard."

He spooned me from behind then kissed my neck. His touches were always gentle. While they felt nice, I wanted something harder. I wished he would bite my collarbone and spank my ass at the same time.

But he never did.

He moved his lips to my ear. "Do we have time?" He squeezed my ass then kissed the shell of my ear.

"We always have time for that." I got on all fours and grinded my pussy against his shaft. I moved my hips and stroked him up and down, from his balls to his head.

Jason gripped my shoulders as he moaned. "You're unbelievable, you know that?" He pointed his head at my entrance then moved inside me with one quick motion.

I rocked into him hard, wanting to get off before I went to work. Every round of sex didn't end with an orgasm, but one-third of them had a happy ending. Maybe today I would get lucky.

My ass begged to be spanked, and I wished Jason would wrap his fingers around my throat. I wanted to be bound and gagged and fucked mercilessly into the mattress. I wanted it rough and hard, just the way Crow used to give it to me. "Spank me."

He slowed his thrusts. "You want me to spank you?"

"Yeah." I wiggled my ass.

He slapped his palm against my cheek, but it was pitiful. It wasn't even a slap. It was a mere tap.

"Harder."

He did it again, but like the last time, it was lame.

"Goddammit, Jason. Spank me hard."

He slapped his palm across my cheek, but it still wasn't good enough. It felt like a light tapping. "Like that, baby?"

"You call that hard?"

"I'm not going harder than that. I'll hurt you."

"I want you to hurt me." Why didn't he get it?

Jason didn't spank me again. He thrust into me quickly until he came with a loud moan.

Unsatisfied, I felt him pull out of me.

Awkward because of the last thing I said, he left the bed and walked into his bathroom. The shower started to run, and the water hit the tile at the bottom.

The area between my legs burned with devastation, and I had to force myself out of bed. I knew Jason was irritated with me because he didn't walk me to the door like he usually did. I threw my clothes on and walked out without waiting for an explanation. If he was annoyed with me, I didn't give a damn.

***

I walked into my apartment and tossed my purse on the counter. I hadn't been there all weekend because I always stayed at Jason's. He had the bigger apartment and the second bathroom for me to put my things.

I showered then got ready for work. The nice thing about my job was my wardrobe was casual. I usually went to work in jeans and a t-shirt. I pulled my flats on before I opened the fridge and tried to find something to throw together for lunch. But, of course, there was nothing in there. I couldn't remember the last time I went grocery shopping.

I grabbed my backpack from the counter and noticed something strange beside it. Two buttons lay on the surface, one bright gold and the other identical to a pearl. Gold metal crested the edge. They both caught the light, looking vibrant in my dull apartment.

I froze.

Where did they come from? Were they in the pocket of the pants I wore on the plane? Did I bring them all the way from Italy and they fell out? But how would they wind up on the counter?

My blood turned ice-cold.

There was only one explanation.

Crow.

Buttons and Pain

Chapter Six

Pearl

I arrived at my apartment after work. The keys were in my hand, but I didn't insert them into the lock. My heart warned me about what was on the other side. Somehow, I could feel it through the door.

I knew he was in there.

I stayed in the hallway and strengthened my nerve before I inserted the key into the lock. I had no idea what he wanted, but I didn't care. He would say what he needed to say then he would disappear.

Unless he was there to capture me again.

And remind me of the debt I still owed him.

When my key turned in the door, it didn't click. It was already unlocked.

Now my heart kicked into overdrive.

I turned the knob and walked inside, my keys still in my hand and ready to be used as a weapon. The lights were off, and the apartment was dark. The city lights came through the small window in the living room.

I quickly turned on the kitchen light so I wouldn't be blind.

A man's shadow came into view from the living room. With strong shoulders and a formidable build, he sat in the chair in front of the TV. His fingertips rested on his lips, and he didn't move. He didn't even turn to look at me.

I didn't need to see his face to recognize him.

My heart pumped at full speed, and my chest immediately expanded from the deep breaths I was forced to take. I was nervous and scared, frightened by the man I thought was gone for good. But I felt the familiar excitement between my legs. The second he was in the room with me, my panties became wet.

I hated him.

"Breaking and entering is a crime, you know. I'm not sure how they do it in Italy."

He didn't flinch.

I stayed at the counter and refused to get close to him. He broke in to my apartment to purposely catch me with my guard down. He wanted control of the situation. He wanted control of me.

But I wasn't going to let him have it.

"Is there something I can help you with?"

He slowly rose to his feet and stepped out of the shadows. In dark jeans and a black t-shirt, he emerged into the light. His five o'clock shadow was prominent, and his intense eyes held more rage than I'd ever seen. He looked terrifying but painfully beautiful. He stopped a few feet away from me, his thick arms hanging by his sides. He hadn't changed in the few months that passed. His hair was the same length, and his build hadn't changed. The only thing that seemed to be different was his insanity.

He looked livid.

I refuse to admit I was scared. The situation was dire and threatening. His intentions weren't clear, but they weren't pleasant either. I held my ground and opened the drawer beside me. Inside was a steak knife, so I pulled it out and held it on the counter.

He glanced at it before he gave me a look of murder. "Drop it."

"No." I kept my grip on the handle.

He took a step closer to me. "Drop it, or see what happens when you don't." He reached the counter between us and gripped the edge with his powerful hands. The veins on the surface protruded from underneath the skin. The muscles contracted, and his knuckles turned white.

I didn't want to give in, but I knew I'd already lost the battle. I tossed it in the sink. It made a loud clatter as it bounced against the stainless steel. Once it stopped moving, silence returned to the apartment. Only the distant sound of street traffic could be heard. "What do you want?"

He stared me down.

I held his look and didn't give in to the fear. I'd spent nearly a year of my life with this man, but he still frightened me. More than two months had come and gone, and I didn't hear a word from him. So why did he show up now? "I asked you a question."

He pulled his hands away from the edge and stepped around the counter.

I moved the opposite way, keeping the counter between us. "Don't. Touch. Me."

"Don't. Run. From. Me." He moved around the counter, this time picking up speed.

I sprinted to the bedroom and slammed the door behind me. My hands shook as I worked the lock. Adrenaline was coursing through me, and I couldn't keep my body still. I got the door locked just before he reached it.

Buttons and Pain

I stepped back and wrapped my arms around my waist. I felt the panic emerge, and I couldn't control my breathing.

He was silent on the other side of the door.

Did he leave?

A loud boom sounded through the apartment as he broke down the door with his shoulder. In one swift move, he broke the lock and made the door swing hard on its hinges.

Now there was nowhere for me to go.

He clenched his fists by his sides as he walked toward me, that same angry look on his face.

"Don't touch—"

He threw me on the bed and pinned my hands together above my head. He kept me against the mattress with his weight. His knee kept my thighs pinned down, and he used his free hand to keep my hips in place. "Let me go."

"No." His face was just inches from mine. He stared down at me with a heartless expression. He glanced at my lips before he looked into my eyes again. "Who the fuck is he?"

"Who?" I fought against him, but he was too heavy. We were a year into the past, and I was trying to run from my tormentor—before I fell for him.

"The fucker who lives on Park Avenue."

How did he know that? "Have you been spying on me?"

He squeezed my wrists together. "Answer the question."

"No!" I tried to knee him in the groin, but he was too strong.

"Are you fucking him?"

"None of your goddamn business."

His eyes burned with rage because he could see the answer written all over my face. "Who is he?"

"Jason."

His eyes narrowed in recognition. "The asshole that took your virginity?"

"He's not an asshole. He's one of the greatest guys I've ever known. And yes, he was my first. Now get off me."

He moved farther on top of me, constricting my wrists. "You aren't seeing him anymore."

Buttons and Pain

"Like you can tell me what to do." I twisted my wrists so I could get free. "I've been gone for two months, and you never gave a damn. You never tried to call me or get me back. You just let me go. I've gotten my life back on track, and I'm not letting an asshole like you screw it up."

"You and I have a misunderstanding."

"No. You're just an idiot."

He pushed my hands deeper into the mattress and pressed his face closer to mine. My body automatically reacted to him, not recoiling but tensing. His breaths fell on my skin, and they still smelled like wine. His cologne was the same, and his lips were still kissable. "I gave you a break. There's a difference."

"A break?"

"You never paid off your debt. You still owe me."

"I don't owe you shit."

"I beg to differ." His hand moved to my jeans, and he unbuttoned them. "You still owe me thirty buttons. Thirty."

"Fuck you, Crow."

He unzipped my pants and yanked them off my legs. "You're about to fuck me."

My thighs trembled with longing, and the area between my legs grew wet. I didn't know what the hell was wrong with me. I was terrified of this man and how maniacal he was, but my body still yearned for him. "I'm not doing anything. I don't owe you a damn thing."

He undid his own jeans and kicked them away. When he was in his boxers, he inserted two fingers into my panties and immediately shoved them deep into my pussy. The moisture flooded around him. "You still get wet for me, Button."

I broke eye contact for the first time out of humiliation.

He pulled his boxers off then positioned himself between my legs. My hands were still pinned above my head, and I was vulnerable to whatever he wanted to do to me. "You're mine. Not his. Mine." He pointed his tip at my entrance.

Despite what my body wanted, I didn't want this. I'd spent the last two months of my life getting back on track. I finally started to think about him less and was looking to the future. If I got swallowed up in this all over again, I would be lost. "Crow, no."

He shoved his head inside me.

Buttons and Pain

My head rolled back because it felt good. But I still didn't want it. "I said no."

That didn't stop him either.

I tried to think of the safe word, but I was drawing a blank. But then I finally remembered it. "Fire."

He immediately stopped and pulled the tip of his dick out. He released my hands and moved away, pulling his boxers back up to his waist. He eyed me with the same anger but kept his hands to himself.

I covered myself with the comforter and looked away. His eyes were too terrifying for me to look at anymore. "Crow, help me understand. Why are you here?" He found out I was sleeping with someone else, and he grew jealous. But that didn't make sense. He was the one who let me go to begin with. When I told him I loved him, he was the one who didn't say it back.

He sat up on the edge of the bed and rested his elbows on his knees. "I told you."

"We both know I don't owe you anything."

"Quite to the contrary. I had to give up my revenge because of you. You owe me every single button that's due."

"You didn't seem to care for the past two months."

"I've always cared." He stared at the ground, his shoulders tensed. "And you're going to pay each one back."

"I'm not doing anything." There was nothing he could do to make me cooperate. I knew he wouldn't take me against my will or hurt me, so he had nothing to threaten me with.

"You love this guy?"

I refused to answer.

"Do you?"

"It doesn't matter."

"It does," he pressed. "Now answer me."

"No." It was slightly insulting that he assumed I could fall in love with someone else so quickly.

"But I'm sure you don't want him to die, right?"

I turned his way, feeling the threat in the air. My blood ran cold at the insinuation. I knew Crow was a dark man, but this was a whole new level. "Excuse me?"

"If you don't work off the rest of those buttons, I'll kill him." He turned my way, and the threat was in his eyes. He meant every word he said—to the last syllable.

"Leave him out of this."

"No. He got involved the moment he touched you. And you aren't his to touch."

"What the hell, Crow? You can't have it both ways. You can't forget about me for two months and fuck an endless line of beautiful women, but then throw a hissy fit once I move on with someone else. It's childish, even for you."

"I haven't fucked anyone." He rubbed his knuckles with his thumb.

"Like I'm supposed to believe that."

"Believe what you want, but when have I ever lied to you? We don't lie to each other, remember?"

Even after all this time, I still trusted him. If he said something, he meant it. The fact didn't make me feel better, it just confused me. I shouldn't care whether he'd slept with anyone else or not.

"What's it gonna be?"

"What?"

"Are you going to pay off your debt or not?"

"No."

"Then I'm gonna kill him." He massaged his knuckles while he held my gaze. "I hope you don't think I'm bluffing. I've killed a lot of men. He's just another name on a list."

"But you don't kill innocent people."

"Innocence is subjective. He's guilty in my eyes. He touched something that didn't belong to him."

"I'm not yours."

"You've always been mine. And you'll always be mine."

When my heart skipped a beat, I looked away.

"I'll give you a day to think about it." He rose from the bed and pulled on his jeans. Then he walked out of the bedroom. "But if you screw him during that time, I'll kill him anyway."

Buttons and Pain

Chapter Seven

Crow

I didn't handle that well.

When I saw the GPS coordinate spending the weekends at Park Avenue, I connected the dots and realized exactly what she was doing. She was sleeping over for the weekend then going home Monday morning.

So, she was sleeping with someone.

Mr. Park Avenue.

Fucker.

I'm not sure what happened to me. All rational thought left my mind, and I turned into a psychopath. Red tinted my vision, and adrenaline saturated my blood to dangerous levels. My hands wouldn't stop shaking, and they kept balling into fists.

Before I knew it, I was on a plane to New York.

I shouldn't have ambushed her like that, but again, I wasn't thinking clearly. All I knew was I had to put an end to her relationship with Mr. Park Avenue. I had to stop it before she fell in love with him. Because if that happened, I would be too late.

I was at her apartment when she came home from work. She obviously expected me to be there because she didn't react when she saw me on the couch. She set her backpack on the counter and grabbed a bottle of water from the fridge.

"How was work?" I watched her stand at the counter in her t-shirt. It was tight across her chest and slender stomach. It highlighted the deep curve of her waist, making her hips more pronounced. She was even more beautiful than I remembered.

"Good. How was sitting in my apartment?"

I loved it when she talked like a smartass. I found it oddly entertaining. "Good. I went through your underwear drawer. Nice selection."

She rolled her eyes. "You better not have. I'll kick your ass."

"I'd like to see you try." When she fought against me yesterday, I was so hard. I wanted to pin her to the mattress and fuck her until she screamed. I'd never gone so long without getting laid. The withdrawals were killing me. When my fingers felt how wet her pussy was, I almost ignored the safe word and fucked her anyway.

At least she still wanted me.

Buttons and Pain

"Why are you here?" She left the bottle on the counter and walked into the living room. She wore skintight jeans that hugged her long, thin legs. I'd never seen her in jeans before. She always wore dresses at my estate. "Why don't you just knock on the door like everyone else?"

"You know why I'm here." I ignored her second question. "What's your answer?"

She crossed her arms over her chest, pushing her tits closer together.

If she wasn't careful, I'd bend her over the couch and fuck her then and there. "Don't make me repeat myself." I rose to my feet but didn't take a step closer to her. This time, I would give her space. I went overboard yesterday. My feelings were haywire, and I couldn't contain my rage.

"No."

I should have known she wouldn't make this easy. "You think I'm bluffing."

"Yes."

"I'm not." It was unfortunate she didn't believe me. "I'll make it look like an accident. Accidentally slipped and hit his head in the shower. And when you move on and start seeing some other guy, I'll do the same."

When she heard the sincerity in my voice, her fire died down. The strength that constantly coursed through her veins turned into a simmer. "So I'll never be able to move on with my life because you'll kill every guy I like?"

"Exactly."

"You're despicable, you know that?"

"Yep."

She shook her head and stepped away, flustered. "Even if I work off those buttons, you're just going to keep doing this."

"No."

"Are you kidding me?" she snapped. "You flew all the way here the second you found out I was seeing someone. You threatened to kill him if I touched him again. Do you have any idea how crazy that sounds?"

"I told you I wasn't a good guy. Not sure why you're surprised."

"You're better than this."

"Nope."

Buttons and Pain

She released a growl of frustration under her breath. "So, I work off the rest of those buttons, and you just disappear? Because the second we're done, I'm going back to Jason—"

"Don't say his name."

"I'm going back to him once we're finished."

That's what she thought. "Yes."

She narrowed her eyes in suspicion. "Why don't I believe you?"

"When have I not kept my word to you?"

She rolled her eyes, knowing I was breaking my word by just being here. "I only have thirty buttons. That won't last long."

"I'll take what I can get." Did that mean she was agreeing?

"Alright. Fine. But once this debt is paid, I don't want to see you again."

Fuck, that hurt. "Fine."

"Okay."

The deal had been set. She was mine again. She was mine until I ran out of buttons. "Pack your things, and we'll leave."

"Pack my things?" she asked blankly.

"We're going home."

"To Italy?"

"Yes."

"I'm not leaving. Crow, I have a job."

"I'll give you money in compensation."

Her eyes narrowed at the insult. "I don't want your money. I want my life."

I had work to do and business to oversee in Italy. "I can't stay here."

"Well, I can't leave."

This was a problem I hadn't foreseen.

"Looks like this isn't going to work after all."

No, it was gonna work. "Pack your things. We're staying elsewhere."

"What?" she asked in confusion. "I said I'm not going to Italy."

"And that's fine. But you aren't staying here."

"Crow, I live here."

"Not anymore. Now, do as I say."

"What makes you think I'm ever going to listen to you?" She crossed her arms over her chest and stared me down. That fire I loved was bright in her eyes.

Buttons and Pain

"I'm not fucking you in that bed." I wasn't going anywhere near the place she'd screwed Mr. Park Avenue. I wanted a clean slate, a place where she and I could start over. "You can come back here in your free time, but you're sleeping with me every night. For the last time, pack your shit and let's go."

Penelope Sky

Chapter Eight

Pearl

We arrived at his hotel room. It was on the top floor of The Plaza, and it was as big as a mansion. Floor-to-ceiling windows took up one wall and gave a brilliant view of the city. It had a full kitchen and dining room, laundry machines, a private pool, and several bedrooms.

It was too big for a single person. "They didn't have anything smaller?"

Crow set my bag on the couch and ignored my question. "Do you want a drink?"

"No."

He poured himself a glass of wine.

I couldn't believe I was in this hotel room—alone with him. I couldn't believe I gave in to his demands. At first, I didn't because I didn't believe he would really hurt Jason. But when that maniacal gleam didn't disappear from his eyes, I realized he meant every word.

So, I didn't have a choice.

"Help yourself to anything you want."

Buttons and Pain

"Okay." I already felt like I was back in Italy. The only thing missing was Lars.

Crow finished his wine before he crossed the living room and stopped in front of me. His eyes were dark with longing, and he wanted to get down to business right away. His hand snaked around my waist, and he pulled me into his chest. His forehead rested against mine, and he closed his eyes.

Then he just held me.

The innocent touch was unexpected, and I closed my eyes to enjoy it. His hands gripped me tightly, but they were loose enough that I could slip away if I wanted to. His breaths came out deep and even, and he seemed to reach a moment of peace. "I missed you, Button."

The nickname brought me two months into the past. I remembered the last time we made love in his bed. He thrust into me with my legs wrapped around his waist, and he gave me passionate kisses that made my spine shiver. I fell hard for him in that moment. So hard I could never get back up.

Emotion caught in my throat, but I refused to say it back. I confessed my feelings once, and he walked out. Our relationship was never the same again. He viewed me as a slave, a piece of property.

And I viewed him as so much more.

When I didn't say it back, he opened his eyes and looked into mine. He searched for an answer in my expression but was unable to find one.

I let my walls come down when I shouldn't have, and I got my heart broken. I refused to let that happen again. He coerced me into this, and I was only cooperating to keep Jason out of it. He was a great guy and shouldn't be dragged into the nightmare that was Crow Barsetti.

Crow's fingers glided to my cheek, and he felt the soft skin before he cupped my face. He leaned in and brushed his lips past mine, teasing me. Our lips never fully collided, just touched slightly. Then he went in for the real thing, fisting the back of my hair as he closed his mouth over mine.

And I felt it. I felt that scorching heat and intense desire. I felt my body come to life like it always did when his lips were on me. I felt both alive and dead, existing in a different dimension that no one else could understand.

Nothing compared to his kiss.

Buttons and Pain

He tilted my head back with a yank of my hair to get more of my mouth. He sucked my bottom lip slowly before he slipped his tongue into my mouth. A quiet moan escaped his lips as the passion burned between us.

I moaned too.

His other hand squeezed my waist, claiming me as his all over again. His fingers stretched to the top of my ass, and he gave it a firm squeeze, pulling me farther into him. He devoured my mouth with his wine-soaked lips and guided me toward the bedroom in the back. His cock was rock-hard and pressed against my stomach. I knew exactly how it would feel once it was inside me. I would never forget that delectable stretching that sent me to the stars.

He pushed me onto the bed then pulled off his t-shirt. His body was exactly the same as I remembered. Lithe and toned, his muscles were long and exaggerated. His skin looked chiseled from stone, and his narrow hips led to a stomach harder than concrete. He was perfect.

He unbuttoned my jeans and slowly pulled them down my legs. When they were at my ankles, he gave them a firm tug and pulled my ass to the edge of the bed. After they were on the ground, he kneeled at the edge then kissed my inner thighs.

I'd already forgotten I hated him.

My head rolled back, and I gripped the sheets as I felt his mouth migrate to the apex of my thighs.

But then I realized exactly what I was doing and why it had to stop. "Fire."

Crow immediately pulled his hands away and stood up. He took a step back, giving me more space than necessary. If I didn't say the safe word, he would have pushed me until I broke. Nothing would stop him from taking what he wanted. But once the word was said, he took it seriously. "What is it?"

I sat up and pressed my thighs together. I was half naked with Crow and riddled with guilt. "I need to talk to—"

"Don't say his name." The veins in Crow's neck were thick like cords.

"I need to talk to him."

"Why?" Crow kneeled down again.

"I need to break it off with him first. This is wrong."

He bowed his head in irritation, his chest rising and falling with pent-up aggression. "Didn't realize you were so serious with him."

"I'm not. I wouldn't even say we're dating—just hooking up."

His jaw clenched tighter.

"But I should give him the courtesy before I do this. He's been so good to me, and he deserves better."

"Good to you?" His hands moved to my thighs, and he gripped them tightly. "Do you care to explain that?"

"He was the one pushing the investigation. He was the one who told the authorities to look for me in Tuscany. He did his research and never gave up." I would always be indebted to Jason for that. There wasn't a single person on the planet who cared about me the way he did. He was the closest thing I had to a family. "So, I can't do this until I talk to him."

Crow released the tension on my thighs then pulled his hands away. When he bowed his head and remained silent, I knew he didn't have an argument. He couldn't disagree with my sense of loyalty. "Okay."

My lips still ached for his. I wanted the kiss to continue all night and the following morning. That was exactly the kind of affection and attention I craved. I missed the scorching heat of his body as it kept me warm during the night. I missed having my leg hooked around his waist as an anchor. I missed everything.

"I need to ask you something."

"Okay." I met his look.

"Did you sleep with him out of obligation?"

The assumption stung. "Of course not. I did it because I wanted to." That wasn't the answer he wanted to hear, but I wouldn't lie to make him feel better. "Two months is a long time to go without some physical contact."

Crow looked away, clearly annoyed by the answer.

"You have no right to feel jealous. If you slept with someone, it wouldn't bother me."

He closed his eyes in the form of a cringe. "Not even a little?"

"No."

"Not after everything we've been through together? You wouldn't feel a damn thing?"

Buttons and Pain

I cocked my head to the side and examined him with new eyes. "I told you I loved you." The emotion entered my voice without any warning. I felt the words burn all the way out. My eyes watered with tears that emerged from nowhere, and I felt the excruciating pain all over again. "And you said you didn't feel the same way. That was when I understood you were never mine. That's when I understood the true nature of our relationship. So, no, Crow. I don't give a damn if you sleep with anyone."

***

I grabbed my bag from the couch. "I'm going back to my apartment."

He leaned against the wall with his arms across his chest. "Why?"

"There's no point in me staying here."

He slowly walked to me and pulled the backpack out of my hand. "I disagree."

I extended my hand. "I don't care."

He set the backpack on the other couch. I could only get to it if I moved through him.

"Fine. One button." I wasn't working for free. If he wanted something from me, he had to work for it.

His eyes narrowed at my request. "No."

"Then I'm leaving." He could keep the bag if he wanted it so badly. I had other stuff at my apartment.

Crow realized he had to play the game or forfeit. "One button."

"Deal." I extended my open palm. I wanted those buttons as soon as possible so this could end. I had to guard my heart tightly this time. Last time, he stole it without me even realizing it. I was in a better state of mind, and I wanted to keep it that way.

He fished the button out of his pocket and dropped it into my hand.

Once I had the token of payment, I walked to my backpack and placed it in one of the pockets. One down and twenty-nine more to go. We couldn't have sex, so I wasn't sure why he wanted me to spend the night. If he planned on seducing me into sleeping with him anyway, he was going to be disappointed.

"Have dinner with me." He came up behind me and pressed his chest into my back. "There's this nice place just down the block."

Once I felt him against me, my breathing hitched. With every breath, his chest expanded against me. I started to count the number of times he took a breath. I used to do the same thing when he was asleep. I'd stare at his handsome face and count his heartbeats. "I don't have anything to wear."

He wrapped his arm around my waist and pressed a kiss to the back of my neck. "I have something for you."

***

Crow ordered the wine and our entrees before he handed the menus over. He wore a black suit with a teal tie. The color of his tie always contrasted against the other dark colors he wore. It was his signature move, making him stand out more than he already did.

I couldn't believe I was sitting across from him.

Going months without a single conversation was a long time. When I first came to the city, I felt alone. Living in Crow's beautiful house without a care in the world was the most freeing experience of my life. Falling in love with a man who fixed me after I'd been broken was the only thing that put me back together. Without him, I would have been screwed up for the rest of my life.

But I would never admit that to Crow.

Weakness wasn't my strong point, and it was a side of myself I rarely showed. The last time I allowed it to happen, Crow broke my heart. I opened myself to him completely and said three little words I wished I could take back. It was one of the most humiliating moments of my life.

"You look beautiful tonight." He stared at me with a gaze that was both intense and frozen. His eye contact never broke, and he stared at me with both hostility and interest. It was his form of intimidation—and it always worked. I noticed both he and Cane did it anytime they walked into a room. Perhaps it was a Barsetti thing.

"Thank you." I didn't give him a compliment in return because he already knew he was beautiful—and deadly. And he knew exactly how attracted to him I was. "How's Lars?"

"He's good. Misses you."

"He said that?" That sweet man always took care of me, and he did so with a smile. He'd become an essential part of my life in Italy. I saw his face every morning and every night.

"Not in those words. But yes."

"Well…I miss him too." I missed everything about that place. It was a magical gem in the middle of nowhere. The vineyards were just as beautiful as the glorious sunsets over the hillsides. The smell of grapes always entered my nose when I opened the window in the morning. The food was always perfect, but nothing could beat the company of Crow Barsetti. "How's Cane?" He told me Crow loved me, but that turned out to be a cruel joke. I hated Cane all over again.

"A shithead, like always."

I chuckled at his choice of words. I'd never heard him say something like that before. "And work?"

"The winery is doing well. We just finished our harvest, so that was a big project. My business with Cane is the same. We had a shipment last Monday that was a success." He swirled his wine before he took a drink.

"Any news on Bones?"

"Cane and I have been trying to track him down, but he never stays in one place too long. He must know we're after him."

"Who was that woman who kidnapped me?" When I left Italy and got on the plane to America, I never called Crow to tell him I was okay. But then again, I didn't have his number. I didn't even have his address. There was no way for me to get in touch with him. And I had to admit, I was hurt when he never contacted me.

"A bounty hunter. Bones dispatched a ton of them to find you."

I shivered involuntarily at the thought. That man was obsessed with me in an unhealthy way. I'd been gone from his clutches for a year, but he still searched for me. "I see."

Crow rested his fingertips around the stem of his glass as he watched me. He examined every reaction that I gave, seeing the emotions underneath. "When I found them, I killed them. You don't need to worry about them."

He'd read my mind, like always. "You didn't need to kill them."

"If I didn't, they would have told Bones where they found you. It had to be done." He spoke with no remorse, like it was just business. "I don't mean to scare you, but Bones will never stop hunting you. He'll figure out where you are, and when he does, he'll take you again."

I covered my unease by taking a large drink of wine. I'd rather die than be imprisoned again. If I had to go through that torture again, I'd put a gun to my head and pull the trigger. I lived through it once, but I couldn't live through it again. "I'm not going to live in fear. If that happens, I'll kill myself."

That wasn't the response he wanted to hear. His eyes narrowed in offense. "No. That's not the solution."

"Then there is no solution."

"If you come home with me, you'll never have to worry about it."

I stared into my glass.

"Button." His voice came out gentle, the exact opposite of how it sounded just a moment ago. "I'll keep you safe. You have my word."

"Like how you kept me safe from those bounty hunters?"

"I would have gotten you back. I was just one street away when you ran for it."

"Why didn't you stop me at the airport?"

"There wasn't time. Airports have strict security. For someone on the run, that was the safest place for you to be."

A part of me hated him for not stopping me. A part of me hated him for letting me go. His indifference hurt just as much as his cold rejection. "Why haven't you contacted me?"

"I assumed you didn't want me to."

"But then you show up when I start seeing someone…"

His expression didn't change. It was just as cold and stoic as before. "For the past few months, I've…been lost. When I sleep at night, I still stay on the left side of the bed even though you aren't there. I stopped taking my meals in the dining room because you weren't sitting across from me anymore. I still haven't gone into your bedroom since you left. Lars had the window repaired, but I haven't checked on it. When I go to work, I can't concentrate. I kept telling myself this feeling would go away. But it hasn't."

I held my breath as I listened to every word. It was a confession I didn't expect to hear. He actually felt something for me—whatever it was. He wasn't indifferent to my absence. Our time apart was difficult for him like it was difficult for me.

"Lars said something to me…and I haven't stopped thinking about it. And then I watched your GPS coordinates obsessively. Based on your movements, I figured out your routine. When you started spending every weekend on Park Avenue, I figured it out...and I couldn't handle it."

I wondered what Lars had said, but I didn't dare ask.

"I admit I didn't approach you in the best way. If you shot me, I wouldn't have blamed you. But I was just so...angry."

"Like how I was when I saw you kiss Jasmine." I'd looked out the window and saw her kissing him in the fields. Rage like I'd never known took me. I'd never been heartbroken like that. The betrayal hurt me to the core.

"She kissed me," he corrected. "And yes, that's exactly how I felt."

"Looks like we're even."

"No. Not even close." Tension filled the space between us. It hung heavily in the air, reminding me how betrayed he felt when I slept with Jason. "I've never been jealous before." He took a long drink to mask his anger.

"Why haven't you slept with anyone? Three months is a long time..." Crow was a man with specific needs. If he didn't unleash his dark urges, they would consume him.

He swirled his glass but didn't take a drink. He set it beside his water, the dark wine half gone. When he turned his eyes on me, they were impossible to read. He didn't seem angry or annoyed with the question. "I didn't want to."

I waited for him to elaborate because that answer wasn't enough.

His thin lips remained closed, refusing to speak another word.

"You didn't want to?" I didn't believe that for a second. Maybe he did miss me, but sex wasn't emotional for him. It was just about getting off. He could use anyone for that, not just me.

"No."

My eyes narrowed. "And that's it?"

"Why is that hard to believe?"

"I don't know…maybe because Jasmine was at your beck and call whenever you wanted her." I was sure she'd figured out I was gone and tried to get under his sheets more than once. Why would he turn her away if I wasn't there anymore?

"You know my type. I like smart, strong, and proud women. She's none of those things."

"But you slept with her before."

"That was before my tastes changed." He gave me a knowing look.

"Then why didn't you look for someone else with those traits?"

He rested his hand on the table, and his slender fingers thudded gently against the tablecloth. "Like I said, I didn't want to."

My eyes narrowed in annoyance. "You made it very clear you were never mine."

"I wasn't."

Everything he said contradicted what he'd said in the past. My neck was sore from the constant pull back and forth.

"But now I am."

The frustration left my limbs, and my stomach tightened in response. My eyes automatically searched his face for a trace of a lie. Did he really say that or did I just imagine it?

He rested his arms on the table and leaned forward. His voice came out low, so no one else could overhear us. The look he gave me was terrifying but beautiful at the same time. "And I want you to be mine again."

***

Penelope Sky

When we entered the bedroom, he came behind me and unzipped my dress. It was black with a lacy pattern. It fit the curves of my body perfectly, like he knew my measurements offhand.

It fell to the floor at my feet.

He immediately unfastened my strapless bra and let it fall to the floor. His lips found my shoulder, and he kissed it gently. The scruff from his chin caused the right kind of friction I'd missed. He slowly moved closer to my collarbone.

And I anxiously hoped he would nip at me.

His tongue licked the skin right over the bone. Then he nicked me with his teeth, giving me a nibble just like he did when we were in bed together.

I couldn't help it. I moaned.

His hands moved around my waist then trailed up my stomach. He gathered my tits in his hands and massaged them aggressively. His mouth moved to my ear, and his breaths filled my canal. "Button." My nipples hardened, and he gathered them in his fingertips before he pinched them lightly.

My back arched into his chest, immediately reacting to the aggressive touch. I said I wouldn't sleep

94

with him tonight, but my resolve was quickly slipping away.

His hand continued to grope my tits while the other moved down my stomach. Slowly, his fingers glided over my belly button and into the lace of my panties. Gently, they migrated to my throbbing clitoris then pressed against it.

I arched my back again.

"This is mine. Do you understand me?" His lips moved against my ear, his heavy breaths igniting me.

"Crow…" I gave in to his control and said his name when I shouldn't have. I missed this so much. I missed it more than I would admit to myself. He took control of the situation and made the decisions for both of us. All I had to do was enjoy it.

"You missed me as much as I missed you."

"Yes…"

He pulled his fingers out of my panties then yanked the fabric down my thighs. When I was naked, he undressed behind me, removing his suit and tie. His boxers were stripped away and kicked across the floor.

As much as I wanted to do this, I knew I couldn't. "I said no."

He turned me around until we were face-to-face. His hand fisted my hair aggressively and gripped the steep curve in my back. I was pulled so close to him that my chest pressed against his every time I took a breath. "Your mind and body are at war with each other. And I know who's going to win." He lifted me off the ground then lay me on the bed underneath him. His hands rested against either side of my head, and his thighs separated mine. "You've already kissed me. You've already touched me. What difference does it make?" His fingers interlocked with mine, and he pinned my hands to the mattress.

"It does make a difference."

He bowed his head until his nose brushed against mine. His quiet breaths fell on my face, the hunger obvious in the way he gripped my hands. He was the hunter, and I was the hunted. He stared at my lips for several heartbeats before he kissed me. The embrace was softer than the one we'd shared before. He concentrated on the feel of my lips, giving me purposeful kisses that were both delicate and passionate.

My lips immediately moved with his like they had a mind of their own. I tasted the bitter wine on his lips and felt my body tighten underneath him. My ankles met around his waist, and I wanted a night of unbridled passion. The moment reminded me of all our nights together, making love in front of the fireplace.

He pulled his lips away until there was just an inch of space between us.

I almost whimpered because the withdrawal was painful.

"I miss hearing you come." His intense gaze met mine, desperate and powerful at the same time.

The area between my legs immediately throbbed. He hadn't been inside me for so long, and I craved that feeling. I wanted the connection we once shared. I missed it more than I would ever admit.

He gave my lips another kiss before he slowly moved down my body. Kisses were placed on my tits and my stomach. His large hands widened my legs as his mouth drew closer. He ran his tongue along my hips then kissed the inside of my thighs.

Oh god.

I should've put an end to it, but I didn't. Instead, I gripped the sheets underneath me and prepared for that warm mouth against my heat. His eyes locked with mine as he kissed the skin surrounding the area, purposely teasing me. He never looked sexier than when his face was pressed between my legs.

Finally, his mouth sealed over my folds, and he gave me a scorching kiss.

"Oh my god…" My back arched, and I dug my fingertips into the mattress. Ecstasy shot through my body immediately, making my toes curl and nipples harden. Without any embarrassment, I widened my legs because I wanted more of that handsome mouth.

He kissed me again, and this time, he circled his tongue around my clitoris. He used forceful pressure to bring me to life. He kissed and sucked the area, giving me the delectable head I missed so much. He sucked my clit again before he gripped my hands on the sheets and interlocked our fingers. He kept me in place, so I couldn't move. "You want me to stop?"

My head was in the clouds, and I couldn't think about anything besides that warm mouth around my pussy. "No." No one could hold it against me. I had a gorgeous man between my legs, and it seemed like he enjoyed it even more than I did. It was the perfect fantasy. "No."

He moved his mouth between my legs again and kissed me harder than before. His tongue did magical

Buttons and Pain

things, and I found myself writhing and moaning for the man who broke my heart.

He used his tongue to circle my clit harder, hitting me in the right spot so I'd go over the edge.

"God...right there." I twisted against his hands, but they were locked in place. My hips immediately tilted upward as the collision hit me like a freight train. It was powerful and blinding. It was so good that I couldn't believe I forgot just how amazing it felt. "Crow..." I didn't even realize I'd said his name until the damage was done. I was a slave to this man all over again.

His kisses softened as the high left my body. Slowly, I started to relax. My hips came down, and my fingertips stopped squeezing his. My breathing returned to normal, but my nipples were still hard, and my chest was covered with sweat.

Crow crawled up my body until we were facing each other. The residue from my body was smeared across his lips. Seeing my arousal shine on his mouth made my legs automatically squeeze his hips.

My hands glided up his chest, feeling the grooves of muscle. I wanted to sink my claws into him and never let go. Instantly, my body allowed him to possess me. That invisible cord that once bound me to him was tight around my throat. My heart was made of steel and would never let him in again, but the rest of my body bowed to him.

"I want you." He moved his body against mine, his thick cock pressed against my tender folds. He slowly grinded against me, his throbbing dick desperate to be inside me. He leaked pre-come onto my already drenched pussy.

It took all my strength to combat the powerful desires in my body. I'd already done too many things with Crow that I regretted. The damage was already done. But sleeping with him would only make things worse. I had to be strong. "Tomorrow."

He growled against my face, his eyes shining with defiance.

"Tomorrow," I repeated.

He finally pulled away and lay on the bed beside me. His hard cock still lay against his stomach, thick and ready to plow me if I changed my mind.

I wasn't sure if I could lie beside him all night while keeping my hands to myself. He'd have to put on some clothes if he wanted to make that happen.

Buttons and Pain

He turned off the bedside lamp, and the bedroom fell into darkness. Then he wrapped his arms around me and pulled me hard against his chest. He hooked my leg over his waist and rested his forehead against mine.

Thinking with its own mind, my arm wrapped around his neck, and I closed my eyes. I could feel his gaze on me, the burn of his eyes as they stared at my face. I didn't look at him because I didn't trust myself to see into those haunted eyes. I hung on the precipice of temptation. If I strayed too far, I'd fall headfirst into the abyss known as Crow Barsetti.

His deep voice came into my ear. "Good night, Button."

"Good night, Crow."

Penelope Sky

Chapter Nine

Pearl

I dreaded the conversation I was about to have with Jason. He would be upset with me, and he had every right to be. The guilt was eating me down to the core of my soul, and I couldn't shake the feeling. He'd been so supportive, and I felt like I betrayed him. We weren't in a relationship. In fact, we hadn't even gone out to dinner together. But I still felt like I had done something wrong.

He answered the door with the same cold expression he wore the last time I saw him. He was in jeans and a t-shirt, and his hair was damp since he'd just gotten out of the shower. When he didn't speak, I knew he was still irritated with me.

"Can I come in?"

"Sure." He walked into the kitchen and stood at the counter. His arms were across his chest. The muscles of his arms were tight, and his usually bright eyes were dark.

I stood on the opposite side of the counter and felt his hostility seep into my pores. "Jason, we need to talk—"

"Yeah, we do. And I think I should go first."

Buttons and Pain

He was already pissed at me for the way we left our last argument. When I dropped this new bomb on him, he would be even more pissed. "Okay."

"I don't know what we are, but I think we should take a step back. After the other night, I just don't feel comfortable moving forward."

I didn't change my expression, but I was definitely surprised. We had a tense moment, but I didn't realize it bothered him so much. "Can you be more specific?"

He leaned against the refrigerator, keeping miles between us. "Every time we have sex, it moves to something else. You want me to spank you or tie you up... I know you went through a lot over the past year. You never talk about it, but I can imagine how horrible it was. And...I feel like you're projecting these experiences onto me, and it makes me uncomfortable."

"Jason, that's not what I was doing. I just...I like stuff like that." The best sex I'd ever had was with Crow. In the beginning, I didn't like the twisted things he did to me. But now, vanilla was my least favorite kind of sex. I wanted the kinky stuff, the dark stuff.

"But you didn't like that stuff before."

"Things change, Jason. We haven't been together in years. You aren't the same in bed either."

"But I'm not doing weird stuff."

I swallowed my offense and let it go. "It's not weird. I like it, and I'm not ashamed to admit it."

"Well, I don't. And I can't stop thinking about...you know."

That hurt the most. Crow never looked at me like I was damaged goods. He fucked me like I was the sexiest woman in the world. In his eyes, Bones had never touched me. Crow refused to allow me to feel sorry for myself. He expected me to be the strong woman I'd always been. "Jason, you need to stop looking at me like a rape victim."

"Look, I can't help it. I try not to, but it's difficult. If you didn't ask me to spank you with my belt or tie you up, I'd be able to look past it. But I can't."

I hated it when people viewed me as weak. What happened to me wasn't my fault, and to hold it against me was simply wrong. Maybe Jason didn't understand, but it was the most hurtful thing he could say to me. "I'm still me..."

He bowed his head, and a quiet sigh left his lips. He closed his eyes for a moment before he reopened them. His arms fell to his sides, and he came closer to me. "I know. Pearl, I still love you. I will always love you. But I don't think I can handle this."

"I understand." Maybe only a man like Crow could deal with my past. Maybe only someone just as scarred and ruined could look into my eyes and see everything below the surface. When he moved inside me, it was only the two of us. We didn't think about the men and women before each other.

"I'm sorry... I hope I didn't hurt you."

"Don't feel bad, Jason. You're being honest, and I completely understand."

His hand snaked to mine on the counter, and he gently brushed his thumb across my knuckles. "I still want to be friends. I still want to see you."

He may not feel that way after I told him about Crow. Even though Jason broke up with me and things felt distant for a while, my actions were still inexcusable. "I would love that. But there's something I need to talk to you about too."

***

Jason sat across from me at the table. He was speechless, saying nothing for nearly two minutes after I finished talking. He rubbed his chin with his fingertips and stared at the surface of the table.

"I know it's a lot to take in... I don't expect you to understand."

"So this guy captured you and kept you as a prisoner for a year...but you fell in love with him?"

When someone else said it, I understood just how ludicrous it was. "Yeah."

"But he didn't feel the same way."

"No." That cold reminder made me feel like shit all over again.

"And he's here now?"

"Yeah."

"And you kissed him?"

I nodded. "Yeah." After months of silence, I thought I would be able to resist him. But like no time had passed, I was his prey all over again.

"Okay..." He continued to rub his chin. "You're right. I don't get it. It sounds like Stockholm syndrome."

"It's not." Crow had never done anything harmful to me. He didn't even make good on his threat to rape me. He took care of me when he could have done worse things. I respected him because he deserved it.

"Does that mean you're seeing him again?"

I couldn't mention the button system. Jason would never understand it. "No, not really. He's here, and we've talked, but we aren't getting back together."

"Then why is he here?"

Jealousy. Possessiveness. Insanity. "To check on me."

Jason narrowed his eyes in suspicion. "Couldn't he have just called?"

"Yeah, but he likes to do things in a specific way." My relationship with Crow could never be explained to a man like Jason. After the ordeal I suffered through, I wasn't normal anymore. And normal people would never understand me. "So...are we okay?"

"What do you mean?"

"I kissed him and fooled around with him last night. You and I weren't serious, but...I still felt guilty for doing it. I hope I didn't hurt you."

"No, it's okay," he said quickly. "Like I said, I've been unsure of this relationship for a few days now. You don't need to feel bad."

I was glad we talked this out and preserved our friendship. "I'm glad to hear that. You're my only friend, Jason. I don't want to lose you."

His eyes softened from across the table. His hand snaked around the surface until it reached mine. "You could never lose me. Friends forever, alright?"

I smiled. "Friends forever."

"But as your friend, I have to say this thing with Crow is beyond my understanding. I'm not sure if spending time with him is such a good idea. Honestly, he sounds like a psychopath."

I tried not to chuckle. "I'm not getting serious with him again. He'll be here for a while, and then he'll leave. I'll probably never see him again."

Jason nodded. "So...are you still in love with him?"

The question caught me off guard, and there was nowhere to hide. "It doesn't matter if I am or not. It doesn't change anything."

***

After Jason and I had dinner, I returned to my apartment. When I walked in the door, I almost collided with a concrete wall. "Shit. Can you just wait outside like a normal person?"

Buttons and Pain

He shoved me against the refrigerator then pinned my hands above my head. His grip was ice-cold and powerful, and he crushed me with his strong chest. "Did you end it with him?"

"Uh, hello to you too."

He squeezed my hands.

"I didn't end it with him because I didn't have to."

His eyebrows furrowed as his eyes narrowed. He pressed me farther into the fridge. "What does that mean?"

"He broke up with me." I twisted out of Crow's grasp and moved away. I was suffocated against the fridge and needed some air. I tossed my purse on the counter.

He didn't crowd me again, but his eyes followed me closely. "Elaborate."

"I asked him to do certain things in the bedroom he wasn't comfortable with. So, he thought it was best if we stayed friends."

Crow clenched his jaw at the subject.

"So, I didn't have to do anything."

"Did you tell him about us?"

Penelope Sky

"Yes. I said you were in town, but you would be leaving soon." The sooner Crow got out of there, the better. I gripped the edge of the counter and looked out the window to the city beyond. My conversation with Jason replayed in my mind, and I couldn't ignore the pain it caused.

Crow watched me silently, reading the sadness in my eyes like a billboard. "You're hurt."

"Yes…"

He came closer to me but didn't touch me. He stood beside me, his eyes burning into the side of my face. "Talk to me, Button." His fingers moved to my cheek, and he tucked my hair behind my ear.

"He said he couldn't stop thinking about the fact that I've…you know." Jason didn't look at me with genuine eyes. All he could see were the scars other men had inflicted. I wasn't desirable because I'd been used.

Crow wrapped his arm around my waist then steered me into his chest. He rested his lips against my forehead while his strong arms formed a steel cage around me. With his protection, he kept all the pain and suffering out. "He was never good enough for you, Button." His lips moved against my forehead as he spoke. "A real man doesn't think about the men before him. He erases them."

I already felt safe with this man. He said the right things and touched me the way I needed to be touched. I already felt myself falling deeply into him again, relishing the strength and power he radiated constantly.

"You know what I see when I look at you?" He fisted my hair and pulled my head back, forcing me to meet his gaze. "I see a strong woman who refuses to give up. I see a resilient fire that can't be put out. I see the sexiest and most desirable woman on the planet. If he can't handle your past, he doesn't deserve your future." Crow cupped my face and kissed me. "Don't let him bring you down, alright?"

All I could do was nod.

"Because the woman I know doesn't let anyone tear her apart—not even me."

Chapter Ten

Crow

"Pack your things." I tossed an empty bag on her bed.

She stood in the doorway with her arms over her chest. "Why?"

"Unless you want to be naked all the time, I suggest you bring a few things." I opened her underwear drawer and took a peek. "But if you just want to pack some panties, I'm okay with that too." I winked before I shut the drawer. I was finally getting what I wanted, and I couldn't contain my good mood. The last few months of my life had been hell without her. I finally admitted it to both her and myself. Now, I wanted her underneath me, her legs wrapped around my waist. Her pussy tasted better than I remembered, and my cock wanted a taste too.

"Jason and I aren't seeing each other anymore, so there's no bargain to fulfill."

I was her crutch when she lost her resolve, but the second she defied me, I was her enemy. "You're incorrect."

"I'm not sleeping with him. So the deal is off."

Buttons and Pain

I walked across the room until I was face-to-face with her. She kept a strong expression on her face, but I knew she was trying to hide her fear. I made her tense when she didn't even realize it. Her body naturally reacted to mine, doing a quiet dance we both felt. "Work off your remaining debt, and he doesn't die. That's the deal."

"But I'm not seeing him anymore."

"Does that mean you don't care if I snap his neck?" I crowded her personal space and forced her back against the doorframe. "Because I will, Button. I'll kill that piece of shit with a snap of my fingers. If that's not what you want, then pack your shit. Now."

That rebellious fire burned in her eyes, highlighting the beautiful features of her perfect face. Her lips automatically tightened, and her shoulders became tense. Her nipples hardened inside her blouse. I couldn't see through her shirt, but I understood her body language so well I knew exactly what was happening. "I don't believe you."

My hand immediately wrapped around her throat, and I gave her a threatening squeeze. "If you think I won't kill the man who fucked you, you don't know me very well." I dropped my hold before I actually hurt her. The violent side of me emerged the moment I didn't get my way. I wanted her back in my bed and underneath me—where she belonged. "Don't make me ask you again."

She remained by the door for nearly a minute, her fingers touching her slender neck. There wasn't a bruise, but she still felt the pain. She confessed she'd asked Jason to do the same things I did to her in bed. There was no denying she still wanted me. And her wet pussy told me the same thing last night. Finally, she cooperated and packed her things.

I watched her, victory in my eyes.

***

The second we entered my hotel room, I lifted her onto the counter in the kitchen and stood between her legs. Nothing held me back anymore, so I gripped her waist and kissed her harshly on the mouth. My kiss was so violent I nearly bruised her lips.

But she kissed me back—with the same desire.

The world disappeared, and Button was the only thing that remained. I forgot about my lonely existence back at the estate. I forgot about all the scotch I drank and the regret that festered in my chest cavity. It was the first time I'd felt at peace in months.

Buttons and Pain

I fisted her hair and recognized the familiar softness. It was longer than it used to be but contained the same smell of vanilla and orange. That scent stayed in my bedroom for weeks after she left. But one day, it disappeared—and I felt lost.

My blood pounded in my ears, and my heart swayed as it beat in time to hers. And that's when I finally felt whole for the first time in months. All the pain, the regret, and the anger disappeared.

I severed our kiss and looked into her face. "I won't kill him."

With puckered and red lips, she stared at me.

"But I'm not going to leave until you work for every single button." I would never take her freedom away. There were countless times in the past when I wanted to chain her to a wall and own her completely, but that fire in her eyes stopped me. She commanded my loyalty with only her silence. She had more power than she realized—and I hoped she'd never figure it out.

"When I pay the debt, you'll leave?"

I died a little inside when I heard the hope in her voice. "Yes."

"Why do you want me to repay these buttons at all? I don't understand."

Because every single day was torture without her. My life flashed by in a meaningless blur. I lived in the most beautiful place on the planet, I had the kind of luxury people only dreamed about, and I could have any woman I wanted.

But none of that mattered after she left. "Because I want you."

"And that's all?" she whispered.

Maybe if I had her again I would get her out of my system so I could move on. Maybe things didn't end the way they should have. "We never had a chance to say goodbye. I wasn't prepared for you to leave when you got on that plane. I wasn't finished with you."

The desire in her eyes slowly started to fade. If there was something else she wanted me to say, I wished she would tell me. "I'll get the last of those buttons. And then I never want to see you again."

I ignored the sting as it stretched across my skin. The burn was hotter than ash, and it scorched me through the inside of my body. My expression remained the same, and I swallowed the hurt all the way down to my stomach. I knew where her pain came from. She said three little words to me that I never said back. And she would never forgive me for that.

But perhaps I could change her mind.

Perhaps I could make her fall for me all over again—and she would give some of those buttons back in exchange for my affection. And she would be mine until the end of time. "Okay."

***

"What do you want?" She stepped into the bedroom and slowly undressed. Her fingertips played with the top of her jeans before she finally undid the button and the zipper. Slowly, she pulled them down her long legs and stepped out of them. Her hips swayed from left to right as she moved, and without even trying, she looked like the sexiest woman I'd ever seen.

My cock was hard in my jeans, and it pressed painfully against the zipper. It was desperate to be free, to rub against her slick pussy until it slipped inside. I wanted to stretch her and erase the memory of the man who didn't deserve her. If that guy saw her as a lost cause, then he'd never truly looked at her. He didn't see what I saw. If he'd bothered to pay attention, he would have noticed that fire in her eyes that never dimmed. He would have treasured the unmistakable sexuality that exuded from every inch of her skin. He would have begged her to stay the moment she wanted to be with me.

Fucking idiot.

It was the first time my jealousy waned. When I saw the hurt in her eyes after Jason rejected her, I wanted to fix everything. I wanted to convince her he was the problem, not her. All her life, men had disappointed her, and frankly, I was no different. I was the first man she allowed to take care of her, provide for her, and to protect her.

And then I hurt her.

I couldn't blame her if she never trusted me again.

Button turned around and faced me, standing in her t-shirt and black panties. The shirt hugged her waist and rib cage, showing off her naturally sexy curves. Her wide hips slimmed down to an hourglass figure. When I stared at her from behind, her curves looked even more prominent. To my cock, it was the mecca.

Buttons and Pain

She locked her gaze on mine with proud confidence that made her innately sexy. No other woman could pull that off without looking conceited. A woman who understood she was a perfect ten immediately became a zero. But a woman who never scored herself to begin with was a perfect ten.

Button pulled the shirt over her head and stood in a black bra. It was a push-up, and it pressed her perky tits together tightly. It was a landing strip for my dick, so she could be tit-fucked until her chest was sore. "You never answered my question." She walked closer to me, her authoritative gaze never leaving mine.

My eyes moved to her slender neck and the hollow of her throat. My lips ached to press endless kisses there, to scorch her body with my marks. How I let this beautiful woman walk away was a mystery to me. I'd spent my evenings beating off like a teenager because I couldn't have the real thing. "And what question was that?"

Her slender arms wrapped around her torso, and her fingers undid the clasp that held her bra together. It immediately came loose, and the straps fell to the front of her body. Slowly, gravity took its toll until the bra fell to the floor with a quiet tap.

I missed those tits. Fucking gorgeous.

My tongue suddenly felt too big for my mouth. It wanted to lave her nipples in painful kisses before it sucked them raw. I'd already seen her beautiful body more times than I could count, but now that she was submitting to me, my cock was in a rage. Having her bow to me, give me the control, was the biggest turn-on of all.

She was finally mine.

She grabbed the straps of her thong before she pulled them down her long and exquisite legs. The heaven between her legs was perfectly maintained, and the nub was calling my name. "What do you want?"

Her tits were hard, and her lips were parted. I couldn't decide what I wanted. I wanted everything all at once. I wanted that pretty mouth around my dick, but I also wanted to be ten inches deep inside her.

She closed the distance between us with her panties still in her hand. Her fingertips moved to my jeans, and she slowly unbuttoned them. When the zipper came down, my cock was finally free of its restraints. It pressed against the front of my boxers, reaching out to her like it had a mind of its own.

Buttons and Pain

My arms stayed by my sides despite how much I wanted to touch her. Her act was sexy as hell, and I wanted to see what else she would do. She took the lead tonight, and I actually liked handing over the reins.

She pulled my jeans and boxers down to my ankles then rose to her full height again. She was significantly shorter than me, my cock level with her stomach. But her height didn't make her weak. She was the tallest person in any room she entered.

She placed her black panties against my length then massaged my shaft, using the soft lace to stimulate the hard skin of my cock. Some of her wetness was in the fabric, and I could feel it spread from my balls to my tip.

Fuck.

She moved up and down with slow movements, focusing on the feel of every second rather than the stimulation of going as fast as possible.

Damn, did she understand how sexy she was?

"What do you want?" She pressed her lips to the corner of my mouth but didn't give me a kiss. She teased me, hovering her kissable lips just inches from my mouth.

My cock ached because the fantasy was better than I ever could have imagined. It was the same as it was in Italy—but somehow better. I had complete dominion, and I didn't truly understand the awesome responsibility until now. "On your knees." The power grew in my spine, starting from my groin and spreading to the back of my skull. I finally had this woman, and she was mine to enjoy—exclusively.

She dropped to the hardwood floor and never complained about the pain on her knees. She kept her small hand around my shaft, the panties bunched near my balls. Her fingertips slowly played with my sac, massaging them tenderly.

"I'm gonna fuck your mouth." I gathered her hair in my palm then held it tightly against the back of her head. The panties were still bunched in place, but I wouldn't remove them. I loved feeling the slickness of her pussy from the delicate fabric.

I grabbed the base of my cock then rubbed my tip across her soft lips. Immediately, she started to kiss it, her tongue emerging and rubbing over the sensitive skin. Her eyes were bright like fire, and I knew wetness was beginning to soak between her legs. She still loved my big cock in her mouth.

Some things never changed.

Buttons and Pain

I inserted myself inside her, moving far down her throat until every inch was deep within. Like the pro she was, she took it without gagging. She held her breath because her throat was blocked. Once I pulled out to the front of her mouth, she took a deep breath. Then I shoved myself back inside.

The feel of the blow job wasn't even the best part. Nothing could beat the view. This woman was my obsession, and to see her on her knees like I was her king did amazing things to my ego. It just made my cock thicker.

I fucked her deep in the throat for a few minutes, preserving the moment in the back of my mind, so I could treasure it later. This was something I would beat off to when she wasn't around. I just hoped I didn't have to use it.

I pulled my cock out of her warm throat then commanded her to lie on the bed. "On your back. Head on the pillow." I pumped my dick as I watched her obey me. My cock throbbed in my hand because I was so eager to be inside her.

She lay on the bed with her head on the pillow. Like a slave, she waited for my next command.

I crawled on top of her then placed another pillow under her head. Her neck curved, and her face was nearly upright. She stared at me with slight confusion, but she didn't ask a single question.

I groped her tits and laved the valley of her breasts with wet kisses. My cock hung forward, dangling just an inch over her stomach. Once her chest was wet with my spit, I positioned myself on top of her. "Press your tits together."

She did as I asked, creating a distinct seam between them.

"Open your mouth."

She did as I commanded.

My spine shivered at her obedience. Her mouth fell open with the snap of a finger, and her eyes didn't show her hatred. She was just as aroused as I was, wanting my dick between her tits.

I pressed my cock between her gorgeous tits until my head emerged on the other side. It entered her mouth and rested on her tongue. "Button, keep your tits tight together." I thrust my hips forward and backward, sliding through her wet boobs. She kept them tight like I asked, and her tongue kissed my tip every time it reached her. I stared at her the entire time, watching her tits shake over and over. I'd never tit-fucked her before, and I enjoyed it immensely.

She kept her tongue out as a landing strip, prepared for my dick every time I gave it to her. Somehow, she was a better submissive than ever before. There was no fight in her because she wanted me to conquer her.

The ecstasy began distantly in the bottom of my shaft. I could feel the euphoria creep to the tip, the explosion slowly approaching over the horizon. I wanted to let go and give in to the carnal desire to come all over her face, but I stopped myself.

I removed my cock from between her beautiful tits and grabbed her by the hips. I pulled her underneath me and widened her legs. My cock rested against my stomach, gleaming with a mixture of her saliva and mine. It twitched with anticipation, ready to bury itself deep in this woman who stole my entire focus.

She gripped my forearms, and her long nails dug deep into my skin. She almost drew blood with the steel-like grip. The harder she clung to me, the harder I wanted to fuck her. She kept up an act of indifference when we spoke, but now that we were naked together and ready to fuck, she was anything but indifferent.

I positioned myself on top of her until my face hovered just inches from hers. Her lips gleamed from the saliva that she stroked onto my long cock, and her white teeth could be seen through the slight parting of her mouth. I'd seen that look a hundred times and knew what it meant.

She wanted me to kiss her.

I held my weight on my arms and slowly sank into her until our mouths touched. Like I'd never kissed her in my life, a fiery explosion erupted deep inside my chest. It was a growl that vibrated across my skin and emerged deep in my throat. All the muscles in my body tightened in reaction, and I fisted the sheets underneath me.

She gasped quietly into my mouth, getting the exact touch she craved. Her lips trembled against me as if she'd been stung by a fire ant. Her legs wrapped around my waist, and her ankles hooked together like an anchor. She pulled me tighter against her, wanting me inside her now—not later.

Her hands cupped my face then drifted into my hair. She fingered the strands with such force she nearly pulled my hair out of my scalp. Her body rocked with mine, and her hips grinded against me, anxious to feel me inside her. "Crow...fuck me."

Buttons and Pain

Fuck.

I adjusted my hips until my cock pressed against her entrance. Putting my weight into the thrust, I moved completely inside her in one swift movement. Her pussy was tighter than it used to be, but my cock slid in with ease.

Because she'd never been so soaked.

"Yes..." Her hands dragged down my back, and her nails were still sharp as daggers. She panted into my mouth because she couldn't kiss me. All she could do was moan—moan for me. "Crow."

I curled her body until she was a tiny ball underneath me. Her legs were tight around my waist, and her arms were around my torso. With her bent and squirming, I fucked her hard against the mattress like a sailor who had just docked to shore.

My arm snaked underneath her frame until I reached the back of her neck. I wrapped my fingers around the back of her throat and gave her a firm squeeze. With the tight grip, I moved her up and down my length while slamming into her hard from above. "Button..." Her pussy was heaven after the long dry spell I'd been through. But it was worth the wait because this moment was powerful and crippling. The

Penelope Sky

connection we used to share was back in full force. I felt it, and I knew she felt it too.

I couldn't last any longer. Beating off didn't give me the stamina I once had. My cock needed to release inside her, to give her so much come that her pussy couldn't hold it all. I needed to erase every trace of the man who'd replaced me. "Button, come for me." I deepened my thrusts and rubbed my pelvic bone against her throbbing clit. I wanted to watch her come, so I could get off to it.

Her cheeks flushed pink, the distant color of a spring rose just after winter. Her lips turned ruby red in the aftermath of my bruising mouth. Her nipples hardened to daggers, and slowly, her beautiful mouth formed the distinct O I'd been waiting for. Then she let out a scream that nearly shattered my eardrums. "Oh god..." Her head rolled back, and her nails almost cut through my skin. "Yes, that's it."

Her pussy tightened around me, and another wave of slickness surrounded my cock. It grew wetter and warmer between us. My cock thickened in preparation, and I gripped her neck tighter, practically bruising her. "Take. It. All." I shoved myself completely inside her, giving her every inch. And then I released with a moan I couldn't contain. It left my lips and

128

escaped like a growl. My fingers kept squeezing her, and I had to force myself to let go so I wouldn't choke her.

I remained on top of her because I didn't want to leave, not just yet. I used to spend most of my time buried deep inside her, and when she left without notice, I had to face the cold reality that she was gone. She was underneath me now, and I wanted to treasure every moment with her.

Her eyes were full of satisfaction, and her breathing slowly returned to normal. Her thick hair was sprawled across the pillow, and her fingertips loosened their hold on my skin. Her beautiful blue eyes eventually faded from a vibrancy to dormancy. She wasn't only satisfied but exhausted.

I kissed her, giving her a soft embrace to make up for the harsh way I did it before. Now that the passion was gone and it was just the two of us, I wanted to give her a caress that showed more than lust. I didn't just miss her because the sex was great between us. I missed her for a lot of reasons—reasons I couldn't explain.

I pulled out of her, feeling my cock ache in pain from being separated from the heaven between her legs. When I lay beside her, I spooned her from behind, the usual arrangement we took when we slept together. I didn't know what time it was, and she didn't set an alarm for the following morning. She didn't ask for her buttons, and I didn't offer them.

Then we fell asleep.

Buttons and Pain

Chapter Eleven

Pearl

When I woke up the following morning, I instantly smelled coffee. The scent was unmistakable. It was rich in aroma, and the distant sound of the brewer landed on my ears. The light from the window hit my eyelids, and I knew the sun was rising.

And that meant I had to go to work.

I got out of bed and snatched the first shirt I found on the floor. It was Crow's, and it reached past my knees because it was a zillion sizes too big. I felt the fabric in my fingertips and immediately remembered doing the exact same thing every morning when I lived with him a lifetime ago.

I walked into the kitchen and saw Crow sitting at the table. Shirtless and gorgeous, he read the morning paper. Only his boxers were on, and his muscled and toned thighs reached out beneath the table. "Breakfast is on the stove. Lars didn't make it, but it's edible."

I scooped the eggs onto my plate and poured a cup of coffee. The cream and sugar were already sitting out because Crow knew exactly how I took it. I sat down in the seat across from him and glanced at the clock. I still had an hour before work, so I could take my time.

Crow read his paper and didn't look at me once. If the window behind him didn't show the Manhattan landscape, I would have assumed we were back at the estate in Tuscany. His five o'clock shadow was coming in strong, and his lips looked slightly chapped from all the hot kisses we shared last night.

God, last night was so good.

Jason never satisfied me like that. It wasn't dark, but it was certainly intense. Crow treated me like a piece of meat, but he did it right. I never felt more wanted and desirable. Jason always treated me like glass, like I would break at any moment. I must have had the best orgasm of my life because it knocked me out immediately.

"How did you sleep, Button?" He put down the paper and turned his amused eyes on me. His hair was messy from rolling around the night before, and there were scratches on his chest from the way I sank my claws into him. Somehow, all those things made him sexier.

"Good." Fucking fantastic, actually. I hadn't gotten a night of sleep like that since I shared a bed with him. I usually tossed and turned in the middle of the night, the old nightmares of Bones haunting me. Sometimes I would lay absolutely still but feel the rocking of the ship from my journey across the Atlantic. Sleeping with Jason didn't make anything better. Everything was exactly the same. But with Crow, it was nothing but calm serenity. When his arms were locked around me, nothing could hurt me. I would never admit it out loud, but he was the first man who made me feel safe. "You?"

"Like a rock." He drank his coffee then rubbed his fingers against the scruff coming in along his chin. It was thicker than usual because he hadn't shaved the day before. I'd never seen him with a full-grown beard, and I wondered how it would look on him. Would he look even more beautiful? Or just deadly?

Now that we were sitting across from each other civilly and our appetites had been satiated, I needed to get down to business. "Five." I laid my open palm on the table so he could deposit my payment onto it.

He never took his eyes off mine.

I kept my hand there and waited for my debt to be paid. I wasn't there because I wanted to get sucked into this nightmare again. I wanted to sever our ties forever so we could move on and never see each other again. The sex was amazing, and it felt incredible when he held me. But my heart had been smashed once before, and I wouldn't let it happen again. I kept it hidden deep inside my chest where he couldn't reach it. I could keep it safe for thirty buttons—but no longer than that.

He stared at me with narrowed eyes, uncooperative.

"Pay up." I beckoned him with my fingers.

"Two."

"Two?" I asked incredulously. "I said five."

"That was worth two, and we both know it." He drank his coffee with his elbows resting on the table. His stern expression told me this was nonnegotiable.

I guess I should have settled the payment before we fucked—like a whore. "The night before was worth one. So how was last night worth two?"

"It was vanilla. If anything, it should only be worth one."

Maybe restraints weren't used, but it was still long and aggressive. I felt like that night was worth a lot more than he gave me credit for. He didn't realize that those buttons represented more than mere payment. They represented the layers protecting my heart from his coldness.

"Two."

"Five."

He shook his head slightly. "Button."

I couldn't believe I was about to cave. But I recognized a dead-end when I saw one. "Fine."

He pulled two buttons out of his pocket and passed them to me across the table.

They were shiny and metallic. One had an image of a bow while the other was plain silver. I'd collected hundreds of buttons since I'd been captured by him, but I had nothing to show for it. These would be added to my hidden collection. "I have to go to work."

Crow didn't argue, but he wasn't happy about it. "I'll see you when you're off."

"I'm not coming here, Crow."

He crossed his arms over his chest, warning me not to defy him.

"I have plans. I'll see you tomorrow." I had to keep space between us. If I spent too much time with him, it would just make everything harder. I had to pace myself—take it slow.

"What plans?"

"I'm getting drinks with my coworkers."

"Do you normally do that?"

"About once a month."

His eyebrows furrowed in annoyance. "I'll join you."

"No," I snapped. "You aren't a coworker."

"I own you."

Those words hit me like a palm against my face. I rose to my feet and gripped the edge of the table. "You don't own me, Crow. I'm not your slave anymore, so I can do whatever the hell I want." I stormed off, leaving the buttons on the table behind me. After a great night, I was already pissed off at him. One minute, he'd pushed me away because I'd confessed how I truly felt, and then the next minute, he'd possessed me like he couldn't live without me. It made no sense, and I was fed up with it. He couldn't have it both ways.

I put on the clothes I was wearing the night before and stormed out of the hotel room.

Just when I got to the front door, he stopped me. "Button." He pressed his hand to the door, so I couldn't open it. His heavy mass blocked the way, and I was trapped.

"I'm going to be late." I still had plenty of time, but I was desperate to get away from this psychopath.

His arm circled my waist, and he guided me against the door. My back was pressed to the wood, and I was cornered like an animal. The predator had caught the prey, and there was nothing I could do except wait for the end. He dug one hand into my hair and forced my chin up, so I looked directly into his face. "Be mine again." His thumb moved across my cheek until it rested at the corner of my mouth. "Let me own you. Let me possess you. Let me have you." His lips hovered near mine, tempting me with a kiss.

"No." Every moment I was in his presence tore me down. A part of me wanted to go back to what we were. My life was much simpler then. I belonged somewhere. I had a home. I had a man who was brutally scarred just like me, and those cuts bound us together like family. Staying in that estate in the middle of Tuscany was the best therapy I could ever get. Even if I'd never been sold into slavery, I wasn't ever happy in America. I hadn't been happy with Jacob or anything else in my life. Crow gave me something I'd been searching for my entire life. But then he took it away. "You had me, and you didn't want me, Crow. You can't just change your mind about that."

"I've never not wanted you." He pressed his body farther into mine. "You know that."

"A few months of silence says otherwise." When I was alone for those months, it was easy to lie to myself and pretend I wasn't hurt. But as the words left my lips, the betrayal felt like a fresh wound he'd just given me. He broke my heart worse than I could have anticipated. He shattered me into infinite pieces—and this time, he couldn't put them back together. "I'm only doing this to settle the score. I'm only doing this so you'll disappear. So don't pretend we're back in Italy and everything is what it used to be. We can never go back to that. And don't you dare call me a slave ever again. Don't you dare say you own me. Because you don't deserve to own me."

***

I was in a ferocious mood all day.

I hated Crow for the way he'd emotionally tortured me, and I hated myself for being head over heels for him. Yes, he was sexy and smoldering. Yes, he was compassionate but not weak. But he was still a heartbreaker underneath that pretty package.

Buttons and Pain

I wouldn't get sucked into that again.

I couldn't believe it'd happened to begin with.

When I was working, I focused on the project that had been handed to me weeks ago. The best thing about my job was how easy it was to get lost in it. It was complex and challenging, and that kept my focus, so I didn't think about anything else.

After work, I got drinks with some of the guys. They mostly talked about sports and what they were going to do on their next vacation. I drank my beer and wished it were Tuscan wine. Then I went home, so I could be alone. If Crow was lurking inside my apartment, I would kick his ass.

Seriously.

I stepped inside then flicked on the lights. There was no food in my fridge, so I had to order a big-ass greasy pizza for dinner. I wished I made more money at my job, so I could hire Lars to work for me.

As I feared, that arrogant son of a bitch was there.

I tossed my purse on the counter and snagged a wooden rolling pin from one of the drawers. It wasn't a baseball bat, but it would have to do. "Asshole, I said I wanted the night off and—"

"Listen to me, and then I'll go." He stayed on the opposite side of the counter wearing a gray t-shirt and jeans. His face was cleanly shaven, and his hair was styled to perfection. The usual watch he wore was missing, but he still looked like an executive.

I didn't want to listen to whatever it was he had to say. "Make it quick."

He came around the island and moved closer to me.

I immediately stepped back, not in the mood to be touched. "There is good." There were two feet between us, but that still wasn't enough distance. I crossed my arms over my chest and closed my body off, making it clear he wasn't welcome.

He stood with his arms hanging by his sides, and his eyes told me he wanted to be closer. His hands were always on me every chance they got, and being denied that luxury was testing his patience.

I continued to stand there, waiting for whatever he had to say. Whatever it was, I was sure I wouldn't like it. The man was void of all emotion because he was a hollow shell. It was stupid of me ever to think he would change—especially for me.

"I finally understand how much I've hurt you."

Buttons and Pain

That was the last thing I expected him to say. I tried to keep my face expressionless, but the moment those words came tumbling out, my mouth softened from the grimace it'd been holding. My arms became weak against my chest, even my knees didn't feel as strong as they had a moment before. And all he'd said was a single sentence.

When he realized my walls had started to crumble, he stepped closer to me. His hands remained by his sides and he didn't touch me, but the yearning to grab me was obvious by the desire in his eyes. "I see what I've done to you, and I hate myself for that."

I hung on to every word, feeling my body pull toward his like a magnet. My mouth already wanted to kiss his, and my hands ached to grip his hard flesh. All the emotions I'd tried to battle came flooding out. The power he had over me was so strong, it was terrifying.

"Come back to Tuscany with me. I'll give you a home to call your own. I'll give you a life full of luxury, beauty, and respect. My bedroom won't just be mine but ours. You'll be the lady of the estate, just as entitled to it as I am. You'll have everything you could possibly want. Whatever it is, I'll give it to you."

"What exactly are you saying, Crow?" It sounded too good to be true, and I needed clarification before I made any hasty assumptions.

He closed the gap between us, and his hand immediately wrapped around the back of my neck. He looked down into my face, his darkening eyes taking in every reaction my features gave. "I'm yours, Button. I'll be devoted to you. I'll protect you. I'll give you everything you want. Come home with me. Home."

My hand wrapped around his wrist, feeling his powerful pulse. I counted the number of times it vibrated against my fingertips. The veins in his forearms protruded from underneath the skin because of the pronounced muscles that were strung so tight it was as if they were made of steel. "How long?"

His eyes narrowed when he didn't understand the question. "Forever."

I closed my eyes because that sounded like a dream come true. I wanted to spend every day under the Tuscan sun with this man. Despite his intensity and rage, he was the other half of my soul. I'd convinced myself I didn't love him anymore so I could move on with my life, but I knew that wasn't true. My lies weren't strong enough to fool me. "Crow, do you love me?" I didn't open my eyes because I didn't want to see his reaction. I didn't want to watch him say the painful word.

When he didn't say anything, that was my answer.

I opened my eyes and looked at him, feeling stung all over again. The same pain was written on his face because he hated himself for hurting me. He hated himself for not saying the words I wanted to hear.

"Then what's the point?" I whispered. "You want me to live with you, but for how long? You'll get tired of me and want someone else, someone new. And then I'll be shipped back here to start over once again. I can't do that, Crow."

He cupped my face with both hands, looking me straight in the eye. "I'll never get tired of you, Button. I've never felt this way about someone. If I go back without you, I'll just be miserable. I need you in my life. Without you, there is no me."

How could he say those things but not feel anything more? "I don't understand, Crow. You say these beautiful things to me, but you still don't love me. I can't give up everything to be with you unless we

143

feel the same way." Now my cards were on the table. I'd admitted I still felt the same way as I did before I left Italy. I hated myself for giving up that information so easily.

He lowered his hands to my shoulders while a quiet sigh escaped his lips. "I told you I don't feel love. I told you that I can't love anyone. It's not that I don't want to. I'm just incapable of feeling it." His hands moved to my waist, his head bowed. "But I can give you everything else besides that. I can give you my fidelity, my loyalty, my honesty, my wealth, my home—everything else. That should be good enough."

Maybe it would be enough for someone who didn't love him. Maybe it would be enough for a woman looking for security, wealth, and protection. But I didn't need any of those things. "Crow, I loved living with you because of you. I loved sleeping in that beautiful mansion because you were beside me. I loved looking out that window because I could watch you run through the fields. I loved Lars because I saw his devotion to you. When will you understand that it's not the things you offer me that keep me beside you?" My hands moved to his chest, resting over his heart. "It's just you."

Buttons and Pain

Chapter Twelve

Crow

The scotch they had at the hotel wasn't nearly as good as the stuff I had at home. But it had the same effect, so I kept drinking it. I sat on the couch in the living room and looked out the window to the city beyond. Button was probably in her tiny apartment eating a bowl of mac and cheese and watching cable.

She could be living in a mansion with me while staring across the endless grape fields.

I downed the rest of my glass before I refilled it. The last conversation we had kept playing in my mind like a broken record. She never said the words specifically, but she told me she still loved me. She refused to settle for part of me because she wanted everything.

Now we were at a stalemate.

I could lie and tell her I loved her just to get her to come home with me. But I would never forgive myself for lying to her when I vowed I never would. It was a promise we made to one another a lifetime ago. When it came to Button, I kept all my promises.

I really thought offering her everything else would be enough. If she were any other woman, she would have jumped on the offer like she'd won the lottery. Other women would spend my money on expensive clothes and jewelry, and lounge under the olive trees while reading a book in front of the pool. Whether I loved them or not, they wouldn't care.

But Button cared.

I could drug her and bring her back to Tuscany against her will. I could lock her up and keep her for my own amusement. The idea was tempting, so tempting that it made me hard in my jeans.

But I would never do that to her.

My cell phone rang, and I immediately grabbed it in the hope she was calling me. Maybe she'd changed her mind and had agreed to the terms. But I saw Cane's name on the screen instead. He hadn't called me since I arrived a week ago, and for my brother, that was unusual. I took the call, probably because I was drunk. "What?"

"Hello to you too."

"What?" I repeated.

"When are you coming home? We've got shit to do."

"I don't know…" I couldn't leave without her, but I couldn't stay in America much longer. Work required my attention back at home. I had a whole life of business waiting for me. But I couldn't leave her behind when I didn't know if she would be safe.

"What's taking so long? You said you were going to get Pearl and come home."

"She doesn't want to come with me." The sadness broke through my voice, and I felt my chest ache. I must have been really drunk if I was telling Cane this. I didn't even like my brother most of the time. He was a childish and irrational human being.

Cane paused over the line, knowing the conversation was much more serious than he'd anticipated. "What do you mean, man?"

"She said she doesn't want to come with me. She's done with me."

"I don't believe that," he said calmly. "There's something you aren't telling me."

The liquor took the lead, and I started rambling. "She'll only come back with me if I tell her I love her."

"Then just tell her," he snapped. "Problem solved."

"But I don't love her, Cane. You know that."

"Bullshit." His anger rose over the phone, reaching powerful volumes against my ear. "I've known you my entire life, and I've never—not once—seen you act this way with another woman. You don't just love this woman. You're head over heels, pathetically and stupidly, slit-your-own-throat in love with her. Don't lie to me and act like that isn't true."

I dragged my hand across my face, feeling the frustration burn deep inside my chest. "Cane, I don't."

"What the hell is wrong with you? Why won't you just admit it? If you're afraid to look like a pussy, you already look like a pussy by lying about it."

"Shut the hell up, Cane."

"No. I'm being serious."

"Fuck off."

"This is what it comes down to, Crow." He would normally fly off the handle when I insulted him, so the fact that he was staying so calm was a testament to his belief in this. "She's not like all the other women we've met in our lives. She's got a spine of steel and a mouth that rivals our own. I beat the shit out of her, and she survived. No one else would have handled that but her."

"Cane...you're just pissing me off." Talking about the terrible night when he nearly killed her wasn't a good way to convince me to do anything.

"My point is, she's special. You're seriously going to let her go because of your pride...or whatever the hell it is?"

"It's not about pride."

"Then what is it?"

I didn't want to talk about this with Cane. I didn't want to talk about this with anyone. "Just drop it."

"No. We're doing this. We're gonna have girly, pussy talk until we get this figured out. Because you're my brother, and I'm not letting you fuck up the best thing that ever happened to you."

I downed the rest of my glass to cure the migraine that had formed out of nowhere.

"Now, what is it?" he repeated. "What is it, Crow?"

"I just can't love anyone. It's that simple. That feeling people are always talking about when they meet their husband or wife...I'm incapable of that. After Vanessa died...that was it. I loved her with everything I had, and like everyone else, she died. I've lost enough people, and I'm fucking tired of it. She'll just be another name on the list."

Cane was quiet. He didn't speak, which was unusual for him. Normally, he ran his mouth until someone told him to shut up.

"So, I'm not going down that road again. I'm not going to feel anything for Pearl besides fondness. I think she's beautiful, and I love being around her, but that's as far as my affection goes. I'm not going to lie to her and tell her I'm going to feel that someday when I never will—no matter how badly I want her."

He sighed into the phone. "Look, I get it. You're scared to lose her. With the shit we go through every day, I understand. But I don't think losing her now is the right decision either."

"There is no other decision. She wants more, and I'm not giving it to her."

"So, you're prepared to come back and forget about her? Isn't that the exact thing you're scared of? Losing her?"

No. They were completely different scenarios. If she died, I would be heartbroken. But if I loved her…I would be shattered. I couldn't let myself get to that point. If I gave myself entirely to her, I would be screwed in the end. They weren't the same—not in the least. "No. And I'm done talking about this."

"Just listen to me—"

I turned off my phone and threw it across the room. Instead of drinking out of the glass like I should have, I threw it against the wall and listened to it shatter into tiny pieces. Then I started drinking right out of the bottle.

***

I was about to break the lock on her door when I changed my mind. I stepped back until I reached the opposite wall then crossed my arms over my chest, waiting out in the hallway like a normal person. At least, that's what she would call me.

She was supposed to get off work soon, and I'd spent most of my morning recovering from a severe hangover. I drank that entire bottle of scotch alone and got carried away. Cane left me ten voice mails, but I didn't listen to them.

A little after five, she came down the hallway with her hair pulled back into a ponytail. Her prominent cheekbones were visible under the fluorescent lights, and even though she wore no makeup, her face was beautiful. Her eyes still stood out like lights against the fog, and her full lips always contained some form of expression.

151

She snaked her keys out of her purse as she approached the door, her head down. If I were a burglar, she wouldn't even notice. When she finally looked up, her face showed her surprise. She eyed the door before she eyed me. "Is someone already waiting in there?"

I didn't laugh because it wasn't funny. "I'm trying to be normal."

"Normal? I don't think it's possible for Crow Barsetti to be normal." She got the door unlocked and walked inside.

I followed her even though I wasn't invited. I didn't break in to her apartment like all the other times, so she should've appreciated my politeness.

Like every other day, she threw her purse onto the kitchen island and immediately eyed the contents of her fridge. "I don't know why I look in here. I never go grocery shopping."

"I can always take you out to eat."

She rolled her eyes. "I can get my own food. I'm just too lazy to go to the store."

"If you lived with me, you'd never have to go to the store." If there was anything that could change her mind, I would use it against her. I'd pay her off if she would accept it. I wanted her in that mansion with me every single day. I wanted to wake up to her face every morning. If she didn't agree to come with me, I'd have to walk away. And the idea of doing that terrified me because it hurt so much.

"Or maybe I could live inside a grocery store, so I wouldn't have to go either."

Her smartass comments used to annoy me, but now I enjoyed them. They were an innate part of who she was. I missed all the little things she did once she was gone. The estate was never the same when her presence disappeared.

"What do you want, Crow?" Her walls were fully erected once more. She hardly looked me in the eye because she couldn't stand the intimacy. Just last night, we were connected on every level, and now she acted like she hardly knew me.

"I wanted to see if you would reconsider." But it was painfully clear she wouldn't.

She bowed her head before she shook it. "No."

Now I had to go back to that estate without her. Her ghost would always haunt me. When I started seeing someone else, I would always compare her to

Button. The idea was so depressing I lost the will to live.

"I'm sorry, Crow. But I think going our separate ways is the best."

"I don't agree with that." Not in the slightest. We were both fucked up on so many levels, but together, we seemed to fit. My darkness complemented her light. And her fierceness complemented my rage. We both knew we would never find anyone to replace each other.

"Well…" She finally looked at me with blue eyes full of sadness. They weren't fiery like they used to be. They were dead like old moss on a tree. "Sometimes, things don't work out the way you want them to."

"Button, just think about it. You would be much happier with me than you would ever be here alone."

"I know," she admitted. "But that will only last for so long. Crow, I don't want to have this conversation again. It was depressing enough the first time. Again, I told you how I felt, and you didn't say it back. A girl can only take that kind of rejection so many times."

I started to feel like shit all over again. "Maybe I didn't say those words. But I did say a lot of things to you that I've never said to anyone else. You've earned my respect, my affection, and my loyalty. No woman has ever done that before. So, don't focus on what I didn't say. Remember what I did say."

She looked into my eyes, but her expression became masked. She blocked her thoughts from me, closing herself off, so we were distant once more. "When are you leaving?"

"Tomorrow. But I really think you should come with me for another reason altogether. I'm telling you, Bones isn't the kind of man who just gives up. You won't be safe here, Button."

"If he hasn't found me by now, he probably never will."

I narrowed my eyes at her ignorance. "Don't be stupid."

That fire came back into her eyes. "I'm not living in fear, Crow. If he comes, I'll be ready. But I doubt he ever will."

I wanted to stay and protect her, but my life wasn't in America. It was in Italy. My grapes needed to be tended to, and my business with Cane didn't sleep. I couldn't stay here just to watch her. And I couldn't help her if she refused it. "If you change your mind, you know where to find me." I pulled a business card out of my pocket and set it on the counter. It had my cell phone number and my address. "And you're always welcome to stop by for a visit. I would love to see you." Even if she were married with kids, I'd still want to see her. No matter how much time had passed or how many women I bedded, that fact would never change.

She eyed the card without taking it. "Are you leaving in the morning?"

"At nine."

She nodded before she stared at the ground again. "Well, you should get a good night's rest since you have to be awake early."

That wasn't how we were going to say goodbye. This woman came into my life in the most surprising way, and I wasn't letting her leave without something meaningful. A chapter of my life was closing, and I was moving on to a darker part of my life. She was my light for a full year, and I didn't even realize how happy I was until it was over. "You and me. All night." I'd make love to her until the sun came up the following morning. I crowded her into the counter and cupped her face. My fingers immediately grasped her hair, and I tilted her chin up, forcing her to look at me.

Buttons and Pain

She didn't resist me or avoid eye contact. She met my look with the same longing deep in her bones. The only reason why she wanted me to leave was to make things easier on herself. But she wanted me nonetheless. "You and me."

***

I lay on my back and stared up at her. Her hair was pulled over one shoulder, long and soft. Her other shoulder was exposed, and scars from her captivity could be seen even in the darkness. The flaws didn't devalue her skin. They were battle scars that showed her resilience. As disturbing as it was, I found them sexy.

My hands moved to her womanly hips, and I squeezed them gently, my fingertips digging into her soft flesh. My cock was underneath her and anxious to be inside her. Her wetness seeped onto my length, lubricating it so I could slide inside her smoothly.

Her hands snaked up my chest, and she leaned forward, her perfect tits right in my face. Her nails dug into me as she moved, coaxing the monster inside me to the surface. My hands clung to her hips, and I took a breath as I prepared to feel her.

Her hair fell onto my shoulder, and she arched her back, preparing to move her wet pussy onto my length. She bit her bottom lip gently, and she began to move. My cock slowly stretched her, making a smooth entrance that was slightly painful from my thickness. Her breathing quickened, and her nipples hardened to the sharpness of diamonds.

My excitement got the best of me. I sat up and hooked my arm around her waist, pulling her the rest of the way down my length. I was balls deep and buried inside the most amazing woman in the world. My lips sucked her tit into my mouth, and I gripped the back of her neck as I held her firmly on my lap. "You're fucking gorgeous, Button." I pressed kisses to her chest then the hollow of her throat. Ecstasy swept me away, and I got lost with her. Our bodies were hot and covered with sweat, and we slowly began to move together. Her pussy took me over and over, and I wanted to come inside her so many times that I'd start to shoot blanks.

She gripped me by the shoulders then pushed me back onto the bed with the kind of force that turned me on. I loved it when she was rough with me, taking the control like a woman who thrived on it. She rolled her hips dramatically and took my length over and over, her wet clit rubbing against my pelvic bone as she moved.

My fingers dug into her thighs, and I rocked into her from below. Her tits bounced in my face, and I could see the reflection of her ass in the mirror on the walls. This was the bed she screwed Jason on, but I was wiping away any trace of him. I was leaving my mark for all the other men who came into her life. They could try to erase me but would never succeed.

She bit her bottom lip again, telling me she was about to come.

"Button." I moved her hips forward and backward, giving her extra friction against her clitoris. I felt her pussy tighten around me, constricting around my dick until she nearly bruised it.

"Crow." She bounced on my dick harder, her tits jiggling with the movement.

I knew this was a memory I would beat off to later. "Come on, sweetheart. You're already there." I pinched both of her nipples to give her the kind of pain she needed to get off with blinding pleasure.

It worked instantly, and her hips bucked with the orgasm I just gave her. She cried and moaned loudly, her breath coming out as a whimper. She continued to grind against me as she rode the high for as long as possible.

She didn't need to squeeze out every drop because I would give it to her many more times before the sun rose. I hooked my arm around her waist before I rolled her onto her back. Underneath me was exactly where I liked her. Her legs immediately wrapped around my waist, and she dug her fingers into my hair. "Crow…"

I ran my tongue along her neck and continued rocking into her. Her pussy was still tight from the orgasm that had just passed, and I wanted to fill her until she was so full my come dripped out. My ass contracted with every move I made. I pressed her slowly into the mattress, her tits shaking with every thrust. I didn't want to fuck her hard tonight. This was perfect.

I held my weight on top of her with my hands on either side of her head. I watched her reaction every time I moved deep inside her. Her lips always formed that distinct shape like she might come all over again. Her lips were irresistible, so soft and sweet. I pressed my mouth to hers and kissed her gently.

Then everything slowed way down.

Her hands were all over me. She touched me everywhere she could, memorizing the feel of my body. She breathed into my mouth between kisses, trying to catch her breath as the passion swept us away. She sucked my bottom lip then gave it a gentle bite, the kind that was so sexy it made my spine shiver.

She moved her nails down the back of my neck then pressed her lips against my ear. She breathed into my canal. All the sexy sounds she made were amplified and beautiful. "Crow...you feel so good."

My cock twitched inside her, and a quiet moan escaped my throat. I'd been with a lot of amazing women, but none of them had the sexy qualities Button had. She was sexy without even trying, and she was sexier when she did try.

I crushed my mouth against hers and sucked her bottom lip into my mouth. I loved how full her lips felt when they were tight against mine. She belonged to me. She was mine and no one else's. "Bite me."

She continued to kiss me hard, her hands digging into my hair.

"Button, bite me."

She opened her eyes and looked into my eyes, her mouth still moving against mine. She grabbed my bottom lip between her teeth then bit into the skin, puncturing it until blood came out.

I moved my tongue into her mouth, wanting to give her all of me. I wanted her to have the very essence that kept me alive. My blood was her blood. When I left, we would move on with our lives, but she would still have me. She would always have me.

The taste of my blood set her off, and she tightened around me again. Her nails dug into my skin, and this time, they drew blood. She came all over my dick and moaned into my mouth, her pussy desperate for my come. "God...yes." She panted into my mouth as her lips trembled with pleasure.

Fuck, I would miss this.

"Give it to me." Her hand moved to my ass, and she pulled me farther inside her. "I want all of it, Crow."

This woman was a sex goddess.

I pinned her harder into the mattress and deepened the angle, wanting every inch of my cock inside her before I hit my trigger. She continued to rock with me, our sweat soaking into her sheets. I could feel the explosion forming far in the distance.

Heat flushed through my body, and I knew I was about to give her everything I had.

She pulled my hips farther into her, increasing my pace and making my balls smack against her ass. She widened her legs to allow me room, and she prepared for the moment of ecstasy. She must have felt my cock tighten inside her because she said, "Oh, yes..."

I held her tightly against me as I released, wanting to treasure this high forever. The sex wasn't just good because she was beautiful. It was amazing because we had a connection. Apart, we'd been through hell. And together, we'd found peace. Having to give that up made me more terrified than I'd ever been. I held her tighter to chase away the sorrow. I wanted to hold on to this moment for as long as I could before I had to say goodbye forever.

When I pulled away, her eyes were looking into mine. The passion faded for a moment as the same thoughts entered her mind. Together, we were strong and indestructible. But the moment we were apart, we were equally weak. She missed me before I was gone.

And I missed her too.

***

Neither one of us slept that night. If we weren't making love, we were staring into each other's eyes and memorizing the details to treasure on a different afternoon far into the future. I didn't have any pictures of her because I never took the time to get a photo. Stupidly, I thought she would always be right by my side.

Her hand cupped my face, and she gave me an unexpected kiss. As the hours passed, she became more affectionate with me, giving me all the embraces she wouldn't have the pleasure of giving me later. Her lips were starting to crack from becoming chapped during our nonstop make out sessions, but they still tasted like honey.

When the last hour arrived, she clung to me harder, and every last wall she'd erected came falling down. She rested her hand over my chest and felt the beat of my heart. She used to do the same thing when we fell asleep together. The sound must have soothed her.

I waited for her to change her mind, to realize settling for most of my heart was better than losing it entirely. But the sadness only increased in her eyes as she stuck to her guns, refusing to settle for anything less than what she deserved.

The sun had already crept into the city and pressed against the black curtains covering her bedroom window. I didn't look at the time, but I knew the minute hand was going fast. Our doom was fast approaching, and soon, I'd have to walk out without looking back.

Within the blink of an eye, my alarm went off. I had to stop by my hotel room and grab my bag before my driver picked me up and took me to the private jet waiting at the airport. The alarm continued to sound on the nightstand until I finally silenced it with the swipe of my thumb.

That's when she started to cry.

Button had never cried like that before. She was always so strong and resilient. The only time I saw her break down was when she realized how much pain I was in over Vanessa. She wept because she understood my pain. She carried it with me.

But now, she was crying for her own heartbreak.

"Button..." I cupped her face and pressed my forehead to hers. I wanted her tears to stop, but I also loved watching them. She was so cold when I first came to New York, but she was only trying to push me away because she was as in love with me as she'd always been. This was just as hard for her as it was for me. "Shh..."

She took a deep breath and silenced her tears, swallowing them down her dry throat. She sniffed before she wiped her nose, leaving her eyes red and wet. "I'm sorry."

"Don't be." I hated listening to a woman cry, but it was a different situation when it came to her. I kissed the corners of her eyes and absorbed her tears onto my lips, treasuring them like diamonds.

She blinked quickly to dispel the moisture.

I got out of bed and began the painful task of dressing myself. I pulled on my boxers and jeans then pulled my shirt over my head. They were wrinkled and cold from sitting on the floor all night long. They didn't fit the way they used to, not because they had changed, but because I had.

She pulled on her clothes and stopped her tears completely. Her eyes were slightly red, and that was the only evidence that she had cried at all.

We walked to the front door and faced each other.

Buttons and Pain

I wanted to ask her to come with me again, but I didn't. I knew what her answer would be.

She wrapped her arms around my neck and buried her face in my chest. Nothing was sadder as we held each other in front of the door. Our heartbeats measured the passing moments, and slowly, our connection was slipping away.

We were out of time.

When she pulled away, her eyes were wet again. "I never got the chance to say thank you..."

"For what?" I'd kidnapped her and kept her as a prisoner in my home. Instead of giving her freedom like I should have, I made her work for it. I made her sleep with me in exchange for something she already had the right to—her freedom.

"After what happened with Bones...I was really messed up. You put me back together, Crow. If it weren't for you, I'd be so fucked up in the head. You made me feel strong when I pitied myself. You made me feel beautiful when I thought of myself as damaged goods. For that, I'll always be grateful."

My eyes slowly started to mirror hers, and I blinked to hide it. "Button..." I tried to find the words to respond, but my mouth was dry. She was thanking me for something that I didn't realize I'd done. "You're the strongest woman I know. You never needed me. And you don't need any man to make you feel beautiful—because you're the most beautiful woman on this earth."

Her bottom lip quivered.

I couldn't stay there for another instant. I was about to crack and spill everything onto the floor. Up until that moment, I didn't think I was capable of feeling anything but lust and violence. But now, I was trying to hold back tears. When my sister died in my arms, I didn't shed a single tear. When my parents died, I didn't feel anything. But now that I was walking away from Button, I was about to collapse.

I didn't say goodbye because the word was too harsh. Even if I wanted to, I couldn't say it. I cupped her face and gave her one final kiss. It was wet from her tears, and soon it would be wet from mine. Our lips hardly moved together because we were both numb from the pain. I moved my lips to her forehead and gave one final kiss goodbye before I opened the door and walked out.

I wanted to turn back and look at her one last time, but I didn't. I grabbed the door and shut it behind me, keeping my face averted so I wouldn't catch a glimpse of her. I pressed my back against it and dragged my hands down my face, wiping away the tears that managed to break the surface.

I looked down at my hands and saw the drops smeared across my skin. My fingertips rubbed together to make sure they were real. The last time I cried I was five years old, and Cane had burned my stuffed teddy bear. I felt so pathetic and weak that I vowed I would never allow myself to break down like that again.

But Button broke me.

Chapter Thirteen

Pearl

When he was gone, I returned to bed and closed my eyes. The tears began deep inside my chest, shaking my frame as they tried to get out. For the past few months, I kept busy, so I wouldn't think about the man who didn't just steal my freedom but my heart. But now, there was nothing to distract my mind from the heartbreaking truth. Crow was gone, and I would never see him again.

The tears broke the surface and dripped down my nose. They streaked down my face until they formed a large droplet and fell to the sheets below me. Crow's scent was still all over the bed, and it would take weeks before it faded away. Every time I smelled it, it was painful. But I knew the instant it was gone, it would be far worse.

Eventually, I began to sob. When he came to New York, I did a fantastic job of seeming indifferent, but it didn't take long for that act to disappear. My true emotions got the best of me, and I couldn't pretend this man wasn't my whole world.

Because he was.

Buttons and Pain

He wasn't just my lover, but my closest friend in the world. Not a single person understood me the way he did. He knew exactly what I had been through, and he never allowed my past to change my future. He looked at me and saw the woman I was underneath the scars. He just saw me—Button.

And now he was gone.

I took a deep breath and forced the tears to stop. Sobbing into my bed wasn't going to fix the heartache, and it certainly didn't make me feel better. If anything, it only made me feel worse. I wanted him to come back just to hold me and kiss my tears away.

I finally halted the tears and dragged my hands down my face. I wiped away every drop of moisture and returned my cheeks to the dry surface they'd been before. My eyes still felt red and puffy, but after a hot shower, they would return to normal.

And I could move on with my life.

I walked into the kitchen and saw the business card sitting on the counter. In black embossment was his name and contact information. I stared at his cell phone number and tried to memorize it just to give my mind something to focus on. I would never call Crow, so there was no reason to keep it, but I couldn't throw away something he gave me. It contained a form of his essence, and to toss that aside was like throwing a piece of him away.

I opened the kitchen drawer and dropped the card inside. His name still looked up at me, the font hinting at his profound masculinity and power. The card didn't even explain what he did for a living, but the appearance made it clear it was something important—and dangerous.

I shut the drawer then went back to bed. Maybe if I went to sleep, I would wake up refreshed and with a new start. Maybe this would just feel like a distant bad dream that I could forget about in a few weeks. Maybe it would feel like a new beginning.

***

After I got off work, I went by the grocery store and picked up some food. The only edible things in my house were Top Ramen and stale crackers. Ordering a pizza wasn't an option because I'd ordered so many over the past few weeks I was officially sick of them.

When I approached my building, I saw a tall man with greasy hair standing off to the side of the entrance. He wore a black leather jacket that didn't look like it was purchased in America, and when his eyes landed on me, he gave me a look blacker than coal.

Like he knew me.

I kept walking and pretended I didn't notice anything suspicious. He was the kind of guy that hung out with a bad crowd. There were a lot of ruthless men in the city, so it wasn't strange to see a shady man looking conspicuous, but it did seem strange that his hostility was directed at me.

A name popped into my head.

I took the stairs to my floor and walked down the hallway. The paranoia set in, and I kept thinking about the distinct features that man possessed. He was harder than steel and more evil than the devil. I could feel it deep inside my gut. And something told me he was there for a reason. The look he gave me wasn't coincidental. It was full of purpose.

Bones.

I got my keys in the lock and opened my door. My hands were shaking, and I dropped the bags of groceries onto the tile without any intention of putting them away. A small part of me was convinced I was just being paranoid. After Crow left, I was an emotional wreck. I was so depressed I couldn't think straight. Maybe this was just a side effect of his absence.

But what if I was wrong?

I pulled out the business card from the drawer and grabbed my phone. If I really were in serious danger, the police couldn't help me. Bones was too deadly and powerful. With an endless supply of men and weapons, he was a tank that couldn't be bombed. Crow was my only savior if my hunch was right.

I typed the number into the phone but didn't make the call. If I was wrong about the whole thing, Crow would come back for no reason. And if I had to say goodbye to him again, I'd kill myself. That was hard enough the first time.

"Here." A man's voice came from the hallway. Two pairs of footsteps accompanied him, heavy boots hitting the hardwood floor outside my apartment. "234A."

That was my apartment number.

Shit.

I hit send and placed the phone against my ear. I listened to it ring and waited for him to answer as I held my breath.

Buttons and Pain

The doorknob gently turned but stopped when it hit the lock. They were testing out the door to see if they could just walk inside and find me standing there.

Shit.

I grabbed the biggest knife I could find and listened to the phone ring.

Goddammit, Crow. Answer.

He finally came on the line. "Crow."

I only had a second before I was captured, so I said everything as quickly as possible. "Bones's men are here for me. They're about to break down the door—"

The second they heard my frantic voice, they broke down the door with their massive shoulders and entered the apartment. All enormous and with guns on their hips, I was no match for any of them. I wasn't a match for even a single one.

Crow's angry voice came over the phone. "Button—"

I dropped the phone in the sink and ran for it. I couldn't defend myself and hold the phone at the same time no matter how much I wanted to listen to his reassurances. With the knife gripped tightly in my hand, I ran around the kitchen island so there was an obstacle separating them from me.

One man had the audacity to chuckle like this was a sick game. "Feisty, isn't she?"

"If you think you're going to take me, think again." I kept my defensive posture with my knife held at the ready.

The leader pulled out a pistol and aimed it right at my head. "Drop the knife."

"No." They wouldn't shoot me. Bones wanted me alive. He was a sick bastard, but he probably wasn't into necrophilia. I was useless to him dead, and if he went through all this trouble just to find me, there was no possibility he wanted me harmed—unless he did it himself. "Shoot me and see what happens." I tightened my grip on the knife and stood at the ready. I'd stab the blades through each of their eyes if they came too close.

When the man didn't shoot, I knew I'd called his bluff. "Put down the knife and come with us, or we'll make you come with us. And believe me, there will be a lot of twisting and groping going on."

My nostrils flared, and unspeakable rage rushed through me. I'd become used to the privilege of freedom and the respect of the men around me. Crow became a lover instead of a kidnapper, and he never did anything I refused. But now, I was being hurled back in time to when I was regarded as a slave, forced to do unspeakable things just because Bones got hard when he looked at me. No more than livestock, I was an object without a right or opinion. Forced into submission, I had to do what I was told.

No more of that bullshit. "Walk out the door, or I'll cut your dick off."

The man with the gun chuckled. "Stupid and feisty. Bad combination." He rushed me and aimed the handle of the gun against my skull.

I lashed out with the knife and aimed for any piece of flesh I could find. I sliced through his shirt and hit the skin underneath. Instantly, blood pooled at the wound and soaked into his clothes. I could hear him hiss under his breath, the burn of the cut distracting him enough that the gun fell short.

The other two men came next when my first attacker stepped back and pressed his hand to his stomach to stop the bleeding. One grabbed me by the arm while the other approached me from the other side.

"Drug her," the first one commanded.

Fuck. No. I twisted out of his grasp and thrust the knife into his gut.

The man caught the blade with his hand and sliced his hand open. But he kept the pressure on and protected himself from a deadly wound. He threw the knife onto the tile where it clanked against the hard floor. "Fucking bitch. Put her under." He wrapped one arm around my neck and kicked my knees from underneath me.

"No!" I threw my body forward to roll away, but the grip was too tight. He forced me to the ground and onto my knees, his arm still hooked around my neck painfully.

The second attacker shoved a needle into my neck and inserted a serum directly into my bloodstream. I could feel the vein thicken with the extra liquid. My heart was beating quick like a drum, but it immediately slowed down once the drug took effect. My eyes became heavy, and my train of thought disappeared. Only one word, one name, came into my mind. "Crow…"

***

Buttons and Pain

Loud and constant, the powerful sound of the engines ripped me from sleep. My face was pressed to the black tile of the plane, and when I opened my eyes, I saw the aisle of seats around me. The men were sitting in a pod of chairs facing each other. With black leather jackets and beady little eyes, they talked quietly among themselves.

While I laid on the floor like a pile of garbage.

I didn't stir because I didn't want unnecessary attention. When they realized I was awake, they would either drug me again or use me for their own amusement. All I could do was focus on the shaking of the floor beneath me and the constant hum of the aircraft engines.

They must be returning me to Italy. We were probably halfway over the Atlantic at the very moment. As I listened to the whir of the propellers, I hoped geese would fly into them so we would crash into the middle of the ocean. That was a much better alternative to being returned to the psychopath, Bones.

I shivered just thinking about it.

Crow knew I would be kidnapped, but there wasn't much hope he would find me. I was on a plane, and eventually, I would touch down to the ground. If they hadn't already removed the small tracker in my ankle, Bones would definitely find it when I was back in captivity. I wanted to check my ankle with my fingertips, but I didn't dare move. The lack of pain or soreness told me it was still there, discreetly inserted beneath the skin and impossible to find without a detector.

Hopefully, it was still working.

If the signal was going strong, Crow would see it. And if he moved quickly enough, he may be able to find me before I was under the protection of Bones and his private army. My heart believed Crow was capable of extracting me. Nothing would stop him from saving me. Maybe he didn't love me, but he still cared about me more than he cared to admit. Even if it cost his life, he would get me out of there—safe and sound.

Buttons and Pain

Chapter Fourteen

Crow

"Come near me, and I'll cut your dick off."

I listened to Button's distant voice as she squared off with her kidnappers. Listening to their accents told me exactly who they were. I didn't know them by name, but their origin was unmistakable. They worked for my greatest nemesis.

"Come on, Button." I closed my eyes and concentrated on the muffled conversation. She must have dropped the phone on the ground because it was nearly impossible for me to make anything out—other than the fact that she was fighting for her life. If anyone could get out of that situation, it was her. She wouldn't give up no matter what.

"No!" I heard Button's voice cry out in defeat before she fell silent altogether. Bones would instruct his men not to hurt her and certainly not kill her. Her lack of words could only mean one thing.

She'd been drugged.

I hung up the phone then stood in the aisle of the plane. I was on a private flight back to Italy, and I was nearly halfway there when Button called me. Knowing

I was stuck over the ocean and unable to help her nearly ripped me apart.

I should have stayed.

Or better yet, I should have taken her with me.

Fuck, this was bad.

I opened the tracker on my phone and prayed it still worked. She hadn't removed it, and hopefully, the battery was still going strong. After a minute of waiting for the transmission, her dot appeared on the screen. It was moving through the streets of Manhattan and headed toward the coast. She must be in a car on her way to the airport.

Fuck.

I called Cane.

"'Bout time you called me back—"

"Shut up and listen to me. Bones just took Button. They grabbed her from her apartment, and now they're on the move. I'm on the goddamn plane, and I'm already halfway to Tuscany."

Cane took a moment before he reacted, probably because it was a monumental piece of news. "Shit. What do we do?"

Buttons and Pain

"I'm turning this plane around." If Bones thought he could take Button away from me, he was sadly mistaken. I'd die before I let him lay a single hand on her fair skin. He'd done the cruelest and most brutal things to her, and I sure as hell wasn't going to let that type of abuse continue. I didn't save Vanessa, and I regretted that every single day of my life. I wasn't going to let the same thing happen to Button.

"Wait, don't do that."

"Don't do what?" I snapped. "You think I'm just going to do nothing?" My arms were shaking, and I couldn't stand still. Despite the turbulence on the plane, I walked forward and backward down the aisle, needing to move my feet to vent my frustration. Button was in trouble, and I was powerless to help her. The handicap and hopelessness drove me insane. She needed me, and I wasn't there for her. If something happened to her, I would never forgive myself.

Ever.

"Calm down for a sec and think," Cane ordered. "They're obviously bringing her to Italy. Last time I checked, that's where Bones was. And by the time you turn around, she'll already be halfway to Europe. Just stay where you are."

That sounded impossible at the moment. How could I stand and wait? I hated this feeling. Whenever something needed to be done, I did it. I didn't waste time by pacing back and forth. I was a man of action—always. "What if they take her somewhere else?"

"You have that tracker on her still?"

"Yes." Thank fucking god.

"Just keep an eye on it. I assure you, they're taking her to Rome."

"What makes you so sure?" I'd been in America for the month and hadn't devoted any thought to work. I'd been focused on making Button come home with me—which I'd failed to do.

"Shit went down yesterday. Some kind of arms race. We both know Bones would be involved in that."

Bones never passed up an opportunity for business, and he didn't have someone else conduct affairs for him. He was always a hands-on kind of guy. Cane and I were exactly the same. We had serious trust issues and didn't allow anyone else to handle important affairs. "True."

"I can guarantee you, he's here. And he's not going anywhere until she's on the ground. He's gonna want to—"

"Enough." I refused to let him finish because my mind was already ten steps ahead of him. Images of her naked and beaten flooded my mind like a swarm of wasps. It burned from the inside out. She would be tied up and gagged, and he'd bruise her until she was black and blue. The thought was excruciating enough that angry tears burned in the back of my eyes. I gripped the nearest chair until my knuckles turned white.

Cane pushed through the tension. "Land and we'll pick you up. I'll have all the men ready to ambush Bones and his crew. We'll get her back, man."

"We have to get her back, Cane. I mean it." I wouldn't go on if I failed her. My purpose was to protect her and keep her safe. She'd become such an essential part of who I was, and I understood better than anyone what she went through. The images would never stop haunting me, and I would eventually give in to my own suicide.

"I know. And we will. Just stay calm."

That was impossible. Right now, she was in the hands of evil men. Maybe they wouldn't hurt her yet, but that didn't mean they wouldn't do other things. The idea made me so sick I nearly hurled in the middle of the aisle.

"Crow?"

I sat in the nearest chair because I felt weak. "Hmm?"

"I'll stay on the phone with you." Cane fell silent and didn't say anything more. Men spoke in the background because he was at the rendezvous point. They were arming themselves with weapons and armor. He didn't give me false words of hope to make me feel better. He did the only thing he was capable of doing.

Joining me in my misery.

Buttons and Pain

Chapter Fifteen

Pearl

The plane landed.

I continued to lie absolutely still, enjoying my solitude just a little longer. Very shortly, I would return to the hands of the man who got off by torturing me. He would give me a welcoming celebration with whips and a dildo up the ass.

I couldn't go back there.

I'd never relied on a man to take care of me, but I kept hoping Crow would come to the rescue. He was my only hope for getting out of there. But I knew the second Bones drove off with me, it would be nearly impossible for Crow to get me back.

I had to escape on my own.

Fear burned like a fire in my heart, and my hands possessed a light tremble that couldn't be stopped. My legs felt weak from not eating, and my body had more adrenaline than it could handle. But I needed to remain calm and focus on escaping. There was no time for uncertainty or terror.

I just had to do it.

"Get up." One of the men came to my area in the corner and gave me a light kick in the stomach. "We know you're awake."

I kicked him back out of defiance. Instead of being smart and just doing what I was told, my body automatically reacted and strove to inflict as much pain as possible. I hit him right in the knee with my shin and made him howl in pain.

"Bitch." He grabbed me by the hair and dragged me across the floor. "You wanna be a cunt? I'll treat you like a cunt."

The other kidnapper told him off in Italian and gripped him by the arm.

Immediately, he released me and argued back in the same language.

My scalp felt ripped apart, and the migraine was already starting. Some of my hair fell out and sprinkled the ground around me. I didn't touch my head or give any indication I was in pain. I'd die before I let myself look weak.

He stood over me, brooding like an angry psychopath. "Up. Now." This time, he didn't touch me since he was just disciplined for it.

Buttons and Pain

Now that it was on my terms, I rose to a stand and gripped the chair for balance. I was lightheaded and dizzy, a side effect of the medication and the lack of food. I hadn't eaten since Crow left because I was too depressed. Now, I wished I'd had some sustenance to give me strength.

They marched me off the plane and into a black SUV with tinted windows. Thankfully, Bones wasn't inside. It was just me and three men. The guard sitting on the opposite side of the car had his gun trained on me. "Bones warned me about you. Do anything foolish, and I will kill you."

That was a meaningless threat since I didn't care if I lived or died at the moment. Disappearing into the void sounded much more appealing than becoming a slave to that madman. The only thing stopping me was Crow.

He would never recover if I died.

He barely accepted the fact that Vanessa was gone. If I suffered the same fate, he'd put a bullet inside his brain immediately.

I had to escape.

The SUV drove forward and away from the tiny airport. Soon, we were on the road and headed straight into Rome. Now, I knew my surroundings better than before I left. I spent time studying the geography when I was back in America, not because I thought I would be kidnapped again, but because I missed the place I'd called home for a whole year.

With a gaze full of dullness, I looked out the window and pretended to be indifferent to everyone inside the vehicle. They made the mistake of not handcuffing me, and I would take advantage of their stupidity. They knew I was feisty, but they obviously didn't know I was brave and stupid. I would crash this car into oncoming traffic if I had to.

The minutes trickled by as we approached Rome. Hardly any cars were on the streets because it was some odd hour in the morning. After being drugged and flying across the Atlantic, I had no concept of time.

My eyes glanced at the man sitting beside me. The gun was still pointed at me, but it was slowly lowering as gravity made his hand tired. Instead of looking at me like he should have, his eyes were glued out the front window. The radio wasn't on, and only silence kept us company.

I was going for it.

Buttons and Pain

I leapt across the car and swatted the gun down to the floor. Just as I'd seen Crow do countless times, I pulled my right arm back and slugged him hard across the face. I hit him again until his nose broke then I slammed his head into the window.

The car swerved as the driver realized what was going on. He cursed in Italian and got control of the wheel. The man in the passenger seat grabbed me by the back of the neck and tried to pull me off, but it was no use.

I had this asshole in a death grip.

I pulled the lever on the door, and it flew open to the street below the tires. The man nearly fell but gripped the door and the seat to steady himself. Blood streaked down his face and dripped from his chin. "You bitch—"

I shoved my foot into his chest and kicked him out of the car. His back hit the pavement, and he rolled in the road toward the sidewalk. I didn't have time to watch and see if he survived. Now, I had to jump out and get the hell out of there.

"This cunt is crazy!" The man in the passenger seat dragged me back into the car and pinned me to the leather seats. He yanked my hands behind my back then quickly tied them together with a thick string of rope that chafed against my skin as he tightened it. I didn't cry out in pain despite how much it hurt. He grabbed the gun from the floor and pointed it right at my temple. "Move and you'll die." The door was still open, so he slammed it shut. Neither one of them mentioned their fallen comrade and clearly had no intention of retrieving him.

That was cold, even to me.

He cocked the gun and kept it pressed to my temple. "Now I understand his fascination with you. Always fighting. Always trying." His hand slid around my arm and underneath my body. His long fingers groped my breasts through my shirt and squeezed them hard. "Maybe I'll tit-fuck you before we get there."

I thrust my hips as hard as I could to buck him off, but he weighed more than a cow. My movement had no impact on him whatsoever. "I'm gonna shove that gun up your ass then pull the trigger."

"Dirty talk." He chuckled. "I like it." He found my nipple then squeezed it painfully, getting off on my misery as well as my curves.

Buttons and Pain

My mind immediately went into panic mode, and I nearly had a breakdown right then and there. All the memories of my captivity swarmed back, and I realized I was returning to a place far worse than hell. I would be beaten and raped on a daily basis, and I wouldn't see the sunshine ever again. Like an animal, I would be kicked around and disciplined for any misbehavior. I would no longer have a name but be referred to as a slave. I wouldn't have—

Everything moved in slow motion. The glass window shattered and sprayed across my back. It was cold from its contact with the nighttime air, and it was sharp like the teeth of a monster. The SUV immediately swerved harshly to the right as it fell prey to the stampede that had just been unleashed. The man holding me down flew across the vehicle and slammed into the opposite door. My hands were still secured behind my back, and I couldn't hold on to anything. I flew through the air and slammed into the man's chest, feeling the padding of his body rather than the hardness of the door frame. The world kept spinning until we came to an abrupt halt.

If there was any noise, I didn't hear it. If the engine was smoking, I couldn't smell it. Whatever chaos was going on around me was dulled by the ringing in my ears. I knew I was in a car accident, but I still didn't know what had happened. A cut bled from my forehead, and my entire body felt sore from my collision against one of my captors.

What happened?

The opposite door flew open, and Cane's hard expression met mine. With black hair darker than the night and penetrating eyes just like his brother, he stared at me like a target. "Pearl, you all right?"

Was I imagining this? "What...?"

He grabbed my arm and pulled me out of the vehicle. He wasn't delicate despite my injuries, but he pulled me out of there as quickly as possible. "Get moving. We don't have time for this shit."

It sounded like him. It looked like him. Or was I still imagining this? "Where's Crow?"

"Don't worry about that right now. Come on." He helped me to the ground. "Can you walk?"

"Yeah, I think so." I tested my footing. Despite how weak I was, I could stand. When I turned to look at my surroundings, I finally saw him. With a grimace on his mouth and murder in his eyes, Crow yanked the driver's door open and pulled the man out from

194

behind the wheel. His shoulders were tense like a tightrope, and his body screamed with bloodlust.

Once the man was on the ground, he moaned and tried to get up.

Crow spit on his face before he slammed his foot onto his nose. An audible crunch filled the nighttime air.

I stared at him in shock.

"We don't have time for this, Pearl. Come on." Cane yanked me away, pulling me like a dog on a leash.

Crow kicked the man a few more times then stomped on his chest, making him hurl into his own mouth. "Don't. Fuck. With. Me." Crow finally aimed his gun between the man's eyes and shot him point-blank.

Oh my god.

Cane saw the blood drain from my face and egged me forward. "We don't have much time. Come on."

"Time for what?"

"Bones's men will be here any second." He guided me across the road and into an alleyway. "Stay here, alright? Don't move for any reason."

"What's going on?" I demanded. "How do you know his men are coming?"

"Let's just say it's intuition." He kneeled in front of me with his gun held at the ready. He watched the street as Crow grabbed the other man and dragged him into the center of the road. After he maliciously tortured the man, he finally put an end to his misery by shooting him in the head.

Crow was a ruthless man. But I'd never seen him this brutal.

A swarm of cars sped up the street then fanned out when they spotted the destruction on the road. Crow's men popped up from their hiding places with their rifles held at the ready. Crow took cover behind a car with his handgun cocked.

"Aren't you going to help him?"

"My orders are to stay with you. We should be safe here."

"What about Crow?"

Cane chuckled even though it wasn't the time for jokes. "Believe me, he's fine."

"How can you say that?"

"Did you see him a second ago? He has rage on his side."

Buttons and Pain

The battle took place, and gunshots were fired. The echoing sound hurt my ears. The cacophony of noise echoed in the alleyway, and it was pure pandemonium against my eardrums.

Cane peeked around the corner and fired along with everyone else, but he never gave up his position. I tried to find Crow, but I couldn't see him across the street. I knew he was okay because Cane would be devastated if something had happened to his brother.

The war carried on for nearly five minutes. Bullets continued flying across the neighborhood as each side of the enemy was picked off. Men ran back and forth as they closed the perimeter around each other. It looked like a war zone rather than a street fight. I was back in time and witnessing one of the bloodiest battles in history.

I felt like Helen of Troy.

When the guns finally died down, it turned into man-to-man combat. I saw Crow emerge from his hiding place and push five unarmed men to the ground. They were out of bullets and out of time. Crow's men stayed back, holding their positions in the distance.

"Is he going to execute them?" My voice shook slightly as I spoke. I knew these men were evil, and if they had it their way, they would be dragging me off to be beaten by Bones. I shouldn't have felt sympathy for them, not when I knew they did this to countless women before me. But a small part of my heart tugged in sadness.

Cane finally answered. "Yeah."

Crow put his gun away and pulled out a long dagger from inside his jacket. I could see it gleam under the streetlight because the steel was spotless. He stood in front of the first man and stared him down coldly. He wasn't the man I was used to seeing. This was the version of Crow he'd warned me about.

A ruthless killer.

One by one, he slit the throat of each man. It was so gruesome, even I had to look away. Instead of giving them a clean death with a gunshot wound, he made them suffer until the very end. It was a message to Bones and the rest of the world.

When Crow reached the last man, he put his blade away. The man stayed on his knees and didn't show an ounce of fear. Even as his comrades bled out to death on the concrete, he didn't flinch. His loyalty was just as strong as ever.

Crow stared him down, just as fearless. "Call him."

The man didn't move.

He held up the blade, still dripping with blood. "Do it, and I'll show you mercy."

The man eyed the blade for a moment before he pulled a phone out of his pocket.

"On speakerphone."

The phone rang over the line. The soldier continued to hold it in his hand, but his fingers started to shake.

Finally, Bones's voice came on the line. "Do you have her?" His deep voice sounded just as grotesque as I remembered. It was full of entitlement, brutality, and pure evil. I remembered all the terrible things he would whisper into my ear as he fucked me until I screamed. My blood boiled in a rage, and I struggled to breathe.

Crow stared at the phone, his hazel eyes appearing black. "Don't. Touch. My. Girl." Crow took a step forward and stared down at the phone with venomous hate. Without raising his voice, he possessed the authority of a king. He was powerful and majestic, terrifying and cruel.

Bones gathered his thoughts before he spoke. His silence was an indication that he recognized the voice over the phone. To him, it was unmistakable. "I see that—"

Crow threw the phone on the ground and stomped on it with his foot. It shattered into dozens of pieces and Bones's voice died away immediately. He stepped back and pointed the gun right between the man's eyes. Without another word, he pulled the trigger, and the man crumpled to the street.

Three police cars drove up that instant, their lights flashing and their sirens screeching. They braked hard and threw their doors open. They all took defensive stances under cover with their weapons drawn.

"Shit." Was this all going to come to an end?

Crow turned until he directly faced them, his gun in one hand and the bloody blade in the other. He took a few steps forward without raising his gun. Without an ounce of fear, he stared them down, seeing the dozen police officers stare back at him. "Leave now, and no harm will come to you."

Buttons and Pain

The police held their stance but snuck glances at each other. They didn't exchange a single word, but a conversation happened within their ranks. One by one, they holstered their guns then got back into the cars. The lights and sirens were turned off, and they drove away, heading in the opposite direction of the war zone that took up the entire block. Crow stood his ground and made sure they were completely out of sight before he headed to the alleyway where I was hiding.

I'd never seen him in action and never knew exactly what he was capable of. The only side I saw of him was the softer version, the man who was wise in wine and treated his employees like family rather than workers. He told me about his darkness, but he'd been nothing but gentle with me since the moment we met. I never knew this kind of ferocity and war raged inside him. But the beast broke through the gates once it'd been provoked. The second they took me, he launched into action and showed the kind of brutality he'd warned me about. He stopped being a man and turned into a monster.

Cane turned to me when he saw his brother approach. "And you still think he doesn't love you?"

***

Penelope Sky

Crow walked to me at his normal speed, but his tense arms and clenched jaw told me he wanted to run until his hands were finally on me. The second he reached me, he cupped my face. My hair stuck underneath his palm as he examined the wound on my head. "Are you alright?"

"I'm fine." I didn't care about the bleeding or the fact that my back was killing me after being thrown at full speed against a full-grown man. All I cared about was being safe from Bones and with the man standing in front of me. "I'm sure it looks worse than it feels."

He pulled a handkerchief out of his pocket and wiped the blood away. Like a mother hen tending to her young, he cleaned me up until everything was gone. Some of the blood that was stained on his hands soaked into the handkerchief. I couldn't tell the stains apart. "You want to go to the hospital?"

"I said I was fine." A few weeks in bed would put me back together. The soreness would fade away, and the wound would close up and become a scar to add to the collection.

Crow's hands were on me again, and he pressed his face to mine. He took a deep breath like he was inhaling my scent before he kissed me hard on the lips. His abrasiveness directly contradicted the concern he'd just shown a moment ago, and he kissed me like we hadn't seen each other in years.

Without warning, he pulled away and scooped me into his arms. Like I was seriously injured, he cradled me to his chest as if I were lighter than a feather. He didn't need to carry me because I was perfectly capable of walking on my own, but I didn't resist. Feeling him hold me sent shivers down my spine. After the ordeal I'd just been through, I actually felt safe. My arm wrapped around his neck, and I rested my head against his chest.

He directed Cane with a bark. "Get the car. You're driving."

Cane rolled his eyes. "Whatever you say, boss."

Crow carried me to the back of an SUV, and he placed me in the backseat. The moment he was beside me, he pulled me back into his lap then pressed his face close to mine, our lips practically touching. The car turned on the road, and we headed home.

Home.

He pulled the hair from my face and fisted it with a single grip as he examined me. His eyes rested on my lips as if he could read them before he turned his gaze back on me. Instead of being black as coal, his eyes had returned to their sexy greenish hazel color. "Did they hurt you?"

"A little. But it was nothing I couldn't handle."

His hand squeezed my hair. "I should have tortured them more when I had the chance."

"Not necessary. I pushed one out of the car on the way here."

The corner of his lip rose in a half smile. "That's my girl." He pressed a kiss to my cheek, a nurturing touch that was soft and intimate. It didn't crush me the way his other kiss did. This one had a completely different meaning. "Did they...?" When he couldn't finish the sentence, I knew what he was asking.

I didn't bring up the groping I'd received on the way there. There was no need to mention that and make him feel guilty for not saving me sooner. "No. They were told not to touch me."

He hid his relief as much as possible, but he couldn't keep it from me. "I'm sorry, Button. I shouldn't have left you."

"Don't do that..."

"Actually, I should have taken you with me."

"It wasn't your fault." I was the one who chose to tough it out on my own. I didn't expect to be kidnapped the second Crow left the city. The timing was horrendously poor. "I didn't take your warning seriously when I should have."

"I still shouldn't have walked away." He rested his face against mine and closed his eyes. "I won't make that mistake again." His arms circled me, and he held me closer to his chest. Our foreheads rested together, and we listened to each other breathe on the ride home. There were so many things we couldn't say with Cane in the car. And there were so many things we couldn't do with him in the car.

But as soon as we went home, things would change.

***

Crow didn't say goodbye to his brother when he left the car and carried me in his arms. Cane didn't say anything either, possibly out of anger or maybe he didn't see the point. His brother was clearly more concerned with me than having good manners.

He carried me into the house and through the entryway. Lars stepped out of the kitchen when he heard the front door open and shut.

"Your Grace, you've returned. I'm glad you've brought Miss Pearl with you."

205

Crow kept walking like he hadn't heard a word he said. "We don't want to be disturbed for the night. Leave dinner outside my bedroom door."

Lars didn't flinch at the command. "Of course, Your Grace. Have a good evening."

My arms remained circled around his neck, and I stared at his face as we ascended the stairs. His five o'clock shadow was thicker than usual because he hadn't shaved since the morning before he left. He wore the same clothes from the morning he walked out my front door, and I wondered if they still contained my scent from sitting on my bedroom floor all night. All I could smell was him, masculinity mixed with a hint of mint.

He carried me into his bedroom, and the second we entered, it felt dormant. He hadn't been sleeping there for nearly a month, and the air remained undisturbed. Nothing had changed since I left months ago. The bedding was identical, the curtains were the same, and it was spotless like it'd always been.

He set me on the bed then immediately pulled his shirt over his head. It was stained with blood, mine and the men he'd killed. Underneath the fabric was his chiseled physique. It was identical to the last time I saw him. Abrasions, cuts, and bruises didn't permeate his skin during the battle that raged in the streets of Rome.

His gun sat on his hip, and he pulled it out of the holster and set the safety before he placed it on his nightstand. Sleek and shiny, it reflected the dim light of the rising sun outside the window. I'd never seen him with a gun other than on the night he kidnapped me from Bones. I wondered how many he had stowed away in the house.

He got his jeans off next then removed his boxers. As always, he was hard and ready to go. He leaned over the bed and gently forced me to my back, his hands on either side of my waist. With eyes glued to mine, he removed my jeans and panties until my lower body was naked.

The moment didn't feel sexual in nature. It was a level of intimacy we'd never shared before. With hearts beating as one and the fear still heavy in our chests, we clung together like magnet and steel. He got my shirt off then my bra before he lay on top of me, his naked body hard and defined. His lips brushed past mine as he positioned himself with his arm hooked around my torso until he had an iron-clad grip on me. If he were going to fuck me, he would have already shoved himself inside me. Every minute passed with anticipation, and he took his time focusing on my eyes rather than everything else.

He slid inside me slowly, taking his time like he was in no rush to reach the finish line. His usual look of prevalent darkness was absent. Instead of looking like a man who'd just killed dozens of men, he looked like a man who'd just returned from a venture out to sea. His beautiful eyes were warm as he sank into me with purpose. When he was fully situated inside me, he slowly rocked into me. It was the kind of sex we'd had just before he walked out of my apartment for the last time. Slow and tender, it was about more than just feeling each other in the most pleasurable ways. It was about every touch and every kiss.

It was about so much more.

Buttons and Pain

Chapter Sixteen

Crow

Despite the exhaustion burning behind my eyes, I couldn't sleep. Normally when Button was beside me, I was out like a light. Now, I sat in my study and depleted my supply of scotch and brandy, wearing my pajama bottoms with a black t-shirt.

It was five in the evening, but she was still asleep. After what she'd been through, I couldn't blame her for being wiped out of energy. She was chased down in her own home then drugged before being dragged onto a plane. Then a truck crashed into the vehicle she was in and sent her flying against the opposite door. She was banged up and bruised, and after a day of rest, her injuries were bound to look more gruesome.

She deserved the rest.

Cane walked in a moment later, his files tucked under his arm. He plopped down on the couch and immediately helped himself to my glass of scotch. He downed half the glass before he set the folder on the table.

I poured myself another and ignored his subtle gesture of disrespect. "What's the news?"

"Our people cleaned up the street and disposed of the bodies. We jacked some of their cars. After a thorough cleaning and license plate fix, we'll have more toys for the yard. We got some cool guns too, and they've been added to the collection."

"The police?"

"They came back to check on things but didn't file a report. They aren't stupid."

"You mean, they aren't suicidal." I didn't mess around with cops. They protected innocent people throughout our country and did their jobs the best they could. People like Bones and I were above the law, and just because they got in our way didn't mean there needed to be casualties. With a clear warning, they usually backed off our territory and turned their cheeks. Besides, we were criminals who only killed other criminals. We weren't exactly a threat to the citizens of Italy.

"Whatever." He finished his scotch—mine—and refilled it to the brim. "I haven't gotten any intel on Bones. Have no idea what he's doing."

"Not a thing?"

"Nope." Cane shook his head. "I suspect he's not in Italy. He's probably gathering reinforcements to take us down. After what we did to him, I'm sure he wants our heads on silver platters. I mean, we've taken Pearl from him twice now."

"Maybe if he had a bigger dick, he could keep her around." I wanted to set this man on fire and watch him burn. I had serious blood rage when it came to the people who hurt Button, but there was a special place in my ferocity for that man. I would avenge what he did to my sister, my family, and for her. "We need to take him out once and for all. If we don't, Button will never be able to go home and move on with her life."

Cane was just about to open the folder when he flinched and turned his gaze on me. His look was frozen like the arctic and just as unforgiving. He opened his mouth to say something insulting but then quickly changed his mind. "You know what...forget it." He turned back to the paperwork and flipped through it.

"Forget what?"

He shook his head and didn't answer.

"Cane, if you have something to say, just say it."

He slammed the folder down. "After all the shit we just went through to get that woman, you're seriously prepared to send her back?" Cane said

vicious things to me before, but he never meant them. While his words weren't hurtful, his tone implied paramount hatred. He despised me in that moment—completely and utterly. "You took out a whole brigade of soldiers almost completely on your own then executed the survivors like a general in the Austrian army, and you're still gonna look me in the eye and say you don't love this woman?" That arctic look never disappeared as he stared me down. His hazel eyes, identical to mine, contained only hatred, not affection. My younger brother was actually disappointed in me. "I'm done talking about this. It's pussy shit anyway." He found the map of one of Bones's factories then handed it to me. "I think we should strike here. It produces most of his commodities, and if we trash the place, it'll lure him out. The guy is always on the move, so we should draw him to us."

I stared at the map without really seeing it. My brother's words echoed in my mind long after he said them. "Cane—"

"I'm done talking about it. Do whatever the hell you want. But next time you need help saving her or kidnapping her...or whatever the hell you plan on doing with her, don't call me. Because if you do, I won't help you."

Buttons and Pain

Cane wasn't an emotional kind of guy, and he didn't give a damn about romance. This situation with Button bothered him, but I couldn't figure out why. "Tell me why this is so important to you. And don't say it's because you want me to be happy. There has to be more to the story."

"You don't give a damn, so don't act like you do."

I threw the map onto the table and gave him my full focus. "I do."

He rolled his eyes. "I'm not having this conversation with you. It's girly and stupid."

"Whether it's stupid or not, we need to have it. Now spit it out, so we can move on with our lives." Cane and I didn't have meaningful conversations about our feelings and whatnot. We just worked together and planned our movements of action. Most of the time, he annoyed me, and I annoyed him. But the bond of blood between us kept us closer together than either one of us would admit. We didn't even talk much about Vanessa after she died, but we were going to talk about this.

He rubbed the back of his neck with the same look of irritation still in his eyes. "You can't give me shit for it, alright?"

That was the only thing I knew how to do. "Fine. Just tell me."

"Alright…" He rubbed his palms together as he tried to gather his thoughts. "When you brought Pearl here, I hated her. You knew what I wanted to do with her. You saw what I actually did to her."

I clenched my jaw at the memory. I shot him in the arm after he hurt Button, but that wasn't enough punishment. The only reason we were still talking was because we were family. Somehow, that bond outweighed my hatred.

"But I've learned a lot about her from having her around all the time. She's strong, powerful, and she's got a mouth that would make a soldier feel like shit. She's got that drive, you know? She completes our trio."

I didn't have a clue where this was going, but I didn't ask. I waited for him to spit out his incoherent thoughts until he finally made his point.

"If you married her, she would be a Barsetti."

Who said anything about marriage? I'd never said that word to Cane in my life.

"And…I would like it if she were a Barsetti." He rubbed his palms together again as he stared down at his hands. "Our family just keeps getting smaller. One day, there will only be one of us left. But Pearl can make it bigger. She can make our family grow."

When I finally understood what he was trying to say, I couldn't hide the surprise on my face. It was hardwired into my features and hadn't faded away. Cane wasn't just fond of Button. He wanted her to be one of us.

"She could be my sister. And she could give you kids. Our Barsetti family would grow. Maybe one day, it'll be complete again." He shrugged. "I don't know..."

"If extending our family is important to you, why don't you get married?"

"Because I don't love anyone." He leaned back into the couch and crossed his arms over his chest. "I've never met a woman I could even somewhat tolerate. I'm just with them for the pussy, and that's it. If I ever met someone I couldn't live without, you bet your ass I would marry her. But let's be real, women like Pearl don't grow on trees. I doubt I'll ever find a woman like that."

Button was spectacular. The second I heard her speak, I had to make her mine. There was something about the fire that burned in her eyes that drew me to

215

her. I thought I wanted to hurt her myself, but in the end, I only wanted to protect her. Whatever hold she had over me was powerful. She had more control of our relationship than she ever truly realized. "They're hard to come by."

"So why are you letting her go?"

I'd already explained this to him, but apparently, I had to repeat myself. "Cane, we can't love anyone. If we do, they'll be killed. You know that. I know that. It's just how it goes."

"To me, it seems like Pearl already has a price on her head. So what does it matter?"

I drank my scotch to mask my silence.

"You already love her, and she loves you. What does it matter if you don't actually say it out loud? You proved it a million times over yesterday when you went ape shit crazy on all of Bones's men. Just accept the fact that she's in your life, and not just now but forever. You aren't doing anyone any favors by lying to yourself. Be a man, Crow."

"Be a man?"

"Yes," he snapped. "A real man doesn't lie about how he feels. He tells the world he loves someone and dares his enemies to hurt the woman he adores. A brave man has holes in his armor but goes to war anyway. A fierce man isn't afraid to love someone even though he knows there's an ending down the road. That's what it means to be a real man, Crow. This stupidity you've been holding on to is just pathetic. And that's saying something coming from me."

***

Button turned over under the covers and pulled the blankets to her shoulder to fight the cold. Her eyes were still closed, and her lips were relaxed with peace. Dark strands of hair stretched across the pillow and marked most of the bed as hers. She was a tiny thing, but she stretched out her legs and took up most of the bed on her own.

Her hand stretched out and felt the sheets beside her. Her fingers dug into the fabric, searching for something to grab. When she didn't find what she was looking for, she stretched her arm farther and released a frustrated sigh.

Watching her suffer was too much to bear, so I slid between the sheets beside her and allowed her hand to finally locate my hard chest. Once her fingertips felt the warmth of my skin, she dug her fingertips into it slightly and claimed me as hers.

217

My hand met hers, and I interlocked our fingers together. Her fingertips were petite and soft, and they were nearly half the size as mine. Unlike most women, she never did her nails. Her appearance had always been simple and clean. She hardly wore makeup because she didn't need it. Her fair skin and naturally beautiful eyes were more than enough.

I stared at her thick eyelashes and waited for them to move. Any moment now, the queen of my estate would open her eyes to a new day. Exhausted from the hell that was unleashed yesterday, she slept over twelve hours to recover. I was still concerned she needed to go to the hospital, but she'd assured me that was unnecessary.

Finally, she opened her eyes. Brilliant and bright, they sparkled like a birthstone. Magic and excitement mixed with the fog of sleepiness. Her beauty was unparalleled, and sometimes, it simply didn't look real.

After her eyes took me in, her lips stretched into a perfect smile. Her teeth didn't show, but the grin was just as powerful. She scooted closer to me until she was molded against my side, forsaking her side of the bed and invading mine like a conqueror. She squeezed me tighter then pressed a wet kiss against my chest. Then the most beautiful sigh escaped her lips.

Every little detail floored me, and I was so mesmerized I forgot to breathe altogether. My lungs immediately expanded with the deep breath I needed, and I stared at the woman who'd made me cry just a few days before. Without torturing me or threatening me, she brought me to a level of emotion I hadn't known in my adult life. She stripped me of my armor until I was nothing but skin and bone. She made me less of a man, but at the same time, she made me the strongest version of myself I could ever be.

She turned farther into me and pressed another kiss to my chest. Her upper lip clung to my dry skin before it gently pulled away. Her hair was tousled and messy from the previous evening, but it made her look like a sexy goddess who lived to please me.

She crawled up my chest until her legs hugged my hips and slowly slid her body down until her pussy caught the head of my dick. She gently pushed down until I squeezed through her entrance and stretched her apart.

She made a quiet moan then bit her lip.

My hands immediately went to her thighs, and I gripped her hard.

She lowered herself until I was completely inside her, stretching so far within her that I could feel her cervix. Her tits were perky, and her nipples were hard enough to cut through concrete. Her waist didn't carry as many curves as it used to because she didn't eat much when we were apart, but she was still sexy as hell. She leaned back and ran her fingers through her hair before she started to grind against me, a mischievous look in her eyes.

Fuck.

She bit her lip and moaned as she took my cock over and over, touching herself and looking like every guy's fantasy. Her hands groped her tits before they touched her hair again, and she enjoyed herself thoroughly while pleasing me at the same time.

This was better than any dream.

She grinded her hips against me, digging her clitoris into my pelvic bone. Almost instantly, she came all over me, drenching me with her lubrication and sending me to heaven. Her pussy tightened hard around my dick, squeezing me so she could get every drop that was waiting to explode out of my shaft.

Buttons and Pain

"Button." I hooked my arms under her thighs and guided her hard down my length. Anytime I saw her mouth form that delectable O shape and she nearly screamed because her orgasm was so great, I wanted to follow right behind her and release all the desire built up in my balls.

She leaned forward and gripped my shoulders with her long nails. With confidence in her eyes, she looked straight into my soul as her hips kept rolling and grinding down my length. Her cheeks were flushed from the satisfaction between her legs, and her nipples were still hard from arousal. They dragged down my chest with every move she made.

"So fucking perfect." I squeezed her thighs as I moved into her, my eyes still locked to those beautiful blue orbs. I'd bedded so many women who agreed to the dark desires I'd inflicted on them. There were nights when I lived in pure fantasy with women who were more beautiful than the night itself. But this woman destroyed their memories. With her beauty, strength, and resilience, she chased away the ghosts of every woman who'd ever walked into this mansion. She exerted her dominance in subtle ways, conquering everything—including me. She was the opposite side of my coin, the blood to my heart.

"Give it all to me." She slammed harder into me, taking my cock in that tight little pussy. Her nails dug into my shoulders, and her breathing deepened as my dick thickened inside her. "I want it, Crow."

I groaned from deep in the back of my throat because her words set me on fire. Every time she begged for my come, my body couldn't be contained. My shaft lit on fire with delectable pleasure as it swept through my entire body. I throbbed deep inside her as I released, giving her mounds of my essence. I groaned again because the pleasure was unstoppable. My fingertips dug into her hips as a wave washed over me, the aftershocks still setting my nerves on fire.

She slowly pulled off me then placed her fingers at her entrance. She played with herself until my come dripped onto her fingertips. Like a courtesan, she brought her fingertips to her mouth and sucked them clean.

"Fuck, Button."

***

She stood under the shower, washing her hair and removing the dirt that caked her skin. Distant bruises marked her arms and ribs where she'd been manhandled like a dog. The cut above her brow had stopped bleeding, but it still looked painful.

I pressed my chest against her back and wrapped my arms around her waist. "Are you sure you're alright? I can always have a doctor come to the estate." I pulled her hair over one shoulder and kissed her temple.

"Crow, I'm fine." She turned around and dipped her head back so she could rinse the suds out of her hair. "I've been through worse. We both know that."

She was referring to the time my loving brother nearly beat her to death. "There's no shame in admitting you need help. A doctor can give you something stronger than Tylenol."

"Stop treating me like a doll. I may bend, but I don't break." She stepped out from underneath the water and squeezed her hair dry. The drops fell into the drain while her damp hair hung over her shoulder.

My concern would never disappear. Even if she had a paper cut, it would get under my skin. She deserved a life free of any blemish or worries. The only thing she should ever have to be concerned about is what dress she was going to wear for the afternoon and where we would have dinner. She should look at her countless scars and treat them like freckles.

She stepped out of the shower and dried off before she blow-dried her hair at the bathroom sink. With a towel wrapped around her chest, she ran her fingers through her hair as the warm air blew across her tresses. She concentrated on her movements in the mirror without truly looking at herself.

Instead of washing my hair and soaping down my body, I watched her. My eyes never left her frame the moment she was out of my reach. My level of protectiveness reached an alarming height, and I could barely stop myself from hiding her away in some foreign country where no one would ever find us.

After she finished getting ready, she left the bathroom, and I had nothing to stare at. I got out of the shower and shaved before I got dressed for the day. Button found one of her dresses in my closet, and she looked just as beautiful as she used to when wearing it.

"What do you want to do today?" I came up behind her and pressed a kiss to her shoulder.

"Don't you have to work?"

Buttons and Pain

I kissed her again because my lips were starving. She'd just ridden my cock like a cowgirl, but I wanted more. All I wanted was her—all the time. "No." Work could wait. I'd already neglected my duties this long. A few more days wouldn't make a difference.

"You don't have to stay just because of me." She rested the back of her head against my chest and looked up at me. "Lars will play with me."

I kissed her on the forehead, feeling just as much satisfaction as I did when I kissed her shoulder. Heat flushed my skin like coals in a fire. "I want to play with you."

"Yeah?" She pressed against me, her ass directly on my cock.

I kissed her again in response.

"Can we take a walk? I want to see the vineyards."

"Whatever you want." I took her hand, and we walked out to the path around the grape vines. The harvest had just finished, but the vineyards would bloom with grapes again in no time. The smell was just the same, full of greenery and Tuscan sun. Hand in hand, we walked along the rows.

Button's eyes were enamored with the view around her. Not once did she look at me because she was infatuated with her bountiful surroundings. Wearing that dress, with her long brown strands hanging down her back, made her look like a native-born Tuscan. "I never thought I'd seen this place again...only in my dreams."

"Did you dream about it often?"

Her eyes moved to the hillside beyond where a shadow formed on the grass. A single cloud was in the blue sky and formed the only shadow across the land. Her attention was focused for nearly a minute before she returned to the conversation. "Every night."

"Did you dream about me?" I knew her answer without needing to ask. But I wanted to hear it anyway. I wanted to hear that she adored me and that living without me was too difficult to bear. I broke down on her doorstep, and I wanted her to break down for me.

Her answer was the same as the last one. She stopped walking and turned to me, her vibrant eyes matching the vines on either side of us. "Every night."

Buttons and Pain

Chapter Seventeen

Pearl

The Barsetti estate was a beautiful mansion that possessed the kind of Italian elegance people couldn't even begin to conceive of. Every inch of the estate was purposely decorated in just the right tone to make it come alive. Full of history, power, and beauty, it was one of the most spectacular sights I'd ever seen.

The view from any window was more breathtaking than anything imaginable. The vineyards stretched as far as the eye could see, and the low hills crept toward the sky and made a private valley just for the viewer to enjoy. The air was clean there, scented by sweet grapes and trees.

I didn't just love it because it was a fairy tale.

I loved it because it was home.

It was the first place where I felt like I belonged. Crow was the man I'd fantasized about marrying and spending the rest of my life with. I never thought I could trust a man after what had happened to me, but it was clear I trusted Crow with my life. No matter what happened, he would be there for me.

He would protect me.

The fact that there was someone just as jaded as I was made everything a little easier. I didn't feel so broken when he was broken too. He understood me without asking questions, and he understood how I felt at any given point in the day without me having to tell him.

It was a privilege to return to this beautiful place, even if it were temporary. We hadn't discussed what we were going to do, but I knew I would be there for a while. It wasn't safe for me to return to America when Bones could just extract me again. It seemed like the only place I was safe was wherever Crow was.

And that would have been perfectly fine if he felt the same way I did.

He'd walked out my door without looking back. He'd said his final farewell and was prepared to leave me in the past. If he didn't love me then, he wouldn't love me now. And he would never love me for as long as we lived.

So, I couldn't stay there forever.

One day, I'd have to leave. Until then, I'd planned to keep my heart locked up as tightly as possible. Nothing could reverse the feelings already burning in my heart. The love didn't just exist inside my chest but everywhere else. I couldn't erase it or pretend it wasn't there. But at least, I could stop it from growing.

Crow sat across from me at the table with his morning paper beside him. Eggs, bacon, and toast were placed in front of us along with a side of buttermilk pancakes. The food here was so much better than the stuff I was used to. Everything was fresh and lacked preservatives. The eggs were picked up from the market that morning, and the sugar was pure. It was so delicious that I wasn't sure I could ever go back to America for that reason alone.

Instead of reading his paper like he usually did, he drank his coffee and ate his food slowly. His appetite seemed low today, and he didn't even touch his pancakes. Most of the time, Lars didn't bring him anything sweet, but today, he did.

I eyed the paper. "Nothing good in there?"

"I don't know." He returned his cup to the saucer. "Haven't checked."

I didn't bother dissecting his riddle and continued to eat my pancakes. I was starving when I woke up that morning, and it didn't seem like there was enough food in the world to make me feel full. Now that Crow was back in my life, my appetite picked up because I felt the distant sensation of happiness. "Can I read the comics?"

He raised an eyebrow before he drank his coffee again. "We don't have comics, Button."

"What? Then what do you laugh at?"

He set his glass down and gave me his typical intense expression.

I met his look without reacting. He gave me an unusual amount of attention that morning. He didn't seem to care about the paper or his breakfast. All he cared about was me sitting across from him. "No one cares about world affairs. They only care about how much Garfield hates Mondays, which is ironic since he doesn't even have a job."

"Who's Garfield?"

"He's this orange tabby cat that loves lasagna."

Crow's look never changed. "And that's supposed to be funny."

"It's really funny. I'll try to find some online to show you. You'll get a kick out of it."

He poured more coffee into his mug then took a bite of his egg whites. He went for a run that morning, but he didn't eat more than usual. For a man who hardly ate and committed himself to exercising, I wasn't sure how he was so muscular. "I look forward to it."

"Are you working today?"

"No."

He'd already missed nearly a month of work, and he still hadn't gone back. "You don't need to hang out with me. I'll be fine."

"I know I don't need to *hang out* with you." His eyes held his amusement at my choice of words, something he would never say. "I want to hang out with you."

"Well, what do you want to do today?"

"The choice is entirely up to you."

"Why me?" I asked. "You're the bossy one."

Finally, the corner of his lip rose in a smile. "I guess I don't mind letting you take the lead once in a while."

"I saw a hammock outside."

He rested his hand on the table as he waited for me to elaborate.

"Can we lie in it and read?" I used to spend my afternoons outside while he was at work. The Tuscan sun kept me warm and lulled me into an afternoon nap that carried all my troubles away. By the time I woke up, he'd returned from work, and we got to have our fun.

I expected him to deny the suggestion, but he didn't. His mouth was still formed in a half smile. "Sure."

***

A nightmare made me toss and turn in the sheets, and I begged my mind to wake up. Bones had me, and he was forcing me into a life of submission and cruelty. After a few more turns, I finally gasped and woke up.

The bedroom was dark with the exception of the moonlight entering from the window. It flooded the room with beaming white light and allowed me to see my fingertips and my nose at the edge of my face.

Breathing hard and still terrified, I reached for Crow beside me. I needed those strong arms to form a steel cage around me and protect me from Bones as well as my subconscious. But when I saw the empty bed beside me, I realized I was alone.

He was gone.

I sat up straighter and looked around the room but didn't see him anywhere. The bathroom door was open, but I didn't hear his footsteps from inside. Only the shadows kept me company in the empty room. "Crow?"

The quiet ring of silence answered me.

I got out of bed and quickly pulled on one of his t-shirts before I went looking for him. My first guess was his study. It was full of scotch and brandy, along with a warm fireplace. If he was unable to sleep and wanted to be alone, that's where he'd go.

I entered the hallway and located the door on the left. I turned the knob and stepped inside, and the first thing I noticed was him sitting on the couch. Shirtless with just his pajama bottoms on, he leaned forward with his arms resting on his thighs. His eyes were glued to the dancing flames inside the hearth, and they reflected in the flecks of his eyes.

I shut the door behind me and crept farther into the room.

Not once did he acknowledge me, which told me he knew I was there the second my hand touched the doorknob. "Nightmare?"

"Yeah." I sank into the seat beside him and hooked my arm through his. "They seem to happen when you're gone."

"I'm your dream catcher."

I rested my cheek on his shoulder. "Yes."

"And you're my light catcher."

I raised my head when I didn't understand what he meant. I stared at the side of his face and waited for him to meet my look.

He never did. "You chase away the darkness. You capture the light." When he fell silent, I knew the conversation had been dismissed. A glass of scotch sat on the table with two large ice cubes sitting inside. The decanter was beside it, nearly full to the top.

He was in a particularly sour mood that evening, and I didn't understand what had provoked it. We spent the day lounging in the hammock and having dinner on the terrace. We didn't say much, but just being together felt nice. And now, he was drinking away his soul, alone in his study at three in the morning. "What is it, Crow? What's bothering you?"

He grabbed his glass and took a long drink. He forced himself to swallow like he was sick of the burn down his throat. When he returned the glass to the table, he spilled a few drops on the hard wood.

"Is it Bones?" I whispered. "Crow, we'll figure out a way to defeat him. We just need a strong plan." My fingers moved up his back and to the nape of his neck. I massaged his hair and felt the soft strands move against my callused hands. He closed his eyes for a moment, almost enjoying it. "We'll figure it out."

"It's not that...at least, not right now."

"Then what is it?" My hand stopped moving as I waited for an answer.

He stopped looking at the fire and turned his gaze to the paintings on the wall. The buttons still marked the images of the vineyards, and they were in the exact same place they used to be. The light from the fireplace illuminated the details. "Vanessa... She died two years ago today."

My hand fell down his back the second the revelation entered my mind. I never knew the date of when she passed away, but I'd been with him for almost a year and knew it would be soon. He didn't talk about Vanessa often, and when he did, he didn't say much. "I'm sorry."

"Bones is still alive." He shook his head in disgust. "He shouldn't be."

"It'll happen. Give it time."

"He almost got you, Button. I was lucky that I saved you. It could have gone quite differently."

"But it didn't." My arm squeezed his.

"But if it did…I wouldn't have been able to go on." He shook his head again. "I would have given up then and there and put a gun to my head. I would have pulled the trigger right in the middle of the street. Even if Cane were there, it wouldn't make a difference. Nothing would stop me from taking my own life." He grabbed the glass and finished it before he slammed it upside down onto the table.

I rubbed his arm and struggled to comfort him in any way possible. Words were useless when he was buzzed and depressed like this. Even if I brought the light, he couldn't see it. He was swallowed deep in darkness. "We're going to take him down and get the revenge you deserve. Then I'll be free to go home and live out the rest of my life in peace. Everything will be okay."

He finally turned my way and held my gaze with his own. His eyes weren't warm like they usually were. Now, they were darker than charcoal. Without saying a single insult, he threatened me with a simple stare. "You aren't leaving, Button. Not now. Not ever."

"When he's dead, Crow. Not tomorrow." I'd already known Crow wouldn't let me walk away until it was absolutely safe. After he slaughtered those men,

I knew he'd appointed himself as my full-time bodyguard. There wasn't a single place I could go without him knowing about it. I couldn't set foot outside the estate, and I was always being watched.

"Not even then."

When his meaning settled on my shoulders, the rage immediately kicked in. Crow and I had come to a place where we were equals. I didn't owe him any more buttons, and he couldn't command me like he owned me. I wasn't his slave, his property, or his anything. And he'd better not forget it. "You don't tell me what to do. If I want to leave, I'll leave—"

"I love you."

I halted in midsentence and felt the unbearable pain enter my stomach like I'd been shot with a gun. I couldn't speak because my mouth was frozen, and like I'd always been on the verge of tears, my eyes watered. My lungs ached because I couldn't breathe. I'd heard what he said, but it was too good to be true. It felt so good it actually hurt. It was a tease, a glimpse of my most lavish dreams. "Are you... Are you just saying that?" Crow wouldn't lie to me, but he would do whatever was necessary to keep me safe. If it came down to it, he would say something like that to protect me.

"Never." His hand wrapped around my neck gently and rested right over my pulse. Every time my vein throbbed, I could feel the vibration against his palm. "I lost Vanessa, and it killed me. I loved her so damn much, and the second she was gone, I wasn't the same person anymore. But the idea of losing you…hurts me a million times more. I've been trying to deny it for a while, but I can't do it anymore. I know exactly why the pain is unbearable. I know exactly why it consumes my nightmares…because I love you." He rested his forehead against mine and closed his eyes, his breathing deep and even. "Now, I want you to say it back."

The fire crackled in the fireplace and was the only sound in the house. Our breathing filled the space and our thunderous beating hearts hammered at full speed. To anyone else, it was the sound of silence. But to us, it was the sound of a new beginning.

I never expected him to say those precious words, even if he did feel them. Now that he did, I couldn't stop my vulnerable reaction. Tears fell from my eyes and streaked down my cheeks like two small waterfalls. I didn't understand just how much I needed him to say those words until he'd actually said them. This place was my home—he was my home. He was the only man that ever made me feel complete. He was a dream I never thought I could have, but he finally took down his walls and let me in.

"Button." He pulled away and looked me in the eye, his expression the same as it always was. It was dark and intense, not an emotional wreck like mine. His fingers didn't squeeze my neck, but he gave me a gentle tug of impatience.

I finally got myself under control and wiped my tears away with the back of my forearm. Crying was annoying and a serious waste of time, but I gave in to it. When he'd left my apartment, I did the same thing and humiliated myself right in front of him. After priding myself on being harder than steel, I was crumbling like an old pile of leaves. "I love you too."

His thumbs wiped away the last of my tears, and he stared into my eyes with a new expression. He was still dark and threatening, but different from who he used to be. When I first met him, he was cold and terrifying. He would kill anyone who got in his way, and he was ruthless in his leadership. Desperately trying to remain numb and void of all emotion, he turned to sex and scotch. He refused to let me in even though he was several layers deep inside me. But he'd finally let his walls come down and stepped into the light.

He stepped into the light with me.

Buttons and Pain

Chapter Eighteen

Crow

I woke up early that morning, went for a run, and then had a quick bite downstairs. I had a lot of work to do and not much time to get it done. While I wanted to stay home with Button, I had to leave her warm caresses and kisses and step into the real world.

I had to kill Bones.

I took a quick shower downstairs, and Lars fitted me with a new suit he got in Florence. Made of fine Italian craftsmanship to my exact specifications, I looked like a man you didn't want to cross.

But then again, I always looked that way.

"Your car is waiting, Your Grace." Lars smoothed out the back of my jacket even though it was already crisp then walked to the entryway.

"Thank you. Tell Pearl I'll be back before dinner."

"Or you could tell me yourself." She stood at the top of the stairs wearing my t-shirt and sweatpants. Her hair was in a braid over one shoulder, and one hand was on her hip.

My attempt to sneak out had failed. I walked to the foot of the stairs but didn't meet her at the top. "I have work to do. I'll see you at dinner."

She narrowed her eyes on me, suspicion deep inside. If it were a regular day at the winery, I wouldn't be leaving this early, and I wouldn't sneak out without kissing her goodbye. "What aren't you telling me?"

"Nothing." I put my hands in my pockets and continued to meet her gaze. "I'll see you later." I turned around and headed to the door.

"Whoa, hold on."

I turned back around, not bothering to hide my annoyance.

She walked down the stairs gracefully, carrying herself like she wore a gown rather than my enormous clothes. She took her time because she knew I would wait for her until she reached the bottom. When she arrived, she wrapped her arms around my neck and kissed me. "Don't ever leave without kissing me goodbye."

My hands tightened around her waist, and I felt myself get swept away. My earlier ambition disappeared the second that warm mouth was on mine. Now, I wanted to lift her into my arms and take her back upstairs.

She pulled away, her eyes greedy for my affection. "Do you understand me?"

Buttons and Pain

My spine shivered when I heard the command in her voice. When the authoritative side of her came out, it made me harder than steel. I loved it when she possessed me, controlled me like I was hers to be controlled. "Yes."

She gave me a knowing look before she kissed the corner of my mouth. "I'll see you later."

I melted again, desperate to take her upstairs and pin her to the mattress as I had my way with her. She knew she was teasing me, punishing me for trying to get out of the house, so I wouldn't have to explain anything to her. The second I got home, she would rip into me.

And I looked forward to it.

***

"What the fuck took so long?" Cane was on me the moment I pulled into the base.

"I was running late."

"Doing what?" he snapped. "Just get in your car and drive."

I placed my hand on his face and gave him a forceful shove as I kept walking. My younger brother couldn't talk to me like that even if he was right. I marched inside and turned to the intel center. The guys were at their stations taking care of business as usual.

Cane came in behind me, but he didn't continue the argument. "He's gonna call in two minutes. Are you ready for this?"

Beyond ready. "Yes." I sat at the table where the single landline waited. My cell phone was forwarded to the line so it could be traced easier. If we could pinpoint his location, we could bomb him back to World War II. All he knew was we made weapons, not explosives. He was in for a surprise.

"Keep him on the line—"

"You think this is my first rodeo?"

Cane slammed his hand down. "For a guy getting pussy every night, you sure as hell have a shitty attitude."

"Don't talk about her like that again." My hand balled into a fist, and I threatened him with a mere look. He could insult me all he wanted, but Button was off-limits. "Unless you want me to shoot you in the other arm."

Before Cane could respond, the phone rang.

I purposely didn't answer it on the first ring just to be a dick. There was nothing more disrespectful than wasting someone's time. When I was finally done letting the seconds trickle by, I answered. "Crow."

He paused on the line, wasting my time just as I'd wasted his. "I'm impressed with the way you handled Pearl's extraction. If I weren't so irritated, I might actually applaud."

I stared at Cane as I stayed on the line. He stood with his arms across his chest and the headset over his ears, so he could listen to the conversation.

"I'm not impressed that you fail to do your dirty work with your own hands."

"Oh, I do, Crow. Just ask Pearl."

My hand balled into a fist again, this time nearly cutting my skin.

"I don't need to tell you that I want her, and I'm going to get her. Hand her over, and the feud between us ends once and for all."

"Never." I was never going to give up Button. I would fight until my last breath to make sure she was safe. If he wanted her, he had to come through me. And he would never succeed. "I'm sure there's something else we can compromise on. As I've said in the past, I'm willing to compensate you."

"There's not enough money to replace her."

245

It was the first time we'd agreed on something.

"Then no deal."

"Crow, I'm going to come at you hard until I get her. I will find you, and when I do, I'll fuck her in the ass right in front of you. I suggest you take the easy way out while it's still available. Because if you keep trying my patience, I'll treat her far worse than I ever treated your precious little sister."

I restrained myself from slamming my hand on the table. The mention of Vanessa took the conversation to a new level. My blood was boiling, and I couldn't stop shaking. "She's just a woman. You can always find another to entertain yourself."

"But I want her. And I'm pretty sure you understand why."

I didn't deny the implication because my intentions toward Button were more obvious than the shining sun. "You can't have her, Bones. That's not up for debate. I suggest you settle for something else, so we can call off this war. As a gesture of peace, Cane and I won't make you pay for Vanessa's death." That was the most generous offer I could possibly make, and Bones knew it. It was difficult for us to let Vanessa's murder go unpunished, but she was already gone. Button was still alive, and we had to keep it that way. "That's my best offer."

Bones was silent for nearly a minute. If he was seriously considering the offer, we were making progress. Or he was just drawing it out to make me squirm. "I'm going to get her, Crow. And when I do, I'm not going to kill you. I'm gonna make you watch me fuck her until I kill her. And after you see me slit her throat, I'll do the same to you."

***

When I got home, Button was sitting on the balcony looking over the vineyards. She was sipping a glass of red wine and wearing a dress Lars had picked up for her at one of the shops in Florence. Aqua-colored gems hung from her lobes, and her hair was pulled back in some kind of bun. In her lap was a book. Like she'd never left in the first place, she fell right back into her routine of entertaining herself until I came home.

Instead of telling her I was there, I stood in the doorway and watched her. With my hands in my pockets, I admired every feature I'd come to adore. She had long, thin legs that gripped my hips tightly when we made love. Her toes were always manicured even though she never painted them. Sometimes, she wore makeup, but most of the time, she didn't, which was fine by me. She looked stunning just the way she was. I studied her slender neck and remembered all the kisses I had placed there. I couldn't recall the exact moment my heart softened and let her in. It could have happened the very first time I laid eyes on her when she was fighting to survive. Or it could have been the moment she told me she loved me. I didn't say it back because the feeling wasn't mutual. I just didn't say it because of the heartbreak it might lead to down the road.

But now I couldn't deny it, and I certainly didn't want to.

Button must have picked up on my presence because she turned around and looked at me. "I didn't know you were home." She set her book and wineglass on the table and stood, the dress hugging her curves perfectly. "How long have you been standing there?"

"A while." I pulled her inside and guided her to the bed. A moment ago, I was content with examining her intricate details in an affectionate way. But now that she was looking at me with those sparkling blue eyes, I wanted to do something other than stare.

Buttons and Pain

I yanked her dress up and pulled her hips to the edge of the bed. My pants and boxers were around my ankles, and once her thong was on the floor, I shoved my dick deep inside her and felt her wet channel greet me. The second I was inside her, I stopped and treasured the sensation. Sex had never felt this good.

Button pushed my jacket off my shoulders then undid the buttons at the bottom of my shirt, wanting to expose my chest and stomach. "I want to see all of you." She lay back, her hair a mess on the bed underneath her. It had come loose from her hair tie and was all over the place and easy for me to grab.

I undid the rest of the buttons and dropped my shirt to the floor. I wanted to see her tits underneath her dress, but I was too eager to start thrusting. With my hands on either side of her head, I leaned over her and gave her powerful jolts. Her slick pussy felt like heaven, and with every thrust, I was falling deeper into her. She didn't give me restrained looks of affection anymore. Now that we were honest about our feelings, she gave me all of her. She never held herself back and desperately clung to me like she couldn't live without me. She rocked into me harder than I rocked into her, and she said my name so many times I couldn't keep track.

It was the best.

I leaned farther over her and pressed her feet against my chest. She bent her knees to accommodate me, and she allowed me to dominate her completely. I pinned her right against the mattress and thrust into her so hard my balls smacked against her ass. She became wetter and wetter, and soon, she was crying out my name at the top of her lungs.

Just when I'd pushed her over the edge, I emptied myself inside her, knowing I could do this every single day for the rest of my life. No woman ever compared to the one underneath me. She fought me, adored me, and submitted to me all at the same time. "That's what I want every single day when I come home. Do you understand me?" I gripped her chin and forced her eyes on me. She controlled me that morning, but now it was my turn to control her.

She wrapped her fingers around my wrist as I continued to hold her chin. "Yes. And that's what I want every single day too."

***

Candles burned on the table, and the evening crickets chirped throughout the night. The Tuscan sun had disappeared over the hills just thirty minutes earlier, and now, it was twilight. The land was going to sleep, but it buzzed with so much life long after the sun was gone.

Button sat across from me at the table and finished the remains of her dinner. Her hair was in a braid over one shoulder, and her dress was strapless to show off her toned shoulders. A silver necklace hung around her throat, something Lars had picked out for her.

We didn't say anything over dinner, but instead, made eyes at one another. I didn't say much anyway, but it was nice not having to make conversation just for the sake of it. We were comfortable in our mutual silence, and expectations weren't laid on either one of us. But I suspected she was going to ask me what I had been up to that morning.

And she did. "What kind of work did you have today?" She knew I was doing something in secret or else she would have asked the question in a different way. For one, she wouldn't have specifically asked what kind of work I had done. And two, she wouldn't have been waiting to ask the question so for long unless she was fearful of the answer.

"Stuff with Cane." I wasn't going to mention my conversation with Bones. Button was strong and

251

fearless, but even that would frighten her. He basically told me he would never stop hunting her until she was his slave again. Since she was mine in every definable way, she didn't need to worry about it. Under my watch, nothing would ever happen to her.

"Oh." She sipped her wine before she returned the glass to the table. Another question was on her lips, but she didn't ask it.

"We're working on our plan to take out Bones. We're considering bombing one of his factories, so he'll be drawn out into the open. And when that happens, we'll hit him with gunfire."

"So, you don't know where he is?"

"Not at the moment." But I would find out.

"Do you think he's in Italy?"

"Not right now." As soon as we took out his men, he must have retreated to France or Russia to recuperate. We had the upper hand, and he knew it. It was pure chaos in the street, and if he didn't hear about it from his own men, he'd heard about it from the police.

She swirled her wine then looked into her glass. "So…should we have that conversation neither one of us wants to have?"

Buttons and Pain

I stared at her face and waited for her to meet my gaze. She continued to look at her wine so she could avoid eye contact. It was unlike her to hide away behind something, and I didn't like it. "Look at me when you speak to me."

It took her a moment to comply. She raised her head slowly, irritated by the command but also aroused by it. She hated it when I bossed her around like I owned her, but she also loved it at the same time. She was a strong woman who needed a stronger man.

"What conversation?"

"About us." She moved her glass to the side.

"I thought our relationship was pretty defined." When I told her those three little words, I'd assumed that encompassed everything that needed to be said.

"I mean, in terms of Bones. What are we going to do?"

"I'm going to kill him. I told you that."

"What if you don't? What if you can't?"

My eyes narrowed at the insult. "If I said I'm going to kill him, I will."

"And I don't doubt you," she said with forced calmness. "But what if he's impossible to track down?

What if he's always on the move? Should we leave Tuscany? Should we move somewhere else?"

"No." I wasn't the kind of man to run from a fight.

"How does he not know where you live? He must know you make wine, so he can figure out where your house is."

"Yes, he knows I make wine. But just because my vineyard is here doesn't mean I have anything to do with it. According to the paperwork, the property is owned by a family who bought it from mine. The paperwork is false, but he won't know that. And in regards to my home, this estate isn't even on a map. It's not registered to anyone or anything. All my mail is sent to a PO Box in Florence, and even then, it's under a fake name. He won't trace us back here. You don't need to worry about it."

Like a queen, she held herself with refined posture and elegance. Her hair was pulled back from her face, and the lipstick on her mouth made her lips look fuller and even more kissable. But her confidence and strength gave her the greatest qualities of majesty. I'd always felt like the king of my world. And she certainly was my queen. "So, we're going to continue to live here?"

"Yes."

"And I can live here for as long as I want?"

My eyes narrowed. "Button, you're living here forever." Even if I killed Bones, she wasn't going anywhere. She wouldn't rent a house somewhere in Florence and visit me for sleepovers and dinners. I told her I loved her, and that confession carried more weight than she understood. "This is your home now."

She quickly looked away, but she wasn't fast enough. Just a glimpse of moisture built up in her eyes. She blinked it away like it was never there at all.

I pretended I hadn't noticed. "But it will be dangerous for a while. Until I kill Bones, you need to stay at the estate and never leave."

"Okay." Instead of arguing for her freedom and independence, she let it be. "Can I have a gun?"

"You want one?" She knew how to use one, but I'd never seen her in action.

"No. I need one."

"Consider it done."

She sipped her wine again. "There's something else I want…"

Penelope Sky

I'd already given my queen the world. What more could she want? "What?"

"I want to kill him myself." She held my gaze as she made the demand. "I know you and Cane both need revenge for Vanessa...but I'd really like to be the one to pull the trigger."

After what he did to her, I couldn't deny her request. She deserved it. "If the situation presents itself, yes."

"Thank you," she whispered. "It means more than I can say."

I'd never forget the first time I saw her in that opera. From a distance, I could detect her rapid breathing and flushed cheeks. She was scared sitting next to the most ruthless man the world had ever seen. Instead of succumbing to the grief, she tried to find a way to escape—but she was still scared. At the time, her beauty had no hold over me. I'd seen countless beautiful women across Italy. She wasn't special. But when I saw the fire burning in her eyes, I was lost. "You deserve it more than I do."

"I wouldn't say that."

When I saw her point the gun at her own chest and prepare to pull the trigger, I knew she'd hit rock bottom. Bones had tortured her beyond repair, and death was her only escape. If I hadn't stopped her, she would have done it. There was no doubt of that. Since then, she'd come a long way. It took her months to smile and even longer to finally trust me.

"I want to help in whatever way I can. Whatever you need, I'm there."

I wasn't letting Button anywhere near him. There was no way in hell I was using her as bait or sending her into combat with Cane and me. After the threats Bones had made, I didn't want him even to look at her. "We'll see."

***

When I came home from work, Button was nowhere to be found. She wasn't in the bedroom, on the balcony, near the pool, or in the study. Normally when I came home, she presented herself to me immediately with a kiss.

But now I couldn't find her.

I tried not to panic and jump to the worst possible conclusion. The house was undisturbed, and the staff were unharmed. The gateway to the estate had been closed and locked when I pulled up in my car.

I walked to the bottom floor and searched for my butler. "Lars."

He emerged from the kitchen, his white hair combed back and a warm smile on his face. No matter how angry I looked, he didn't seem to notice. "Yes, Your Grace?"

"Have you seen Pearl?" I wasn't going to resort to calling out her name around the estate. She knew her job was to greet me the second I came home. I'd just made the demand the day before, and she wasn't that forgetful.

"I'm in here." Button stepped out of the kitchen with a red apron around her waist. "Sorry, I lost track of time." Stains were smeared across the fabric, and a spot of sauce was on her cheek. She walked to me while wiping her hands down the front of her apron. "It's a whole other world in that kitchen—"

"Don't pull that stunt again." I couldn't dim my anger in front of Lars. He knew what kind of man I was, so my threats weren't surprising. He crept back into the kitchen and tried to disappear without either one of us noticing.

Button's eyes narrowed to threatening slits. "What stunt?"

258

Buttons and Pain

"What did I say yesterday? When I come home, you either drop to your knees or bend over. Sending me on a wild goose chase around the house is unacceptable. For a second, I thought something had happened to you—"

"I was making you dinner, asshole." She put both of her hands on her hips and darkened her look.

My tongue suddenly felt too big for my mouth. The words instantly died in my throat when I realized just how hostile I'd become in a matter of seconds. She was the only person who could put me in my place like that.

"I lost track of time and didn't realize you were home. But if you want me to drop to my knees and suck you off right this second, I will. Is that what you want?" She raised her voice and was borderline feral.

If I didn't backtrack, this argument would take a deadly turn. When I went head-to-head with Button, I usually lost. She was smart with words and unafraid to make me feel like the piece of shit I was. "When I couldn't find you, I panicked. I thought someone took you... I'm not going to apologize for that."

"No." She crossed her arms over her chest. "You are going to apologize for that. You just insulted me in front of Lars and treated me like a slave. You bet your ass you're going to apologize to me, and you're gonna mean every goddamn word."

My body reacted in the wrong way. My cock hardened in my slacks and pressed against my zipper. Something about her ruthlessness got to me. I'd never met someone so small and fearless. Even when she didn't know me, she wasn't afraid of me. It just made me want to possess her even more.

She kept her stance and continued to threaten me with those full lips. They were pressed tightly together to keep the venom in her mouth. This was a battle she refused to lose, and she would fight until the war was won.

I'd never let anyone speak to me that way—let alone a woman. But she put me in my place so effortlessly and didn't flinch while doing it. I wasn't sure if she really was as strong as steel or if she simply made me weak. Whatever the case, I allowed this to happen. And there was only one woman who could make me do it.

No woman had ever brought me to my knees— but she did it. I took a knee in front of her and looked up at her.

Buttons and Pain

Button couldn't hide the surprise on her face. The ferocity in her eyes disappeared quicker than the snap of a finger, and her lips parted in shock. With just her words and her looks, she defeated me. She managed to tame the most feral beast in the world.

"I'm sorry." I meant what I said, and I didn't care if the staff saw me at my weakest point. Button was my queen, and I'd come to terms with the fact that I wouldn't always be the ruler in the relationship. Sometimes she would be the dictator, and sometimes I would.

She still hadn't recovered from the shock on her face. Countless times, she'd fought me tooth and nail and said the harshest things I didn't want to hear. But she never brought me to my knees the way she did now. It took her a moment to finally speak. "I forgive you."

**

We had dinner on the terrace like every night. The weather was too perfect to be ignored. It was cool with a warm breeze, and the nighttime air wasn't quite so humid at this time of year. Button loved being outside under the sun. Even when she was inside, she sat on the balcony just so she could be closer to nature and all its fruit.

"Thank you for dinner. It was excellent." Actually, it was nothing compared to Lars's cooking, but I appreciated what she did. She did the sexiest thing a woman could do for a man—cook for him. It was something I never had a desire for until now. The idea of her doing anything thoughtful for me was a turn-on.

"Thanks for saying that. I know it wasn't very good, but Lars is teaching me. In a few months, I'm sure I'll be better."

I sipped my wine to dismiss her words.

"It's definitely not easy like mac and cheese." She chuckled to herself at her own comment.

"I've never had it."

"You're never had it?" she asked in shock. "Like, ever?"

"I've had noodles with parmesan, but not the American version you're talking about."

"It's so good. I'll have to make it for you."

It sounded like processed horseshit to me. "Maybe." If she made it for me, I would suck it up and eat it. But I wouldn't be happy about it. European food was so much more palatable than American. Their food wasn't fresh, it was full of pesticides, and it didn't taste nearly as good. In the closest town, there was a local market every morning where Lars bought our groceries. Most of the produce had been picked the day before.

Now that dinner was finished, my mind drifted to my favorite activity. When I'd come home, we spent our time fighting rather than making love. Now that my stomach was full and Button was looking beautiful across from me, that's what I wanted to do next.

She rose from the table then stood a few feet away on the concrete underneath the swaying trees. Twilight was deepening into night, and the lights strung across the patio were blocking out the stars up above.

I stared at her with a raised eyebrow.

She extended her hand. "Dance with me."

I heard her command but didn't understand it. The last time I'd danced with a woman was so long ago I couldn't even recall it. But here she was, asking me to dance to the sound of silent music. If it were anyone else, I would walk inside without giving her a second look. But that excitement in her eyes and that smile on her lips pulled me toward her like a magnet.

I joined her under the strings of lights and took her hand in mine. My arm wrapped around her waist, and I slowly guided her across an invisible dance floor. The movements came naturally to me, but I suspected that confidence came from the woman in my arms. She wanted a dance, and I would give her the best damn dance she'd even seen.

When she smiled, I knew she loved it.

I'd never done romance before, but here I was, dancing with a woman I adored. I said those three little words I vowed never to utter, and I even bowed to her in the greatest gesture of possession. I'd never known this kind of happiness, and honestly, it was a little scary.

It was scary because if I lost her, I'd be done.

She pulled herself closer to me and pressed her forehead to mine. Her eyes stared at my lips, but she didn't kiss me. Completely enamored of me, she was obsessed and devoted. She showed me her love long before she said it, and I loved seeing that look in her eyes.

Something supernatural possessed me, and I suddenly began to sing quietly under my breath. My words were in Italian, and I serenaded the woman in my arms. It was an old love song, something I heard in the village where I grew up. I was too young to understand love, and as I grew older, I knew I would never have the privilege of feeling it.

But I was wrong.

Button pulled away slightly so she could look into my eyes. She listened to every word even though she couldn't understand it. My voice was deeper than the man who originally sang the song, but she had no way of knowing that. I wouldn't consider myself to be a talented singer, but I didn't sound bad either. Her eyes watered slightly, and when the coat of moisture was present, it reflected the white lights above us. They twinkled in her eyes like stars, glowing like the heavens.

She fell deeper into me, so I kept singing. I watched her hang on to my every word without understanding them. Somehow, she knew exactly what I was trying to say, that I pledged my life and loyalty to her, and to her alone. I'd never kneeled for someone. And I certainly had never sung for someone.

Only her.

When I finished the song, the same look was in her eyes. She adored me even more than before, and her love had no boundaries as it continued to grow. Women often looked at me with infatuation and obsession. But the look Button gave me was different. It was more than superficial and physical.

It was unconditional.

I wanted to tell her I loved her, but I didn't. She didn't say it either because it was unnecessary. We'd been saying it to each other since the moment we met—just without words. I knew I would love her for all my life—until the day I left this earth and turned to dust. And she felt the same way.

Button stopped dancing and kissed me softly on the lips. "Let's go upstairs..."

I felt her soft lips against mine, and my cock hardened. I wasn't in the mood for serious fucking. I wanted to continue to dance together on my bed, to move slowly together to music only she and I could hear. My body wanted to combine with hers and make her mine forever.

I grabbed her hand and pulled her to the door. Our dirty plates remained on the terrace, but Lars would pick them up the moment we were gone. Just when we approached the back door, we were blocked.

Buttons and Pain

Cane leaned against the doorway with his arms across his chest. A smug grin was on his face, and his eyes were diabolical. "You guys were so cute I didn't want to interrupt you."

I'd never been more irritated to see my brother. "You're interrupting us now."

He shrugged then stepped back so we could enter the house. "It was such a good show that I couldn't stop watching. Nice pipes, by the way."

I should've been embarrassed that he'd heard me. The teasing would continue for the rest of our lives. But I wasn't going to give in to his taunts. That song was only meant for Button. It was a shame he got to witness it. "What do you want?"

"A conversation." He turned to Button and winked. "If she can spare you."

"No, she can't." I pulled her closer into my side. "We can talk tomorrow, Cane."

"Come on, I'm already here," he said. "It'll just be a few minutes."

I wished I could kill him right on the spot.

"It's fine." Button leaned into me and kissed the scruff along my jaw. "I'll be waiting upstairs." She moved her lips to my ear so only I could hear what she said next. "And I'll slip into something a little more comfortable." She kissed my earlobe before she walked up the stairs.

My eyes immediately followed her and homed in on her perfect ass. The last thing I wanted to do was talk to my brother at the foot of the stairs. I wanted to be buried inside my lover, my woman. When she was gone, I turned on Cane. "What?" I didn't bother hiding my disdain. I hated Cane in that moment, and I wanted that to be perfectly clear.

He continued to grin like a goddamn idiot. "That looked romantic."

I stared him down and kept my hands by my sides. They formed fists the second Button walked away, and I wanted to punch my brother in the face and break both cheekbones.

"I didn't realize you were the dancing and singing type."

I was about to snap. The only reason why I didn't was because Cane was my only family in the world. If he were anyone else, he'd already be knocked out cold. "Cane, spit it out. I have a woman to please." All he had were expensive whores to do the dirty things he wanted. I had a woman who did them because she wanted to.

"Have you thought about our last conversation?"

"Cane, I never think about you unless I'm looking at you."

He took the insult in stride. "Did you tell her how you feel? If you haven't, you may not need to. You made it pretty fucking obvious out there with that serenade."

"Your obsession with my love life is creepy, Cane."

"I'm not obsessed. Now answer the question."

These girly talks were getting old. At least if I told him the truth, they would stop. "It's not any of your business, but yes, I told her I loved her." The words were out of my mouth and into the ether forever. I couldn't take them back, and I didn't ever want to.

A slow smile crept into his face until it was a full-blown grin. "Good for you, man." He clapped my shoulder.

"Can we stop talking about it now?"

"Sure. I'm just glad you stopped acting like a pussy."

"Me?" I asked incredulously. "You're the one who kept pestering me."

"I just want the best for you. And I think she's it. I know for a fact Vanessa would have loved her."

The mention of my sister made me sad all over again. Yes, she would have loved Button. My entire family would have adored her.

"I'm sorry if my prying annoys you. But Ma isn't around anymore and neither is Vanessa, so someone has to do it." He shrugged. "I'm the only family you have left, so it has to be me. One day, when I meet the right woman, you have my full blessing to annoy the shit out of me and make sure I don't fuck it up."

I finally smiled, and the action came easily. "We have a deal."

Buttons and Pain

Chapter Nineteen

Pearl

Crow came home at the same time as usual. He entered the bedroom wearing the same pristine suit he wore that morning, and he looked just as delicious as every other day of his life. His flashy watch was on his wrist, and the tops of his hands were corded with veins. Just the sight of him made every woman wet.

He stopped when he spotted me at the edge of the bed. I stood in black lingerie, a teddy tight around my waist with my tits pressed together, and black stockings that led to a matching lace thong.

His eyes immediately darkened to the same color as my lingerie. Then he noticed the handcuffs dangling from my fingertips. Unable to hide his arousal, he swallowed the lump in his throat.

After a pause, he yanked his tie off and threw it on the ground. He undressed himself with speed as he walked closer to me, getting every piece of clothing off before he stood in front of me, god and man mixed together. His body was a behemoth of muscle, and his eyes showed the dark desires in his heart. His cock was rock-hard and ready to be inside me at the snap of a finger. "On your knees." He immediately took control of the situation, becoming dominant and possessive. Lately, we'd only been making sweet and sensual love. But the need for a hard fuck returned to his body instantly.

"No."

His eyes narrowed when I defied him.

"You've got the wrong idea." I pressed my hands against his chest and guided him to the bed. When the mattress was behind his knees, I shoved him onto the mattress then crawled on top of him. "Sit up." I held the handcuffs, ready to chain him to the headboard.

When he finally understood what was really happening, his desire only deepened. The only thing that turned him on more than controlling me was having a woman powerful enough to control him. He did as I asked and rested his back against the headboard, his eyes locked on mine the entire time.

I slipped his hands through the bars and secured him in place.

He immediately leaned in and kissed my neck, his tongue moving along the skin in a seductive way. His cock was hard against his stomach, and he pressed it against me in anticipation.

Buttons and Pain

I left his lap and stood next to the bed, slowly playing with my panties. I fingered them gently, feeling the lace in my delicate fingertips.

Crow watched me, his eyes glued to the movement of my fingers.

I slowly pulled them down my long legs then kicked them aside.

His eyes immediately went to the nub between my legs, and his lips parted in desperation.

I straddled his hips and rested my folds against his cock. Slowly, I moved forward and backward, dragging my lubrication down his length and to his balls.

He pulled on the cuffs in an attempt to grab me, forgetting he was restrained. A quiet growl escaped his lips in frustration. "Button..." The plea was in his voice, a sign of his desperation to be inside me. He knew just how wet I was because I was smearing his entire length with it.

I gripped his shoulders and positioned myself over him. "You want me?"

"Yes."

"Tell me."

He stretched his neck out and kissed the corner of my mouth. "I want to fuck you."

"Say my name."

He spoke against my mouth, his chest rising and falling anxiously. "I want to fuck you, Button."

I positioned his head at my entrance and slid all the way down until he was balls deep.

"Fuck." Crow pulled on the chains and tried to break free.

Using his shoulders as an anchor, I moved up and down his length. He was so thick and full, and I wanted to give in to my desire then and there. Sex with Crow was unlike anything I'd ever known. It was passionate, scorching, and delectable all at the same time.

"Let me go." He pulled on the chains again and nearly broke the headboard.

"No." I wrapped my arms around his neck and deepened my thrusts. I pushed him entirely within me before I pulled up until only the tip of his cock remained inside me. Then I shoved him inside me again, stretching me once more.

"Fuck, Button."

I kissed his bottom lip and sucked it into my mouth. I gave him a playful bite because I knew he loved the violence. I didn't make him bleed, but I caused him pain.

He breathed into my mouth and tried to fight the pleasure building deep in his balls. He'd come inside me so many times that I knew exactly what he was feeling as he felt it.

I moved my hand between my legs and rubbed my clit aggressively, wanting to give him a show he would never forget.

He watched me the entire time, his eyes darker than the underworld. He pulled on his chains even though it was hopeless. His hips thrust into me from down below, and his neck became corded from the tension.

"God, I'm gonna come." I rubbed my clit harder and took in his length. The pleasure was building over the horizon and quickly approaching. I already knew it was going to be blinding and powerful. It would shatter me into infinite pieces, and I would never be put back together.

"So. Fucking. Gorgeous."

I felt the explosion between my legs, and instantly, I was swept off to the stars. I dug my nails into his shoulders and screamed in his face. His name escaped my throat countless times, and soon, my mouth went dry.

I kept taking his cock deep inside me and dragged my hands down his chest. I felt the sweat under my fingertips along with the muscles and strength. That orgasm knocked me off my feet and sucked all the energy out of my body.

Seeing the pleasure on my face just turned him on even more. "Slap me."

I grinded into his length, moving him against my walls so he could feel every inch of me.

"Slap me, Button."

I lightly smacked my palm against his face.

"Harder."

I did it again, making my palm clap against his skin.

"Harder."

This time, I did it as hard as I could, making his face turn with the movement.

He finally groaned, his eyes closed, and pleasure was written across his face. "Again."

I hit my hand across his face.

He turned with the momentum again, and his cheek reddened. He clenched his jaw and opened his eyes, the satisfaction deep in the look. "One more time."

I did it again, and I hit him even harder.

"Fuck." He tensed underneath me and filled me with his hoard of come. The heat spread between my legs as the weight of his deposit settled deep inside me. I could feel the weight as well as the scorching warmth of his seed.

It took nearly a minute for him to wind down from the pleasure and come back to earth. His cheek was red from the several times I slapped him, and he seemed more satisfied than ever before. "You complete me."

I expected him to say something dirty or issue a command to release him, so the words caught me off guard. Sincerity was in his voice when he spoke, and it was just as sweet as the moment he told me he loved me. "And you complete me."

***

"Let me go!" Tears streamed down my face as I gripped the carpet. I dug my nails into the fabric so he couldn't drag me across the ground. I was reaching for anything to get me to safety.

Bones yanked hard on my leg and nearly broke it. "Shut up, slave."

"Stop!" I kicked my leg as hard as I could. I refused to be enslaved by this madman again. My life would be nothing but torture and pain. "Please let me go."

"Button." Strong hands shook me hard. "Button, I'm here."

That voice fell on my ears and brought me comfort. Out of nowhere, Crow appeared from down the hallway. He grabbed me by both hands and yanked me away, pulling me from the grasp of my captor. But I couldn't stop crying. I couldn't shake the terror.

"Button, wake up." Another jerk and the dream shattered.

I sat up in bed and clutched the sheets. My eyes snapped open, and I only saw the shadows of Crow's bedroom. My breathing was haywire, and no matter how deep I tried to breathe, I wasn't getting enough oxygen. My body was drenched in sweat, and my face was soaked with tears.

Buttons and Pain

"Button." Crow's soft voice came from beside me. "It was just a nightmare. It's over. You're here with me, and you're safe." He didn't touch me, keeping a foot between us. His hands rested by his sides, but his eyes longed to touch me. "You're safe with me."

The tears were still hot, and my body was still shaking. Nightmares came from time to time, but they usually didn't exist at all when I slept with Crow. It was unexpected, and that just terrified me even more. The sobs wracked my chest, and I tried to stop them before they escalated.

"You're safe." Crow repeated his words to bring me back to earth. Instead of telling me to quiet down and gather myself, he was patient with me. He used to prohibit me from crying, but now, he watched my tears with concern instead of irritation. "I will never let anyone hurt you again, Button. You have my word."

I finally found the strength to speak. "I know."

He moved closer to me and wrapped a powerful arm around my waist. His touch was warm, not cold and callous like Bones's. Crow rested his face against mine then ran his fingers through my hair to soothe me. "You can talk to me."

The last thing I wanted to do was revisit the nightmare. I wanted it to disappear into the recesses of my mind where I couldn't visit it ever again. Like it'd never happened, I wanted it to go away. "No." The dream was already painful for me. It would only hurt Crow even more.

"You're with me now. Remember that." He wrapped his hand around the back of my neck and kissed the corner of my mouth. "He can't hurt you as long as I'm alive. Do you understand me?"

I nodded.

"Do you understand me?"

I cleared my throat then swallowed my tears. "Yes."

"Next time you have a bad dream, count backward from three. When you're done, wake up."

I looked into his eyes and silently asked for further explanation.

"I used to have nightmares," he whispered. "Counting backward always works. Trust me."

"What are your nightmares about?" I shouldn't ask the question, but I did. I wasn't in the right state of mind. Half of my spirit was still in Bones's grasp. After

I went back to sleep and woke up again, I would be back to normal.

Crow massaged the back of my neck with his fingertips. "Vanessa. My parents. The men I've killed. The things I've seen. Basically, everything I've ever witnessed in my lifetime."

"I'm sorry..." My nightmare was too much, but I could only imagine how bad his were.

"It's okay. They're more infrequent than they used to be."

"Because you count?"

"No. They've slowed down since you came into my life."

My eyes softened, and I finally stopped thinking about my nightmare altogether.

"They'll go away, Button. Give it enough time, and they will. Until then, just count. It always works."

"Okay."

He pressed a kiss to my forehead before he rubbed his nose against mine. "Would a walk make you feel better?"

"Outside? But it's dark."

"The sun is coming up soon. We can watch the sunrise together."

His bed was warm and comfortable, and the walls of his estate kept us safe. But there's nothing I wanted to do more than hold his hand as the sun welcomed us to a new day. "That sounds nice."

***

"Hey, lovebird." Cane walked toward me wearing one of his expensive suits. Most of the time, he wore jeans and a leather jacket. I wasn't sure what he needed to dress up for. In his line of work, it didn't seem like professionalism was important.

"Hey, shithead."

He immediately grinned at the insult like I'd just paid him a compliment. "You guys have been shacking up nicely."

Despite what he'd done to me, I didn't hate Cane. Somehow, I forgave him for his behavior and actually liked him. He was Crow's only family in the world, so it was impossible not to be fond of him. If Crow ever needed help, Cane would be there in a heartbeat. That was the kind of loyalty you couldn't buy. "Yes, we have." I glanced at the top of the stairs and waited for Crow to appear. He and Cane had business together that afternoon.

"This is the moment when I act like an ass and say I told you so."

I crossed my arms over my chest and glared at him.

"Don't deny it." He poked me in the arm. "I was right. You were wrong."

"About?"

"Don't play dumb with me. I told you he loved you."

"Well, I did believe you. Remember? I told him how I felt, and he walked out of the room. So no, you didn't tell me so."

Cane rolled his eyes. "Crow was being a cunt. That doesn't count."

"It does." I moved all the way back to America for a few months. It sure as hell counted.

"Well, he pulled his head out of his ass and told you. In the end, everyone wins."

That was the only part of this conversation I couldn't argue with. "What are you two doing today?"

"We're meeting with a rogue group of soldiers from Greece. In order for us to get intel on Bones, we need to expand the perimeter and bring more people on board. Crow and I have put a halt to both of our businesses to focus on this."

I was relieved by the announcement. Maybe when Bones was dead, I wouldn't have nightmares anymore. Maybe we could all move on and leave the past where it belonged. "I'm sure we'll get him."

"Definitely. When my brother puts his mind to something, he always succeeds—especially when it concerns you." Cane adjusted his cuff links and glanced at the top of the stairs to search for his brother. "Running late today, huh?"

"We may have gotten distracted..."

He grinned then gave me a gentle nudge in the side. "Please tell me you have a sister."

"Nope. And if I did, I wouldn't let her anywhere near you."

He chuckled and pulled away. "That's probably for the best. At least you're getting a brother." He winked.

Crow and I had never talked about marriage. The last time it came up, he said it wasn't on the table, and

I said the same thing. He'd confessed he loved me and wanted me to live with him. But I knew that was as far as our relationship would go. Maybe it wasn't everything I wanted, but I could settle for what he'd given me. "I don't think that will ever happen. But you feel like a brother anyway."

"You really think so?" he asked with a raised eyebrow. "My brother is head over heels, in case you didn't notice."

"As am I. But he's not the marriage type."

"I don't know about that... He says a lot of things."

"I think I know him a little better than you do."

He grinned from ear to ear and actually laughed. "Whatever you say, sweetheart."

Crow finally came down the stairs in a midnight black suit and a white collared shirt. The tie he'd chosen for the day was deep purple. The colors he chose always accented his dark exterior and brought out his brooding eyes. He adjusted his cuff links just before he reached us. "Ready?"

"Like you wouldn't believe." Cane turned his back and headed to the door to give us some privacy.

"I'll see you when I get home." Crow's arm moved around my waist, and he gave me a soft kiss on the lips.

"Okay. I'm making mac and cheese for dinner."

The corner of his lip rose in a smile. "I'll make sure Lars makes something as a backup."

I slapped his arm playfully. "Don't diss the mac and cheese until you've tried it."

"Diss?" he asked. "Another American slang word I'll never understand."

I slapped him again. "Stop picking on me."

He grabbed my wrist and yanked me into his chest. His voice suddenly turned serious. "I'll pick on you all I want—because you're mine to pick on." He kissed me hard on the mouth and nearly bruised my lips before he abruptly pulled away and walked off. His powerful shoulders moved as he headed to the front door where his brother was waiting. Even his ass looked nice in his slacks.

Warm and slightly out of breath, I began the countdown to when he would return.

***

I stood at the stove and stirred the contents of the pot.

Crow leaned against the counter behind me, his arms crossed over his chest. "Maybe I shouldn't have given Lars the night off…"

"Oh, shut up. It's good."

"I'm not even sure where you found it."

"Lars has his ways." After the powdered cheese and butter was melted, I poured the contents into two bowls.

Crow eyed it, his appetite still dormant. "Anything with powdered cheese can't be edible."

"Stop being a pretentious douchebag."

His eyes narrowed immediately. "What did you just call me?"

"You heard me." I dropped a fork in my bowl and did the same to his. "Now, clear your mind, and give it a try."

He eyed the bowl without touching it. "How is your body so fucking sexy when you eat shit like this?"

"Goddammit, Crow. Just try it." I held the bowl close to my chest and took a bite. "Yum…" The cheesy goodness was incredible. The Italian gourmet food that was cooked for me around the clock was delicious, but sometimes, junk food hit the right spot.

He sighed before he pulled the bowl closer to him. Hesitantly, he scooped some noodles onto his fork then brought it toward his lips. He faltered for an instant, dreading how bad the food would taste or how much it would suck to admit I was right.

"Come on. Or do I need to feed you?"

"We could smear this across your naked body. I'd definitely eat then."

As appetizing as that sounded, I didn't want sticky, processed cheese all over me. "The sooner you do it, the sooner it's over. You're just afraid you're actually going to like it."

"Believe me, I'm not going to like this horseshit."

"I didn't know if I was going to like real Italian food, but I still tried."

He rolled his eyes. "Everyone likes Italian food. Pasta is king."

I nodded at his bowl. "And what do you think is in there?"

He gave me a solid look right in the eye. "Horseshit."

I set my bowl on the kitchen island between us and put both hands on my hips. The small monster inside me came out, claws and fangs exposed. "Take a bite."

"Or what?" His eyes immediately went to my mouth, his thoughts automatically turning sinister the moment things became tense.

"Nothing good."

He fought against the emerging smile and finally took a bite. He shoved the noodles into his mouth and slowly chewed before he did a dramatic swallow. With an unreadable expression, he took his time.

"Well?" There was no way he wasn't going to love it.

He set the bowl down and looked me right in the eye. "Horseshit."

I threw my fists down in ferocity. "You're such a liar." I chased him around the kitchen island and swatted him with a dish towel. "You liked it, and you know it."

He ran around to avoid the bite of the towel. As I chased him, he laughed. It was one of the rare times I actually heard that hearty chuckle come from deep in his throat. His smile was infectious. For a moment, I got a glimpse of what he might have been like as a child. He was playful and happy, the light burning bright in his soul. "Button, I love you. But I don't love your cooking."

"I'll make you regret that." I chased him past the counter and farther into the kitchen. I wound up the towel then struck him right on the ass. He wore snug jeans, and the towel made a loud pop once it hit the denim.

He suddenly turned around and grabbed me by the back of the neck. With the strength of a soldier, he bent me over the counter and threw my dress up in a single motion. The towel was snatched from my grasp before he slapped it across my bare ass.

I tensed as the pain shot down my thighs and up my back. The bite of the material was strong enough to leave a welt, but the shock of the collision made my pussy clench in longing. He hadn't been aggressive with me since I left for America, and I missed that dark side of him. It was satisfying and terrifying all at the same time.

Crow pressed his chest into my back then rubbed my ass with his long fingers. His breaths filled my ear, his excitement evident in every single pant. "Did you like that?"

I didn't let a single second of silence linger. "Yes."

Buttons and Pain

He turned me around then lifted me onto the counter. He wrapped my legs around his waist and pulled my chest to his until our faces were touching. His hands moved up and down my body, feeling me everywhere like I was only his to feel. They grazed over my tits through my bra then finally stopped at my neck. He brushed his lips against mine, slowly teasing me before he gave me the kiss I longed for.

I wrapped my arms around his neck and felt his mouth move against mine. With restrained intensity, he kissed me slowly. His lips felt mine with purposeful touches, and he sucked my bottom lip into his mouth playfully before he released it. He was a god at everything, but he was Zeus when it came to kissing. He could give me the most scorching embraces without even using his tongue. He always saved that for the climax of the embrace. When he released a tiny moan into my mouth, I was immediately soaked for him. Finally, he gave me some of his tongue and brushed it against mine with practiced experience, making my heart flutter wildly in my chest.

Unexpectedly, he pulled away and removed his cheesy lips. With amber eyes dark and rich like a glass of his favorite drink, he stared me down without blinking. He glanced at my lips, the corner of my mouth, then rested his gaze on my eyes. Both of his palms cupped my face as he leaned in. "I love you."

My chest heaved with the deep breath that burned my chest. When he first said those words to me, I cherished them like a holy blessing. He didn't repeat them after that night—not when he went to work in the morning or before he went to sleep beside me. It was a one-time thing, and I hoped I'd have the opportunity to hear that confession again. Thankfully, I did. "I love you too."

***

When I woke up that morning, it was later than I was used to. The sun was unusually bright, and it burned right into my eyelids and forced my mind to accept the fact that it was the beginning of a new day.

The second my eyes cracked open, the sun was blinding and warm. The birds sang from the trees outside, picking grapes from the vineyard and enjoying the fruit from the branches of the trees. The noise didn't alarm me until I realized I shouldn't be able to hear it.

I reached for Crow beside me and noticed the sheets were cold. His large body wasn't there to protect me against my foes and my dreams. "Crow?" I sat up and pulled the sheets over my chest as I looked around the bedroom. Nothing was out of the ordinary. His watch and phone were gone, so wherever he was, he took them along.

That's when I noticed the window was wide open. The shutters were pushed outward, and the deep blue sky was just over the horizon. I used to leave my window open in my old room, but it was a practice I never did in Crow's. He must have left it open just for me.

On the windowsill was something small. It glinted in the light of the room and reflected it like a piece of metal. Underneath was a sheet of paper. The image reminded me of the morning I woke up in this new place. He left me a note and commanded me not to run.

I got out of bed and pulled on the dress I'd been wearing last night. My hair was a mess from the way he'd fisted it the night before, and I quickly tucked the tangled strands behind my ears so I could see. I walked to the window to get a better look at the treasures he left for me.

Sitting on the windowsill was a ring. Made of brilliant gold, the band was thin and sleek. Instead of a diamond on the top, there was a gold button with a pearl inside. It was welded to the material and indestructible. I felt it in my fingertips and noticed how warm the metal was from sitting in the sun all morning. I turned my gaze to the yellow parchment placed underneath it. In Crow's handwriting, there was a note.

Marry me.

My heart stopped in my chest when I read those two simple words. It wasn't a question but a demand, and I heard Crow's voice in my head as I read those beautiful words. My eyes immediately moved to the view out the window, and in the field of grass and flowers stood Crow. In a black suit and a matching tie, he stared up at me with the same intense look he always gave me. He'd been watching me this entire time, seeing me discover the ring and the note.

Without realizing it, tears fell from my eyes.

Crow held my gaze then slowly lowered himself to one knee. He kneeled before me, just as he did once before. He was the kind of man who never yielded to anyone, but he yielded to me. He continued to watch me, his back perfectly straight and the command in his eyes.

"Oh my god…" I slipped the ring onto my finger and noticed it fit perfectly. It was snug enough that it wouldn't slide off, and it was loose enough that it felt comfortable. The button shined brighter than any diamond ever could.

I ran out of the room as fast as I could and sprinted down the stairs while holding the banister. Eternity seemed to pass because there was so much ground to cover. My heart was in overdrive, and my lungs worked at full capacity. I reached the back door and pushed through it until I was finally in the backyard. I ran down the path and rounded the corner to where he stood. My hair trailed behind me as I ran, and when I saw the smile on his face, I ran harder.

I jumped into his arms and hooked my arms around his neck. He caught me effortlessly, his strong arms keeping me positioned against his chest. I pressed my forehead to his, my eyes still streaming with tears. "Yes."

"Yes, what?"

"I'll marry you."

One hand fisted my hair as he looked deep into my eyes. "I never asked, Button."

Chapter Twenty

Crow

Button lay on my chest with her long brown hair framing her face. One hand rested on my rib cage, and the ring I made for her sparkled like a set of diamonds. When I decided to take this step, I knew an expensive ring made of the highest quality jewels wasn't the right fit for her. Button deserved something unique, something meaningful.

A button was the only choice.

After spending most of the afternoon making love with our meals left outside our door, we were lost in each other. Nothing was said because our eyes did all the talking. When I made love to her, her eyes were bright with unconditional love and sexual satisfaction. When she looked into my face, I knew she saw a man strengthened by love.

Marriage was never in the cards for me. I didn't even want a relationship for most of my adult life. But then Button walked in and turned my world upside down. When she was with another man, I drowned in my own rage. When she was taken by Bones's men, I saw more rage than ever before. Button was different from the other women who graced my bed.

Buttons and Pain

Because she was the last one.

I wanted her to be mine forever. I didn't just want to live with her and share my home with her. I wanted it to belong to her as well. She would take my last name, and the world would know we weren't just two people in love—but we were husband and wife.

She trailed her fingers down my rib cage then placed a gentle kiss over my heart. "I want to make love again." She crawled farther up my chest, her tits in perfect view for me to enjoy. Her sculpted shoulders and slender arms held her above me, and her legs slowly straddled my hips.

As much as I wanted to, I'd already come inside her four times. My body needed time to recover. "Give me an hour."

She pouted her lips then leaned forward to kiss me.

I hugged her waist then rolled her over onto the bed. I moved on top of her until she was underneath me, the sparkle of life in hers. Her lips were formed in a permanent smile, and her hair was a mess across the pillow. "Button Barsetti. I like it."

She smiled wider, her happiness infectious. "That wouldn't be my legal name."

"As far as I'm concerned, it would."

"Pearl Barsetti. It sounds just as nice."

I'd never called her by that name once. Button was so much better, so much more possessive. "The only name people will call you is Mrs. Barsetti. So, it doesn't matter."

"I like it." She ran her hands up my chest and to my shoulders. "I didn't realize marriage was something you wanted."

I'd been thinking about it for a while, but I tried to fight it in the beginning. My mind kept picturing her living at my estate until she was old and gray. Sometimes she was pregnant with my child, and other times, she was playing with our kids in the backyard. "I didn't either.."

"What happened to never getting married?"

I rubbed my nose against hers. "I could ask you the same thing."

"I said I wouldn't get married because I would never trust a man. But I trust you, Crow."

I never got tired of seeing that love and devotion in her eyes. The more she adored me, the harder I fell.

"I just hope you understand what you're getting into."

I stared at her and waited for an elaboration.

She massaged my shoulders with her small fingertips. "I'm gonna cook mac and cheese pretty often, so you better develop a palate for it."

The corner of my lip rose in a smile.

"I like to sleep in, so you're going to have to get used to not being up at the crack of dawn on the weekends."

My smile only grew.

"I want to see the world. And you're going to take me." She ran her fingers up the back of my neck and into my hair. "Can you handle that?"

I pressed a kiss to the corner of her mouth. "I can handle anything—even you."

"Good. Looks like I said yes to the right man."

"I never asked, Button. You didn't have a choice." Even if she'd said no, I'd make her marry me anyway. She was a part of my life. She was a part of my soul.

"We both know you always give me the choice." She wrapped her legs around my waist and pulled me closer to her, wanting me inside her again. My cock had hardened during our conversation, and she could feel it pressed against her. But she wanted more.

I always wanted to keep my dominant side because it was the only life I knew. But Button did supernatural things to me. She was right in every assumption she made. I was wrapped tightly around her finger, possessed and owned.

And she knew it.

***

Lars knocked on the bedroom door. "Your Grace, Cane is here to see you."

Button and I lay on a blanket in front of the fireplace. We migrated around the room and made love on every piece of furniture before we took a break in front of the fire. Our naked bodies were wrapped around one another as we stared into each other's eyes. The button on her ring reflected the bright light of the fire, shining like an ethereal glow.

The last thing I wanted was to be disturbed. "Tell him I'm busy."

Lars didn't walk away from the door. "You know your brother, sir. He'll hang around until you find the time."

I loved my brother, but I also hated him at the same time. He never called to let me know he was stopping by. He just came and went whenever he pleased. "I'll be right there."

"Very well, Your Grace." Lars finally walked down the hallway.

Button ran her hand up my naked chest. "Make it quick. Your fiancée is waiting." The playfulness burned in her eyes as she stroked my chest with her fingertips.

I kissed her and pulled her bottom lip into my mouth. I gave her a gentle nip before I pulled away. "I won't keep you waiting long. But you better not start without me." I pulled on a pair of jeans that were sitting on the floor and a t-shirt.

She pulled the blanket farther over her shoulder and lay back on the pillow. "I can't promise anything..."

My cock stirred in my jeans at the thought of her touching herself and waiting for me to return. I'd already fucked her countless times today, but I couldn't get enough. My dick was about to break off, but that didn't stop me.

I left the bedroom and ventured downstairs to the entryway. Cane was sitting on the couch with a glass of scotch in hand. Appetizers that Lars had prepared sat on the table along with a few coasters. I told Lars not to bother when it came to Cane, but he did it anyway. "What do you want?"

Cane downed the rest of his glass before he stood up. "For a guy who just got engaged, you're awfully cranky."

"I said, what do you want?"

"What do you mean?" he snapped. "How did it go?"

"How did what go?" I asked.

"Uh, the proposal? What else could I be talking about?"

Cane was so nosy he could easily be our mother. "She said yes—obviously. Why else would I be upstairs having sex with her all day, every day?"

"So, she liked the ring?"

"She loved it." I sat on the couch and rested my ankle on the opposite knee.

Cane took a seat across from me. "Want to know something funny?"

No. I just wanted him to leave.

"The day we left to go get the ring, she said the two of you would never get married."

Both of my eyebrows rose. "Really?"

"Well, she said you weren't the marriage type. I had to stop myself from laughing right in her face."

"At least I caught her by surprise."

"So." He rubbed his palms together. "When's the wedding?"

"Not sure. We haven't talked about it. It'll probably be in the vineyard or something. Something small."

"I'll be the best man, right?"

Hell no. "We won't be doing that. We'll just get hitched and sign the paperwork. Then we'll go on a nice honeymoon."

"Uh...aren't you forgetting something?"

If he thought he was coming along, he was sadly mistaken.

"What about Bones? Isn't taking him out our priority?"

"Yes. But I'm only going to have a honeymoon once, Cane. You can keep working while I'm gone."

"Just don't make it too long. You don't want someone to see you abroad and tell Bones about it. You'll be vulnerable and alone."

"We'll probably be inside all day anyway." Button and I preferred to explore each other more than our surroundings.

Cane winked. "I feel ya."

I rose to my feet again and dismissed the conversation. "If we're done, I have somewhere to be."

"Oh, I bet you do."

As I walked around the couch behind him, I smacked him across the back of the head with my palm.

"Ouch." He leaned forward and rubbed his head. "What the hell was that for?"

"That was my polite way of asking you to leave."

***

Her ass hung over the bed, and my face was pressed between her legs. I kissed her clitoris and sucked it vigorously into my mouth until she screamed my name. She had the sweetest pussy and the most arousing scent. I could eat her pussy all day—and for the rest of my life.

When she finished, I rose from my knees and leaned over her. With cheeks red and warm, she looked like she'd been thoroughly satisfied for the night. No matter how many times I pleased her, she always wanted more. But maybe she'd finally reached her limit for the night.

"Want to marry me tomorrow?"

She froze at the question, her eyes wide with surprise. "What?"

"You and me outside in the vineyards. I can have a priest come from the next town and marry us."

"Really?" She held herself up on her elbows. The satisfaction slowly faded from her cheeks as she looked at me.

"Why wait?" We never talked about it, but I assumed we wouldn't have a traditional wedding with guests and a feast. I figured it would just be the two of us with Lars and Cane. Something simple.

"But I don't have a dress."

"I'll take you to Rome."

"But you can't see the dress. Maybe Italians do it differently, but in America, it's bad luck."

"Well, you aren't in America," I reminded her. "And I won't go into the shop with you. I'll just stand guard outside. I'll feel more comfortable going with you than letting someone else keep an eye on you."

"Oh my god…"

"What?"

"We're getting married tomorrow." She sat up and gripped the crooks of my arms. "I can't believe it."

A part of me couldn't believe it either. But when I looked at her, everything made sense.

"We better get going then. I have a lot of shopping to do." She hopped off the bed and pulled on her jeans and whatever shirt she could find off the ground. "I'm not even sure what I want. Strapless, not strapless… I don't know."

The corner of my lip rose as I watched her. Seeing her excitement over our nuptials just made me look forward to it even more. "Then let's get going."

***

"Nervous?" Cane stood beside me in his black suit. He had a grin on his face that wouldn't fade, and that knowing look was in his eyes.

"No." I was never nervous.

"Can I take a moment to say I'm right?" He crossed his arms over his chest and looked at me.

"Right about what?"

"About Pearl. You loved her, and I knew it."

Buttons and Pain

Wasn't exactly the ideal conversation to have on my wedding day. "Cane?"

"Hmm?"

"Shut up."

He smiled and rolled his eyes at the same time. "Since it's your day, I'll let that go."

I faced the cedar doors and waited for Button to emerge. A harpist was off to the side to play the traditional Italian wedding song, and the priest was on my other side. I was raised Catholic, and my mom would flip over in her grave if an Italian priest didn't marry me.

Lars adjusted my tie for the fifth time even though nothing was wrong with it. "May I say something, Your Grace?"

"Of course."

"I'm very happy for you. Pearl is lovely, and I know your lives together will be beautiful. I'm honored to witness this day." Lars didn't engage in personal conversation with me often. The only way he showed his emotion was by the detailed way he took care of the house. But he knew he was a part of the Barsetti family.

"Thank you. That means a lot."

Lars nodded before he stepped aside.

Cane continued to stare at the door. "What's taking her so long?"

"She's marrying me, so she can take however damn long she wants." I would wait a lifetime for her.

"Just a heads-up." He leaned toward me and lowered his voice. "I got a peek of her in the house. Let's just say…she looks pretty damn good."

"Shocking." Like Button could look anything but gorgeous at any point in time.

The harpist began to play, and I knew that was my cue to shut up. The wooden door creaked open as Button stepped out in a long, ivory gown. A handful of wild flowers were in her hand, picked from my acres of land, and lace strung with buttons had been beautifully placed in her hair.

The moment she was on the path, her eyes locked to mine, and that same look of everlasting love was there. She walked slowly to the music, taking her time even though she was anxious to get to me as quickly as possible.

Her train dragged on the ground and made a swishing noise as it was pulled behind her. Her makeup was done differently but not overbearing like

I thought it may look. Just as perfect as the first day I saw her, she looked like a vision.

And she was all mine.

She reached me and handed the flowers off to Cane without looking at him. Her eyes were only on me, that gentle smile still on her lips.

"You look beautiful." I took her hand and guided her to face the priest. Her hand was scorching in mine, showing her nervousness for the first time. We stood side by side and performed the ceremony of our marriage. When it was time for the rings, I slipped on the ordinary gold ring next to the one she already wore. Her button on the top took focus over the plain band, and the combination was perfect for her.

Then she took my ring from Cane and slipped it onto my finger. It was the first time I'd seen it, and I was curious about what she had picked out for me. The band was solid black and thin, but on closer examination, I saw the marked holes that looked identical to the kind seen on buttons. That's when I realized the band was made of a combination of buttons, melted down and forged into the wedding ring I now wore.

My eyes immediately moved to hers, and I truly felt moved.

Tears were bubbling in her eyes, but she didn't wipe them away. Instead, she took a deep breath so her emotions wouldn't run wild.

My entire life, I couldn't picture myself wearing a ring, especially a wedding ring. But now that it was on my finger, I didn't want to take it off. It was an integral part of me, something that had been missing until now. It didn't just represent my marriage and devotion to this woman. It represented more than that. I took an emotional journey the moment she walked into my life, and she showed me I was a much better man than I gave myself credit for.

Button knew I loved it just by looking at the expression on my face.

The ceremony was performed in Italian, but Button was able to pick up most of it. When it was her turn to complete the exchange, she said I do in Italian, and I did as well. The ceremony happened in the blink of an eye, and then it was over. It was finally time for the best part.

Kissing the bride.

Button smiled as she waited for it, for the first kiss we would share as husband and wife. That knowing look was in her eyes, like she knew how much I wanted to kiss her, probably even more than she did.

I pulled her closer into my arms then cupped her face. Like I had a hundred times, I kissed her. But this one was different. I told this woman I loved her without saying it with words. I told her I would be nothing without her, that she was the single most important thing in the world. I pledged my loyalty and my life eternally—forever.

Penelope Sky

Chapter Twenty-One

Pearl

We arrived in Mykonos and checked in to our hotel. It was on the tip of the island, curved inwards so we could see the beautiful white buildings with blue roofs that I'd seen countless times in photos and in film.

The flight was short, but so far, the trip hadn't felt romantic. A detail of five guards followed us everywhere we went, trailing behind us with guns stowed away inside their heavy coats.

We entered our room and finally shut the door behind us.

"Is it really necessary to have them follow us around?"

Crow set our suitcases off to the side then gripped my hips with his strong hands. "Just ignore them, Button."

"But don't you think they're drawing more attention to us than if we were here alone?"

He pressed his forehead to mine, his gentle touch scorching me. "If it were just me, I would risk it. But with you, I can't afford to take risks." He kissed my temple before he stepped away, his black wedding

312

ring made of buttons still on his finger. "Do you like the room?"

I snorted because the question was ridiculous.

He turned back and looked at me, an eyebrow raised.

"Crow, the room is beautiful. It's like a damn palace. And this place is beautiful. I just wish it was only us."

"I'm sorry, Button." He opened the back doors and let the sea air blow inside. "Until Bones is dead, this is how it has to be." He stepped onto the spacious balcony and looked across the water. Sailboats and yachts sprinkled the coast, and the sun hit the roofs of the buildings just right, making the sunlight reflect back into the open sea.

I came to his side and looked across the beauty of Greece. "It's beautiful here."

"I'm glad you like it."

"Have you been here before?"

"I've been to the mainland but not this island."

"So, it's a first for both of us."

"Yes." He wrapped his arm around my waist and pulled me close to him. "A first of many." His lips brushed against my hairline before he squeezed my waist. "What would you like to do first? The town has a lot of small shops that you'll like. Or we can go to the beach and dig our feet into the sand."

I wanted to go sightseeing, but there was something I wanted to do more. "How about we just stay in for the night?" I ran my hands up his chest and looked into his loving eyes. We'd just gotten married that afternoon, and I was eager to make our marriage official in this beautiful place. "We can go explore tomorrow."

He didn't smile, but the look in his eyes grew more intense. "Whatever Mrs. Barsetti wants, she gets."

***

I thought Tuscany was the most beautiful place in the world, but I quickly realized how naïve I was. The culture and beauty of Greece were unlike anything in the known world. It was more than just beautiful—it was breathtaking.

Downtown wasn't accessible by cars. Instead, it was lined with cobbled streets for pedestrians as they did their shopping. Antique stores and small shops with gourmet food were condensed into this small area. I had lots of sweets. I even tried their version of a Frappuccino—and it was the best thing I'd ever had.

Crow arranged for a yacht to take us around the island, and we got a more intimate view of the place. Sunsets and sunrises were equally beautiful, and paradise wasn't just a dream but a reality. We dined on fresh seafood, wine, and Mediterranean food that nearly put Italian cuisine to shame.

It was a dream honeymoon.

We had dinner together on our balcony and room service that catered to Crow's specific tastes. Being in the room was the only time when the guards weren't hot on our tail. The privacy was nice and appreciated.

Crow sipped his wine and ate slowly, his eyes on me the entire time. Not once on our honeymoon did I look at him and not see him already staring at me. Like I was steel and his eyes were a magnet, he was stuck to me. He set his glass down then stared at me like he was about to say something.

I waited for it.

"I love my ring."

We hadn't talked much despite how often we were alone together. We were either out doing fun activities, or we were in the room making love—neither required much talking. "I'm glad you like it. Lars helped me make it."

He examined his left ring finger before he returned his look to me. "It's perfect, Button. Couldn't have asked for anything better."

In the process of constructing it, I knew it was a perfect fit. The color suited his cold exterior, and the melted buttons were the tokens in our relationship that made us fall in love. Gold and silver weren't nearly as valuable.

"Maybe we should have talked about this before, but at the time, I wasn't thinking clearly..."

I held my breath as I waited.

"I'm not sure if we should have kids. In my line of work, I'm not sure if it would be a good idea."

Kids weren't on my mind right then. I was still getting used to the fact that I was married. Crow kidnapped me and forced me to work for my freedom. The fact that I fell in love with him was still shocking. "I haven't really thought about it."

"I'm not taking it off the table, but I don't think it's a good idea."

Buttons and Pain

When I thought about my life without children, it made me sad. I didn't want them today or tomorrow, but someday, I would want a son just like his father. I would want a daughter Crow would worship. I wanted the family I never had. "I need to have children, Crow. Not today but eventually."

His eyes were unreadable. He stared at me with an expression trained with indifference. Even now, I couldn't always tell what he was thinking. "Again, I'm not sure if that's a good idea."

"Quit your business with Cane. You have the winery."

"But that business is directly from my family. And Cane is an idiot. He'll run it into the ground."

"What does it matter?"

Crow didn't answer, his eyes still unreadable.

"I think having your own family is more important than helping Cane with the business. It's not like you won't see him all the time anyway." I didn't want to push him into something he didn't want to do, but I didn't want his misplaced loyalty to his family to stop us from being happy. "Cane would understand. And one day, he'll meet someone special and will have to make the same difficult choice."

Crow drank his wine, his eyes still trained on me.

"You don't need to do anything right this second, Crow. But I do want to have children. And not just with anyone, but with you. I think you'll make a great father."

It was the first time he reacted in the conversation. His eyebrows raised with incredulity. "Me? Really?"

"Absolutely. You're loving, protective, and selfless."

He finished his wine before he set the empty glass on the table. "I don't know about that. I love you, but that took me a very long time to come to terms with. I'm callous and cold, and my hatred is something that will never go away. I'll never be the family man you think I'll be."

"I couldn't disagree more with that statement."

Crow pulled his gaze away and looked across the water. "You believe what you want to believe."

I didn't want to have this tense argument on our honeymoon, but I hadn't expected it to turn out this way. "I know you, Crow. I know you better than you know yourself. If I think you can do it, you can."

Buttons and Pain

He dismissed the conversation by remaining quiet. He didn't eat any more of his dinner, concentrating on the view across the ocean.

I did the same because looking at him was beginning to be painful. I knew a lifetime with Crow wouldn't always be easy. He had a lot of issues, a lot of scars. But I was broken too, and in that regard, we completed each other.

Crow broke the silence. "I'll give you children. I promised to love you and make you happy every single day for the rest of your life. You know I'm a man who keeps my word."

It wasn't exactly what I wanted to hear, but it was close enough. "Thank you."

***

By the end of the two weeks, we were both sun kissed and drunk off each other. I already lived in paradise, but I didn't want to leave this new place. Mykonos had an ancient beauty that I'd never experienced in America. I felt like I'd stepped back in time and stared at the world with a new pair of eyes.

Our bed was nearly broken from all the sex we had on the sheets. Instead of handcuffs or whips, we kept it at a vanilla flavor. Crow didn't seem interested in anything more sinister, and I wasn't either. I just wanted him slow and steady, so I could treasure every moment of him inside me. There were days when I was sore, but that didn't stop us from going at it.

The valet collected our bags at the end of the trip, and I nearly broke down in tears at the thought of saying goodbye to this place.

Crow wrapped his arm around me and pulled me close. "We can always come back, Button."

"I know. I had such a great time, and I don't want it to end."

He grabbed the back of my hair and forced my chin up so he could look into my face. "I'll take you to see the world, Button. This is only the beginning."

"I know."

He pressed a kiss to my temple before he walked me out.

***

"How was your trip, Your Grace?" Lars set our bags by the front door so the staff could return them to the bedrooms and get the dirty clothes in the washer. Like bees in a hive, they worked together to give Crow everything he needed.

"Wonderful," Crow answered. "Mrs. Barsetti and I had a great time."

I still wasn't used to my new name.

"I'm glad to hear it," Lars answered. "Is there anything I can do for you? Prepare lunch? Afternoon tea?"

"No," Crow answered. "We're going to shower and retire upstairs for the rest of the day. I'll let you know when we're ready for dinner."

"Of course, Your Grace." Lars gave him a slight bow before he turned to me. "Mrs. Barsetti." It was the first time he gave me the same kind of bow. Then he walked back into the kitchen.

"He doesn't need to bow to me," I said to Crow.

"It's an Italian custom."

"Well, I'm not Italian." I wasn't going to let some cute old man bend over backward for me. He seemed to love his job, but that was beside the point.

Crow turned around and looked at me, the fire in his eyes. "You are now." He grabbed me by the hand and walked up the two flights of stairs and past my old bedroom. Ever since I'd left this place, I still hadn't gone inside. My bedroom had been Crow's, and I never ventured anywhere else.

We entered the bedroom just as Crow's phone rang. While we were on our honeymoon, he didn't take any business calls. Even Cane didn't call him, which was astounding. That guy seemed more obsessed with Crow than I was.

Crow answered without checking the number, knowing he had work to do now that he was home. "Crow."

I was standing right beside him, so I could hear every word of the exchange.

"Crow." The deep voice rang through the phone, terrifying me without making a single threat. The tone and cadence of the voice were eerily familiar and frightening. It was unmistakable, and I could recognize it anywhere—even from a few feet away.

Crow stilled noticeably, knowing exactly who it was.

"Long time, no talk, huh?" Bones chuckled into the phone like he'd made some kind of joke. "Cane tells me you were just on your honeymoon with my slave. How interesting."

My blood froze, and I couldn't breathe. I didn't understand what was going on, but whatever it was, it was bad.

Buttons and Pain

Crow didn't lose his composure once. "We had a great time. Thanks for asking."

Bones chuckled even though Crow's statement wasn't funny. "Your brother talks, but he doesn't talk enough. When I asked where I could find you, he refused to give up that information—and I tortured him mercilessly."

I closed my eyes as the pain shot through me. What Cane did to me was in the past, and now I loved him like a brother. The idea of him being in pain nearly broke me. And I could only imagine how much that hurt Crow.

Crow didn't seem affected. His expression was exactly the same. "It's called loyalty, Bones. Something you would never understand."

This time, Bones didn't chuckle. "My original plan was to have Cane lead me back to Pearl. But after weeks of endless suffering, he still won't crack. So, I have a new plan."

"I'm sure it won't work either."

I didn't have a clue how Crow could remain so calm when his only family member was being tortured at this very moment. Only a man with concrete in his veins could manage it.

Penelope Sky

"It's pretty simple," Bones said. "We make a trade. Pearl for Cane."

"I remember how our last trade went," Crow warned. "You have no honor or integrity. Therefore, I don't trust you."

"Are you willing to gamble your brother's life on it?"

"He's already dead anyway." Crow's voice didn't break with emotion. He accepted it without any reaction. "And I would never make that trade, Bones. You know it. Kill him and be done with it."

"Wow, even I'm surprised at your coldness. Your brother refused to crack for you, and you don't care if he dies?"

"He understands."

This was a nightmare that just wouldn't end. Cane was locked up somewhere, and Bones was about to put a bullet in his head. Crow would lose his only family left in the world.

"I'm not just going to kill him, Crow," Bones warned. "I'm going to torture him until he goes into shock. And then I'm going to keep every single bone and add them to my collection. I'll give you forty-eight

324

hours to think about it." He hung up before Crow could say another word.

Crow listened to the line go dead before he tossed the phone on the bed. With his arms resting at his sides, he just stood there. His breathing was even, and his expression didn't change. Whatever he was feeling was far below the surface.

I didn't say anything because I couldn't breathe. My lungs ached from the pain, and my heart was about to give out because it was working at full speed. The adrenaline was killing me. "Crow..." I couldn't fight against my tears as they came pouring out.

Crow finally looked at me, his expression still cold.

I sat on the bed and pulled my knees to my chest, still sobbing. "No..."

Crow slowly approached me, his eyes darker than ever before. "Button, shh."

"We have to save him, Crow. What are we going to do?"

He stood at the edge of the bed, his hands still resting by his sides. "I'll organize a search, but I don't think it'll help. I'm sure Bones is in an untraceable place."

"Then you have to trade me. You have to save Cane." Nothing scared me more than being in Bones's possession, but I couldn't let Cane suffer. He was Crow's only living relative. Bones was after me, so Cane shouldn't suffer. It wasn't fair.

The look Crow gave me was terrifying. "No."

"Crow, you have to—"

"Pearl, I said no."

I froze on the spot when I heard what he said. He never called me by my real name—ever. It was a warning—a terrifying one.

"I'm not trading you, and Cane would understand. He knows I'm not coming for him. He accepted that the moment he was captured. I hate this as much as you do, but I'm not giving you up."

"He's your brother…" How could he do this to him?

"And you're my wife," he whispered. "You're my family now. Cane would prefer it this way."

Tears streaked down my face. "We can't just accept his. We can't let him win."

"I'll try to get him back, Button. But I don't think I'll succeed. Bones knows what he's doing. He'll have covered his tracks by now."

I pulled my knees to my chest and continued to sob. "I'm so sorry... This is my fault."

"Don't say that ever again."

"But it is. If it weren't for me, none of this would be happening."

"And I would have been miserable my whole life." He kneeled in front of me and gripped my arms. "I'm sorry this has happened. It kills me as much as it kills you. But don't ever say that."

I sniffed then wiped my tears away. "Crow, find him. Please. I won't be able to live with myself if we don't rescue him."

"Button, I know." He pulled my forehead to his. "I promise I'll do everything I can to get him back."

"Okay." I gripped his wrists and tried to slow down my breathing. Right now, I was just a mess. As a victim of Bones, I knew exactly what his torture was like. I would never wish that on anyone else, especially my brother.

"It'll be alright, Button. We'll get through this."

Chapter Twenty-Two

Crow

"What about the catacombs?" I'd been searching for Cane nonstop for twenty-four hours. I didn't sleep, I hardly ate, and I drank as much caffeine as I could find. I kept up an air of indifference to Bones and Buttons, but honestly, I was fucking terrified.

I had to find him.

Cane pissed me off most of the time, and he got under my skin like no one else. I always had to clean up his messes, and he hurt my woman in an unforgivable way. But that didn't change the innate feelings deep in my chest.

I loved my brother.

Bones was a man of his word, and if he said he would kill Cane, then he would. If Buttons were anyone else, I would hand her over in a heartbeat. But she was off-limits. In my heart, I knew Cane would understand that. He would understand I had to protect my wife against everything because she was a part of the Barsetti family now.

At least, I hoped he understood.

One of my men responded. "Clean."

"What about Rome?" I asked. "Any of his headquarters?"

"They're all clean," the man answered. "We checked everywhere, Crow. Wherever he is, it's below the surface. We can't get any readings anywhere. No signatures. Nothing."

"What about tracing the call?" Bones would call again tomorrow.

"We can try," he answered. "But I doubt it'll do any good. I'm sure Bones has covered his tracks like a pro."

How did he capture Cane to begin with? What was Cane doing? "When was the last time you saw my brother?"

"Ten days ago," he answered. "He was at work like normal then went home."

"Did he say he was going anywhere?" I asked. "Florence? Rome? Or just home?"

"He didn't say," he answered with a shrug. "Cane doesn't talk about his personal life much."

I kept hitting one dead end after another. "Fuck." I rubbed the back of my neck and felt the anxiety take over. I always remained calm around my men and

Penelope Sky

Button, but now I was losing my resolve. The lack of sleep and the terror were getting to me.

"I'm sorry, sir."

"No, I'm sorry." I wouldn't be able to find Cane in time, and I knew it. If I hadn't been on my honeymoon, I might have noticed he was missing sooner, and I could have done something. But now, it was too late.

Cane was going to die.

***

The second I got home, Button smothered me.

"Did you find out anything? Do you have any leads?"

I ripped my shirt off as I walked into the bedroom, feeling suffocated by the fabric. "No." I bowed my head in shame. After everything I'd learned in my line of work, my skills didn't help when it mattered most. Bones killed my parents, Vanessa, and now he was about to take Cane. That man had ripped everything from my life, and I was powerless to stop it. I sat on the bed and hung my head, feeling like a failure.

Button sat beside me. "There has to be something we can do."

"If there were, I would have found it." I clenched my jaw and tried not to snap at her. She was only trying to help, but her constant questions were only reminding me of my inadequacy.

"Can you offer him money?"

"He won't take it."

"Well, you should try."

"I offered twenty million for you, and he still didn't want it," I snapped. "You don't understand how this guy works."

Her eyes narrowed on my face. "Excuse me?"

It was a stupid thing to say, and I knew it. "That's not what I meant." I rubbed the back of my neck because I didn't want to fight. Arguing would get us nowhere.

"What are you saying? There's nothing we can do? That we give up?"

I stared at the floor and tried to ignore her hostility.

"Crow?"

"Hmm?"

"Please don't tell me we're going to do nothing."

"Button...I don't know what to do. I'm out of options."

"Agree to the trade—"

My words came out as a roar. "I'm not going to trade you. That's final."

She backed away at my hostility. "If you would let me finish, I was going to say we should agree to the trade and try to break Cane out without actually going through with it."

I shook my head. "Too risky."

"This is your brother we're talking about. Risky is okay."

"No. That means I have to bring you and show you to him. Unless he sees you, he won't cooperate."

"Then bring me."

"No." I ground my teeth together. "He's setting us up. I know how he his. He's going to kill Cane anyway. He'll never make the trade fairly. When we tried to get Vanessa, he took our money and killed her anyway. I can't trust him."

Her shoulders sagged under her grief. "Crow...we have to think of something."

Buttons and Pain

I left the bed because I didn't want to be close to her anymore. "Button, if there was something I could do, I would do it. If I could forfeit my own life to save his, I would. But none of those options is available. I can't proceed with the trade because he'll cross me. I know how he is." I dragged my hands down my face because my eyes were dry and exhausted. I hadn't slept in so long I couldn't even think. "I just… Leave me alone." I walked into the shower and turned on the warm water, letting the grime from the afternoon wash away. Every time I closed my eyes, I saw my brother's face. He was cold, alone, and bleeding to death. Images from our childhood replaced the current ones, and I felt the urge to cry. I hated myself for allowing this to happen, but the hatred wouldn't make it go away.

I dried off then walked to bed. I set my phone on the nightstand and pulled back the covers. I was too exhausted to talk to Button or make love. All I wanted was a few hours of sleep, so I could start thinking clearly again. Maybe when my brain had a rest, I could come up with a decent plan.

Button wasn't in the bedroom. Pissed off, she left and probably went outside to get away from me. I would apologize to her when I woke up. I set an alarm on my phone, and the second my head hit the pillow, I was out cold.

I didn't even have a dream.

***

My alarm didn't wake me up.

It was supposed to go off in two hours, but the annoying beeping never came. I opened my eyes and realized it was dark outside. Instead of taking a short nap, I slept for most of the day. My hand reached for my phone to see the time, but I couldn't find it on my nightstand. I kept groping in the dark but couldn't find it. Irritated, I turned on the lamp.

My phone was nowhere in sight. Instead, there was a note.

And Button's wedding ring.

I nearly jumped out of bed as I grabbed the note and read the words in her beautiful handwriting.

Crow,

I'm sorry. He's your only family in the world, and I can't let this happen. I know you hate me right now, but please understand I did this for you.

I love you for always,

Buttons and Pain

Button

My hand shook as I read the note, and a loud scream issued from my throat. I grabbed the nightstand and threw it across the room until it shattered against the wall. Her wedding ring fell to the floor with a distinct clank. That wasn't enough to satisfy my rage, so I destroyed everything in the bedroom, everything that was hers and mine.

I couldn't believe this.

I couldn't.

Penelope Sky

Chapter Twenty-Three

Pearl

I drove down the road in one of Crow's cars and was thankful they drove on the right side of the road. Otherwise, I would be completely clueless. Tears were still pouring from my eyes after I left Crow sleeping in the bed we shared every single night. I kissed him on the brow and told him I loved him even though he couldn't hear a word I said.

Then I took off my wedding ring and set it on the nightstand.

If I took it with me, Bones would just destroy it. He would decimate it and burn it. I loved that ring as much as Crow, and I couldn't stand the thought of its destruction. I would much rather leave it behind.

I completely understood my actions, and while I was scared, I knew it had to be done. Crow picked me over his brother, but I understood how much he needed Cane. He pretended to be indifferent, but I knew he was a wreck deep down inside. He loved his brother as much as he loved me—he just showed it differently.

I wouldn't be the reason he lost the last Barsetti.

Buttons and Pain

I wiped my tears and kept driving, pained at the feeling of leaving my husband behind. Crow would do everything he could to find me again, but I had to figure out an escape myself. I wouldn't stop until I found a knife or a bat. I wouldn't stop until I was free again. And I wouldn't stop until I'd killed Bones myself.

Crow's phone rang, and I answered it. "Pearl." I kept my voice steady and refused to give in to my tears when that fiend could listen.

"On the road?"

I hated speaking to him. My intestines tied up in knots and made me sick. "Yes."

"Alright. You know where the meeting point is?"

"Yes."

"This is what we're going to do—"

He spoke like he controlled the situation, but he was wrong. I controlled the situation. "No. This is what we're doing." I silenced him with a single sentence. "You're going to meet in front of the church on Plaza Street. It's old and abandoned. When I see Cane released and inside the car, I'll come out to you."

"No. We do this my way."

"I don't trust you," I snapped. "If you want me, we do this my way."

"And why should I trust you?"

I gripped the steering wheel until my knuckles turned white. "Because a Barsetti's word is law. And I'm a Barsetti." I tried not to cry again.

Bones paused over the phone. "Fine. We'll do it your way. When will you be there?"

"Ten minutes."

He hung up.

I set the phone down and felt the tears flood all over again. By the time Crow woke up and realized what happened, it would be too late. The exchange would be over and done with. I would never have the chance to tell him I loved him again. And the last time we spoke, we fought. It wasn't the way I wanted to say goodbye.

My phone rang a moment later from a number I didn't recognize. My gut told me who it was. With a shaky hand, I answered it. "Pearl."

Crow's voice came over the phone with restrained ferocity. He didn't yell, but his tone was just as terrifying. "Turn. The. Fuck. Around."

I kept my foot on the gas and the wheel straight.

"Button, do as I say, or I swear to god—"

Buttons and Pain

"I'm sorry. I have to do this."

"No, you don't. He's going to kill Cane anyway. You're sacrificing yourself for no reason."

I kept my voice calm because I didn't want our last conversation to be this terrible. "Crow, I'm going to do this. I have to save him. I'm sorry you don't approve, but frankly, it's my choice. But while I have you on the line, I want to tell you I love you, and I'll do everything I can to escape."

"Button..." His rage disappeared, and his voice shook. I'd never heard that kind of emotion in his voice. He might be crying. I didn't know. "Don't do this to me."

"I'm sorry..."

"Button."

"I love you, Crow." I muffled my tears with my hand and remained as silent as possible. This conversation would be the death of me.

"Please turn the car around."

"I have to go."

"Button—"

"Tell me you love me before I hang up." I gripped the steering wheel tighter, so I wouldn't crash off the side of the road.

Crow gave in because he knew he wouldn't get his way. "I love you, Button. And I'm going to get you back."

I had no doubt those words were true. All I had to do was fight and never give up until he rescued me. I did it once, and I could do it again. I would do anything for this man and his family—because his family was my family. "I know."

***

I arrived at the abandoned church and parked the car on the opposite street. The keys were left in the ignition, and the phone was left in the cupholder. The church was mostly rubble, caused by an earthquake that happened nearly a decade before. The community didn't want to tear it down because it was still a historical relic for the city. I thought it was the perfect site for the exchange because there were many places to hide.

The phone rang right on cue.

I answered. "Where is he?"

"The question is, where are you?" Bones's voice was full of hunger, desperate to sink his claws into me. I could feel his arousal through the line, his desperation to claim me as his all over again. He wanted to wash away any trace of Crow that lingered on my skin.

"Parked on the south side. When Cane makes it to the car, I'll get out."

"If you drive away, we'll blow up the car."

"I know." Actually, I knew that was a lie. Bones would never hurt me, not when I was more valuable alive than dead.

"I'm looking forward to seeing you. It's been too long."

"I wish I could say the same." Around the corner, I saw greasy men with rifles and machine guns. In the center was Bones, wearing a black suit and looking like a nightmare. Cane stood with his arms tied behind his back. He spotted me in the car and shook his head.

"Now we make the trade."

"I'm waiting." I wasn't getting out of the car until Cane was safely in the passenger seat. Crow told me not to trust Bones, and I took his advice very seriously.

The man holding Cane untied him then shoved him forward, practically making him fall to the ground. Cane was thinner than he once was and much weaker. He slowly walked to the car, sporting an obvious limp in his stride. His face was covered in cuts and bruises, the aftermath of ten days of torture. After an eternity, he finally reached the car and got into the passenger seat.

I stared at him, taking comfort in knowing he was alive.

He stared at me like he hated me. "What the fuck are you doing?"

"Saving you."

"You shouldn't have done this," he hissed. "I'm not worth it."

"You are to me."

His eyes immediately softened. "Sis, don't do this."

"You're the only family he has left. I had to."

Cane shook his head. "You're his family too."

"It's not the same."

"Pearl…" He shook his head, tears in his eyes. "Don't do this. You don't deserve it."

"I know. But sometimes...life isn't fair." I wrapped my arms around him and gave him a hug. "I'll escape. Somehow, someway."

"Crow and I will get you. I promise."

I pulled away then turned my gaze, so I couldn't see him. Saying goodbye to Cane was much harder than I thought it would be. "Drive away. When you're gone, I'll walk over there."

Cane didn't agree, but his silence was agreement enough.

I finally got out of the car and shut the door behind me. I stared into the driver's door and waited for Cane to scoot across the console and start the engine. He did a moment later, and after a sad look, he turned around and drove away. Once he was a safe distance away, he would get a hold of Crow and tell him where I was. If they acted quickly enough, perhaps I could be spared.

Now, there was nothing else to do but fulfill the bargain.

Bones whistled and beckoned me to him like a dog.

And I wanted to kill him right then and there.

"Now your end of the deal." He snapped his fingers and pointed to the road underneath his feet. "Get your ass over here."

My legs didn't want to comply with his disrespectful manners. What I wanted more than anything was to stab him in the heart and watch him bleed out and die. The sight of blood wouldn't gross me out. The thought of being alone with a corpse didn't scare me. In fact, it thrilled me.

I began the long walk across the battlefield, taking my time and enjoying the last moments of freedom before I was a slave all over again. Bones's eyes grew in size the closer I came, his desire taking over his logical thought. I was close to being in his grasp, and he could hardly breathe.

I despised him more than before.

I finally ended the long walk and came face-to-face with the culprit of my nightmares. He was just as grotesque as I remembered, terrifying and sinister. His face was thicker from the weight he'd put on, and the look in his eyes was just as evil as before. He'd probably entertained himself with a line of hookers and slaves before he claimed me once more.

Buttons and Pain

"More beautiful than I remember." He grabbed me by the arm and dragged me until I was against his chest. He crushed his mouth to mine and gave me the most disgusting kiss I've ever had.

I pushed him off then kicked him in the balls. "You're disgusting."

He bent over and cupped his balls, moaning at the pain in his groin.

His men immediately grabbed me and hooked my arms behind my back.

Bones recovered after a moment, but a sinister smile was on his face. "I'm going to enjoy training you again. And after the way you tricked me, I'm going to love getting my revenge for that."

"Crow will save me. And when he does, he's going to make you suffer." I knew Crow would never give up until he found me. He would search day and night, Cane alongside him, until I was returned to my rightful place in our home.

"Not where we're going." He motioned to his men. "Search her, and make sure she's not packing."

The men ran their hands down my body, groping me as they searched for hidden weapons and knives. They wouldn't find anything, but they did a thorough examination, even feeling the area between my legs through my jeans.

I shoved them off. "If I had something, you would have found it by now."

Bones smiled at my feistiness, growing hard in his slacks. "Gentlemen, let's go home. Pearl and I have a lot of catching up to do."

Buttons and Pain

Chapter Twenty-Four

Crow

"FUCK!"

I'd never been this furious. Not once in my life had I been this destructive. If I had access to nuclear weapons, I'd be a threat to this country and the entire world because my rage was doing all the thinking for me.

I piled every gun I had in the back of my SUV and the back seat for easy reach. A bulletproof vest was attached to my chest so a flying bullet couldn't stop me from getting my wife back.

I was going to kill Bones.

My car screeched into the driveway at eighty miles an hour before Cane slammed on the brakes. The vehicle was just inches from running me over, but the proximity didn't faze me. If it collided into me, I would have totaled the car without a scratch on my body.

Cane hopped out without turning the car off. "Did you know—"

"Found out ten minutes ago. She snuck out when I was sleeping." I shoved a pistol into the holster at my hips. "Where did they keep you?"

Penelope Sky

"I don't know. I was blindfolded when they moved me."

I grabbed him by the neck, and I squeezed him so tightly he could barely breathe. "My wife's life is on the line right now. You will tell me every goddamn detail you can recall. She sacrificed herself for you. And you better be worthy of that." I threw him back against the hood of the car. "Now, speak."

Cane didn't bother with a smartass remark because now wasn't the time. Every minute counted. "Concrete everywhere. Every room I was in was made of concrete. My meals were brought in on Styrofoam with plastic utensils. The pipes for the toilets and sinks moved up, not down. The men were different from Bones's usual crew. They looked Russian or German. The men tortured me while suspending me from the ceiling. They never broke my body but tried to break my mind. My cot was made of plastic, not cotton." He finally fell silent when he ran out of details. "That's all I can remember."

I shifted through the information in my head and tried to draw a conclusion. "Russian, German… Concrete… Pipes go up."

Cane waited for me to crack the case.

"It sounds like you were underground."

Cane nodded. "The walls were made of solid concrete with the exception of the pipes."

"German or Russian... It was probably German. During World War II, they built barracks here."

He raised an eyebrow. "How do you know that?"

"I just do," I snapped. "They're probably holding her in a barrack where she can't be seen by satellite. That would explain why I couldn't find you."

"Don't you have a tracker on her?"

My eyes snapped open so wide I nearly passed out. I wanted to shoot myself in the head. "Please tell me she left my phone in there." It was synced to her tracking device and couldn't be accessed any other way.

Cane retrieved it from the cupholder and tossed it to me.

I quickly opened the app and prayed her little red dot was somewhere on the map.

But it wasn't.

"What does that mean?" Cane asked.

"They either removed the tracker, the battery died, or the signal can't be detected." I shoved the phone into my pocket and tried not to have a meltdown.

"I doubt they've already removed it. I just left the meeting."

"Then that means she's underground."

"And the barrack is within thirty miles of the church."

I rubbed the back of my neck and tried to think.

"What do we do now?"

I pulled out my phone and called the only high official German I knew. "I might have a plan."

***

It cost me a fortune, but I got the coordinates to the last working barrack in Italy. It was purchased by a private citizen nearly ten years ago, and the name of the buyer remained anonymous.

It had to be Bones.

We rounded up all of our men and dispatched them to the coordinates. Breaking in to the underground base wouldn't be easy. We couldn't break down the walls and just walk inside. If we pulled from underneath, the whole facility would collapse on itself—killing Button.

Buttons and Pain

The thought of her made me want to scream.

He could be touching her right now—fucking her. It made me so angry that my hands shook. My throat went dry, and I couldn't breathe. I had an anxiety attack right then and there—something I'd never experienced before.

It was Vanessa all over again.

Every person I loved wound up dead—and Button was next.

Cane glanced at me as he drove to the coordinates. "We'll get her, Crow."

I stared out the window and purposely avoided him. If I talked about her, I would snap. My emotions were already all over the place, and I couldn't think clearly. If I lost her, I would kill myself right then and there. I found someone I couldn't live without, and that idea was terrifying. Without her, there was no me.

"Don't forget how strong she is," Cane said. "If anyone can get through this, it's her."

I clenched my jaw and stared out the window. Waiting for the vehicles to finally arrive was the worst part. I needed the cars to go faster. I needed to get there quicker. I needed to save my wife from being a plaything to a monster.

"Crow—"

"Stop trying to make me feel better. Until she's safe, I won't be able to do anything but think about it. So, shut the fuck up and drive."

Buttons and Pain

Chapter Twenty-Five

Pearl

Bones shut the door behind him and locked it before he turned to me. "Two guards are posted outside. So, don't try anything."

The room was made of solid concrete. A bed was against the wall and a private bathroom connected to the main bedroom. Even the floor was concrete. I knew we were underground, so it looked like a war base. "Nice place..." I crossed my arms over my chest and watched him closely. "I'm guessing business has been slow."

He grinned from ear to ear, but not in a handsome way. It was a look of pure and conniving evil. It made my stomach drop because his intent was clear. He was going to pin me to that mattress and fuck me until I screamed. "I just want to make sure we can't be followed. I know your *husband* will stop at nothing to get you back. Well, he'll have a hard time tracking you here. No signals go in or out of this place."

My heart dropped when I realized my tracker wouldn't work. Crow wouldn't be able to find me after all. Shit. "It's not very cozy. I would think a man as distinguished as yourself would have better quarters than this." I had no idea where my courage came from because I was utterly terrified. Crow put me back together when Bones ripped me apart. Would he be able to fix me again, or would I be ruined for good?

"I missed that smartass mouth of yours. It's refreshing." He slowly approached me, his hands by his sides but his face full of eagerness.

I tensed as he came closer, repulsed by Satan himself. "I didn't miss you."

"Well, I'll make you miss me." When he reached me, he grabbed me by the wrists and held me firmly in place. "Shall we get down to it?"

I twisted out of his grasp then kneed him in the groin.

Bones stepped out of the way like he'd been prepared for me to strike. He grabbed my hair by the scalp then shoved me to the bed. My stomach hit the mattress, and he used his weight to pin me down.

Panic rose in my throat, and I had the urge to cry. I was terrified of the things he was about to do to me. I thought I could handle it, but maybe I couldn't. I'd endured months of his torture, and I couldn't endure another moment. "Let me go!" I tried to fight him, but he was heavier than an ox.

He stripped my jeans away while he keeping me pinned then moved for my panties.

"Fuck you!" I tried to buck him off, but I couldn't.

"The harder you fight, the more I want it." He shoved my face into the mattress, and I nearly suffocated. During that time, he removed his own clothes until he was completely naked. "You have no idea how excited I am to fuck you." He rubbed his cock between my cheeks, already marking me.

I couldn't take it.

He fisted me by the hair and pulled so hard the strands nearly came out. "I want to look at you. And I want you to look at me." He turned me around and pinned my back to the mattress. Then he separated my thighs with his until he was positioned over me. His eyes landed on the stitches just above my shoulder. "What happened there, Slave? Was your husband as good to you as I am?"

The use of the word slave set me off like dynamite. I shoved my fingers into the stitches that Lars sewed just the night before. Blood squirted everywhere, and there was a good chance I would bleed out and die. Lars warned me that was a serious possibility.

"What the hell are you doing? I'm supposed to be the one who hurts you." He grabbed my wrist and tried to stop me, but my other hand slipped inside the wound and pulled out the tiny blade I had inserted there. It cut my skin on the way out and hurt more than it did when I initially put it in.

But it was totally worth it.

Bones didn't react because he was in total shock.

I finally got the blade by the hilt, and with all the energy I could muster, I stabbed the knife directly through his chest and into his heart. I pushed with what little strength I had, making sure I didn't miss my mark.

Blood oozed everywhere.

"You fucking…" He felt his chest but missed the knife. Blood squirted from his mouth and dripped down his chin. He coughed and spewed blood all over me.

I yanked the knife out, and he bled even more. Like a gaping hole, everything rushed out. The life left him quicker and quicker. Right before my eyes, he was dying, and all I cared about was making it as painful as possible.

I grabbed him by the back of the neck and aimed the knife again. "That one was for me. But this one is for Vanessa." I stabbed the knife right in his eye and straight into his brain. This time, I didn't pull the knife out. I shoved his corpse onto the floor and watched it twitch until it lay still forever. The blood continued to ooze until it finally stopped.

I stared at him, trying to memorize this moment forever. I would use it to combat my nightmares and remind myself that he was gone forever. He couldn't hurt me again, and he couldn't hurt anyone else.

Now, I had to get out of there.

***

My clothes were soaked with blood, and I was a dead giveaway as a fugitive. I cracked the door open and saw two guards on either side of it. They clearly didn't think all the noise they'd heard was unusual, just some perverted shit Bones was into.

They both stared down the hallway, so I snatched one pistol from a holster before the guard had time to react.

When he realized the weight was missing, he turned around and looked at me. "What the—"

I shot him right in the head and did the same to the other before he could react. Both were dead and on the floor, pouring blood everywhere. Each one wore a bulletproof vest, so I took one and placed it on myself. I was going to have to fight my way out of there, so I may as well get some protection. I took the extra gun and shoved it into the back of my jeans.

And then I jogged down the hallway.

I didn't know anything about underground bases, but I knew the only way out was up. I had to get to the surface and move quickly before they sounded an alarm. All I had to do was find some stairs or an elevator and take it to the top floor.

I moved all the way to the end of the hallway and found a corridor that went left and right. There were no directions posted, so I went left and hoped for the best. My gun was drawn, and I was ready to pull the trigger the second someone gave me a reason to.

The alarm sounded, and commotion rang at the end of the hallway. Someone must have spotted the missing guards and knew I was on the run. "Fuck." I had to get out of there as quickly as possible, so I started to run.

Buttons and Pain

I ran as fast as I could and rounded the corner. I moved down another hallway lined with doors, and once I reached the end, I saw a shadow of a man on the wall. He held a rifle to his chest, and he was moving slowly around the corner, coming right my way.

I pressed my back against the wall and pointed my gun. The second he emerged, I would take him out and move on to the next one.

He finally turned the corner and pointed his rifle right at my face.

But I recognized his eyes. I'd stared into them countless times. I saw them in my dreams and the moment right before I fell asleep. My whole life was in those eyes, the other half of my soul. "Crow?"

He immediately lowered his weapon and sprinted to me. "Fuck, Button." He crashed into me and wrapped his arm around my waist so tightly he nearly snapped me in half. "Are you okay?" He looked down at my blood-soaked clothes. "Are you hurt?"

"No. I killed Bones."

Crow stared at me in shock, the first time he'd ever given me that expression.

"Let's keep moving." I still had a wound under my shirt, and I was losing blood. The only reason why

I didn't tell him about it was because I was afraid of his reaction. He would panic and carry me out of there over his shoulder.

"Stay behind me." He moved back the way he came, leading us to the exit. As we moved farther, I noticed the stacks of dead bodies Crow had left behind. His other men were in the hallway and sweeping the place. Eventually, we ran into Cane.

"You found her!" Cane dropped his gun and hugged me. "Fuck, I'm glad you're alright."

"Yeah…" I felt the strength leaving my body as more blood drained away. I could barely keep my eyes open anymore. Slowly, my knees gave way, and I started to sink down to the ground. Their voices came out as whispers on my ears.

"What the hell is wrong with her?" Cane asked.

Crow ripped open my shirt to reveal my wound. "Fuck. We've got to get her out of here. Cane, cover me."

"Alright."

That was the last thing I remembered before everything went black.

***

Buttons and Pain

The last image I saw was black, but now, all I saw was white. Piercing white light burned through my eyelids. It was powerful and warm, and I immediately recognized it from waking up to it every morning.

I opened my eyes and saw the Tuscan sun. It shone through the window and directly onto my face. It was morning, just after sunrise, and it was the beginning of a beautiful day. The birds chirped outside, and I could hear them singing. It was so peaceful I did wonder how I even got there.

I turned my head and noticed Crow sitting at my side. He was in an armchair, and his hand held mine loosely. His eyes were on the book he was reading, and that's when I recognized his low voice. He read the story in Italian, reading to me while I was asleep.

I didn't interrupt him because I enjoyed listening to it. The only time I heard him speak his native tongue was when he argued with Cane or he spoke to one of his men. Other than that, he always spoke in English.

He finished the chapter and turned the page then snuck a glance at me. He turned back to the page automatically but stilled when he realized what he'd seen. "Button." He shut the book and dropped it on the nightstand. "How do you feel?" He scooted the chair closer to my bedside and brought my hand to his lips. His chin was scruffy from not shaving for days, and the bags under his eyes told me he hadn't slept.

"I feel...really good." I was back at home with my husband. Everything that happened was just a distant nightmare. I knew Bones was dead because I would never forget the way I shoved that dagger into his heart. "How long have I been sleeping for?"

"Two days."

"Oh..."

"You lost a lot of blood. I called a physician, and they treated you here."

That's when I noticed the IV hooked into my arm and the distant beeping sound of the monitor. My blood pressure was being measured as the cuff tightened on my arm.

"I knew you would feel better waking up in your bed with the open window." He kissed my head again then rested his forehead against my knuckles like he was saying a prayer. That's when I noticed my wedding ring had been returned to my hand. "I was so worried..."

"I'm fine. I lost a little blood is all."

"You nearly died, Button. You should have told me you were wounded."

Buttons and Pain

"I thought I could make it." Sometimes, I thought I was stronger than I really was.

He stared into my eyes like a man torn between anger and infatuation. "I'm pissed at you for leaving. That's something I'll never be able to forgive you for. But I'm so grateful you're okay that it doesn't matter."

"I'm sorry I hurt you. But I don't regret what I did." I would do it again a thousand times.

"You got lucky."

"No, I didn't."

He held my gaze while he waited for an explanation.

"I cut myself and inserted a smile knife underneath my collarbone." I pulled down my shirt so I could see the new stitches. "I knew they would frisk me but not pay attention to the wound. So when Bones had me alone, I dug my fingers inside and pulled the knife out. Then I killed him." I said everything without emotion because I didn't feel any remorse. Everything I did made me sound crazy, but I'd never felt more sane. I did what I had to do to protect myself and my family. And now we're free.

He shook his head. "Why didn't you tell me?"

"You never would have let me go through with it."

"And rightfully so. This could have gone quite differently."

"I was prepared for that possibility. But I had to save your brother. He's my brother too."

Crow sighed, his eyes softening.

"Marriage is about selflessness. I know you need your brother. I couldn't let you lose him."

He continued to stare at me, his eyes a mystery.

"Everything worked out in our favor. So, let's just leave the past in the past and be happy."

He clenched his jaw then stared at our joined hands before he returned his look to mine. "I have to ask you something. Whatever your answer is, it doesn't change us. But I need to know…"

I knew exactly what he was asking me. "He didn't rape me. Well, he tried but didn't succeed. I killed him before he could."

Crow stared into my eyes until he saw the truth in my look.

"He got me naked and held me down. But that was the worst of it." At the time, it was terrifying, and

I could barely keep my focus. But he didn't need to know those details.

"How did you sew your own wound?"

I would never throw Lars under the bus. I made him help me against his will, and if I told Crow the truth, he would kick Lars out onto the street. "It wasn't that hard."

He raised an eyebrow in incredulity. "You did it by yourself?"

"Yes."

"How?"

"It's called a mirror." I would lie through my teeth if I had to. Lars did me a favor, and I wouldn't repay him by getting him fired.

Fortunately, Crow backed off. "I didn't know you knew how to do that. Might come in handy."

"Yeah..." Now I'd have to ask Lars to teach me.

He stroked the hair from my face and gave me a long look. "You're incredible, you know that?" Compliments were few and far between when it came to Crow Barsetti, so I treasured it at face value.

"What do you mean?"

"You were brave when others wouldn't have been. You were fearless when you shoved that knife inside your body. And you were courageous when you ripped it from your body and stabbed that asshole in the heart. Button...you're far braver than me and every man put together."

I ran my hand up and down his arm. "Not braver than you. If you hadn't come for me, I would have died."

"No." He leaned in and kissed me on the forehead. "Button, you would have found a way."

***

I sat on the balcony with Crow beside me. A book was in my lap, but I'd stopped reading it a long time ago. Instead, I chose to cherish the view right in front of me. Crow worked on paperwork for the winery. He hadn't gone back to work since I'd been home. My strength had returned, but he continued to treat me like I was fragile.

A knock sounded on our bedroom door. "Crow, when the hell can I see her?" Cane's angry voice stretched across our bedroom and landed on our ears on the patio.

Buttons and Pain

He set the folder on the table before he rose with a sigh. "Pain in the ass..."

I smiled and waited for Crow to retrieve Cane.

Crow opened the bedroom door. "I'll invite you over when she's ready to see people."

"It's been five days," he snapped. "Legally, she's my sister, and I have every right to see her as much as you do."

I could picture the angry look on Crow's face.

"Now, if you'll excuse me..." Cane maneuvered around his brother then joined me on the patio. He pulled up a chair beside me and gave me a look I'd never seen before. True joy was in his eyes, the first time he ever viewed me in that respect. "You look great, Pearl. More beautiful than ever."

Crow growled from behind my chair.

"What?" Cane asked. "I can't call my own sister beautiful? She knows how I mean it."

"Just ignore him," I said. "You know how he gets."

Now Crow growled at me.

Cane pulled me in for a gentle hug and rubbed my back. It was a tender embrace, far better than anything he'd ever given me before. Who knew we could come back from that horrible afternoon when he beat me to within an inch of my life. Now there was nothing but love between us. "Thank you so much, Pearl. If it weren't for you, I'd be buried in a hole somewhere."

"We would never let that happen, Cane."

"No, really." He pulled away and looked me in the eye. "You were so brave. After what I did to you, no one would have blamed you if you did nothing."

"Cane...it's water under the bridge."

"Not to most people. I know that was only possible because you love my brother so much...even though I'm still not entirely sure why."

"You wanna die, asshole?" Crow barked.

Cane ignored him. "I can't thank you enough. I want you to know I'm your man for life. Anything you need at all, I'm here. You want ice cream in the middle of the night when you're pregnant, I'll take care of it. You want me to beat the shit out of Crow when he's an ass, I'm your man. Anything at all, I've got your back. Alright?"

I smiled. "Got it."

"There's no one better to hold the Barsetti name. I'm honored to have you as a sister."

"Cane, I'm honored too."

He hugged me again before he pulled away. "Is there anything I can do for you now?"

"No. I think my husband has it covered."

"Yes," Crow said with a threat in his voice. "Her husband."

Cane stood and rolled his eyes. "Dude, I don't want your woman. If I did, I would have taken her already. So, just chill."

Crow didn't crack a smile.

"Okay...maybe I wanted her a year ago," Cane admitted. "But I don't see her like that...for the most part."

Crow's darkness only grew.

"Alright." Cane clapped his hands. "I'm officially not welcome. I'll see you around, Pearl."

"See you then." I waved as he walked out.

Crow made sure he was out of the bedroom before he locked the door and returned to his seat beside me.

I examined the harshness of his face before I spoke. "You aren't honestly mad at him, right?"

His jaw remained clenched, and that answered my question. "He's flirting with you. I don't appreciate it."

"Maybe that's just his way of being nice."

"Well, I'd rather him not be nice to you."

"Crow, get over it. You need to stop being jealous and possessive all the time—at least when it comes to your brother."

"You don't know what kind of shit he said about you before we got together."

"It doesn't matter. That was a long time ago."

He looked over the balcony and to the vineyards beyond. "Not long enough." After everything that had happened, Crow was more protective of me than he ever was before. His hold on me was strong like steel, and nothing could shake it.

"Well, I like him and would like to spend more time with him."

"Just because he's my brother doesn't mean you have to be involved."

Buttons and Pain

"Crow, I already told you I like him. I've never had a family of my own, and it's fun to have someone that's a brother. Lars kinda reminds me of an uncle, and you're a husband that's overbearing just like a father. It's nice."

His features softened at that comment, and he dropped the argument.

"Can we take a walk?" After days on unnecessary bed rest, I was eager to move on my feet and stretch my legs.

"Isn't the view good enough?"

"Crow, I can manage." Instead of waiting for permission, I rose to my feet and walked inside to put on my sneakers.

Crow sighed audibly, wanting me to understand just how annoyed he was.

But I didn't care.

***

We walked through the vineyards and listened to the crickets in the fields. Away from the house, there was a stronger breeze that moved through the rows. The wind caressed my hair like loving fingers, and it touched the back of my neck just the way Crow did.

His hand closed around mine, and he kept sending worried glances my way even though I was perfectly fine. "Are you doing alright?"

"If I need help, I'll tell you."

"No, you won't," he snapped.

The corner of my lip rose in a smile. "You're right. I probably won't."

Against his will, amusement entered his eyes.

I stared at the hillsides up ahead and wondered what was on the other side. Perhaps it was just more acres of land until the next house came into view. "Who's your closest neighbor?"

"A friend of mine lives right on the other side of this hill. It's a vacation home when he comes to visit."

"Where does he live normally?"

"America."

"So...there was someone who could have helped me right next door?" In the early days of my imprisonment, Crow told me there was nowhere for me to go. The nearest town was thirty miles away. Stupidly, I believed that story.

He smiled. "Yeah. But he's not around often."

"But there's probably a phone inside his house."

He shrugged. "I suppose. But I hope you're happy with the way things turned out." His thumb brushed across my knuckles. "Because if I had to lock you up all over again, I would."

"I guess I would too."

He snuck a glare at me.

I loved teasing him because it was so easy to get under his skin. "You know I'm kidding. Speaking of being locked up, are you ever going to remove this tracker from my ankle?"

"I'd rather not."

"You don't think it's weird?"

"No." He didn't change his pace as he walked beside me, and the overprotective maniac was still deep inside him.

"Since there's no danger around me, I don't think it's necessary."

"There's always danger, Pearl. The wealthy and powerful always have to look over their shoulders."

"Well, I don't want some electronic device under my skin. It's not like I go off on my own anyway."

He wasn't going to budge. It was obvious in the way he carried himself. "It's not going anywhere until it needs to be replaced."

Hell no. "Then I want you to wear a tracker at all times." He wouldn't like that one bit. Crow was a man who operated in the shadows. He didn't want to be traced so easily.

"Okay."

I did a double take when I heard what he said. "What?"

"I said okay."

"No… I was just trying to prove a point."

"Well, you did. If you have to wear one, I'll wear one too. That way you can always see where I am if you're ever worried about me. That's a fair compromise."

"But you're missing the main point. I don't want to wear anything."

"That's too bad." He looked at me with a dictator's gaze, daring me to defy him. "You don't even notice it's there, and thanks to that little tracker, I was able to save you not once, but twice. I'm sorry it's an inconvenience to you, but it's a lifesaver for me. I suggest you get used to it."

Buttons and Pain

I knew I'd lost the battle, and more importantly, I knew this was how the rest of our lives would be. Crow Barsetti was a man who couldn't be refused, and when it came to his family, he was ruthless and borderline insane.

He was right—I needed to get used to it.

"Now what?" I asked.

"What do you mean?"

"What do we do now? Bones is gone, and the world seems like a much simpler place."

"Well, that's entirely up to you. I was thinking we could live the rest of our lives quietly here at the estate. We'll drink wine, make love, and grow old together. What do you say?"

I stared at him and felt my smile widen. "Sounds pretty boring."

He raised an eyebrow.

"And that's exactly what I want. A long, boring life with you."

Epilogue

Pearl

I carried the bowls of mac and cheese to the table. Vanessa was five years old with dark black hair like her father and blue eyes like mine. She had a rambunctious spirit, telling me she would be a handful when she got older—like yours truly. "Hungry, sweetheart?"

"Yum." She grabbed her fork and dug in.

I placed the other bowl in front of Constantine. "Here you are, champ."

Constantine was three years old and still in a high chair. The table was permanently stained with all the food he threw around. Instead of pushing away his food when he didn't like it, he chose to throw it everywhere. Sometimes, he was a pain in the ass—like his father. He picked up the spoon and slowly fed himself, still learning the process.

Julia looked into her bowl and raised an eyebrow. With a distinctly Russian accent, she said, "What is this?"

"It's mac and cheese. It's basically pasta with cheese sauce."

She continued to eye it with dread, like it was the worst possible thing I could serve.

Why did everyone hate American food so much? "It's really not bad. But if you don't want to eat it, I'll make you something else."

Julia picked up the fork and took a bite. "It's actually pretty good." Julia had a hard time acclimating to freedom at the Barsetti estate. After being sold into human trafficking, Crow and I were able to free her and a handful of other women. Most of them had families to go home to, but Julia was an orphan without a penny to her name. She was staying with us until she was ready to get back on her feet.

"I'm glad you like it. Crow hates it, but he's the most stubborn man I know."

She continued to eat slowly, taking her time spooning herself. She was unnaturally thin, and I had to fatten her up as much as possible. I purposely had her spend time with the kids because their happiness was infectious. They could brighten anyone's mood.

Crow walked into the dining room, wearing a dark navy suit with a purple tie. Like a king, he owned the room the second he walked into it. Casting a distinctive shadow on the wall, his power was unmistakable. "Cane, I said no."

Cane followed behind him, talking his ear off. "Look, it's just one gig. I won't ask for your help again, I swear."

"I'm not in the business anymore," Crow answered. "I told you that." He walked right up to me with an irritated look that wasn't meant for me. "Hey, Button." His arm hooked around my waist and he gave me a kiss.

"Hey, husband."

No matter how many times I called him that, the corner of his mouth rose in a smile.

Cane continued to ramble on. "We just get in and get out. No big deal. That's it."

Crow ignored him and turned to the kids. First, he greeted Vanessa with a kiss on the forehead then kneeled so he could watch Constantine for a moment. "How's my little boy?"

"It's a plane!" Constantine scooped up the mac and cheese on the edge of the spoon then flew it into Crow's mouth.

Crow took it then swallowed. "Yum."

I smiled in triumph. "Everyone here seems to love it."

Crow masked his dislike of the food then greeted Julia. "Hello, Julia." He always stayed as far away from her as possible, not because he disliked her, but because he understood how terrified she probably felt when she was close to any man.

Cane continued. "Hey, asshole. I'm talking to you."

Crow turned on him quicker than a snake. "Don't cuss in front of my family. How many times have I told you that?"

Cane rolled his eyes. "Whatever. Are you gonna help me or not?"

"No." Crow didn't show an ounce of sympathy. "I told you, I have a family now. I'm not involved with that lifestyle anymore. You can find someone else."

"But no one has your skills," Cane argued. "I don't trust anyone."

"Too bad," Crow snapped. "Now, drop it."

Cane rolled his eyes again until they landed on Julia. When he noticed her in the room, his interest piqued. "Hey—"

Penelope Sky

"Get the fuck away from her." Crow immediately turned into a pit bull, guarding our guest with teeth barred and his claws extended.

"What happened to not cussing?" Cane argued.

Cane took him by the arm and pulled him from the room. "Knock that shit off." His voice could still be heard from outside the dining hall. "We rescued Julia from that operation in Russia. Don't even look at her wrong, or I swear I'll kill you."

"Geez, give me some credit. You think I'm gonna just whip it out and hold her down then and there?"

Julia purposely looked down at her bowl.

"Don't make her uncomfortable," Crow ordered. "She's under my roof, so she's my guest. I don't want you to even look at her."

"What?" Cane asked. "I thought she was pretty. Burn me at the stake."

"I might," Crow threatened. "Now leave."

"Wait, I was serious about the operation. I need your help."

"Cane, how many times do I have to say this? I'm not in that line of work anymore. I have two kids and another one on the way. I'm not getting involved with that lifestyle ever again."

"Geez, you're boring."

"One day, your life will be boring too. And you'll love it." Crow walked back into the dining room and dismissed his brother. "Sorry about that, Julia."

"It's okay," she whispered.

"You don't need to worry about him," Crow assured her. "He won't bother you again."

She kept eating. "I know."

Crow returned to my side and placed his hand on my small stomach. I wasn't even showing yet, but he was excited that I would have a baby bump soon. Nothing turned him on more than when I was pregnant. That was probably why I accidentally got knocked up again. "How's my little Barsetti?"

"Pretty boring." I rested my hand on top of his. "No kicking yet. I can barely tell they're in there."

"Give it time. Maybe they'll be a kicker like Vanessa was."

"God, I hope not. I didn't get any sleep when I was pregnant with her."

"Yeah, I remember," he said. "But it was exciting to feel her move." His fingers expanded across my entire stomach before he slid his hand around my waist again. "How about we have Lars watch them for the night so we can go out to dinner? Maybe stop by the house on the coast?"

Having two kids made it difficult to have alone time, but Crow and I made it work whenever we could. We loved spending time with our kids, but we loved the times when it was just the two of us too. Two hours a day seemed to be enough to keep us happy. "That sounds perfect."

***

Crow pressed his ear to my naked stomach and listened.

"I'm telling you, there's nothing going on down there. She's sleepy."

"She?" He sat up and looked at me.

"Yeah, it's a girl." There wasn't a doubt in my mind.

"How do you know that?"

"I don't know… I just do."

"But this pregnancy is nothing like the one you had with Vanessa."

"Yeah." She was by far the most difficult pregnancy. "But I just know. Trust me, it's a maternal thing."

He kissed my stomach before he moved farther up the bed. His thighs separated mine, and the dark look in his eyes told me what he wanted to do next. He seemed to be proud of his handiwork in knocking me up, and that stroked his ego and made him want to make love even more. "I want to keep getting you pregnant for as long as I can."

"Uh, no, thanks." Three kids were enough. Even with the help of the staff, I couldn't handle a fourth.

"Come on, it's sexy." He pressed the tip of his cock against my entrance but didn't enter me.

"Yeah, for a while. But you don't have to waddle around the house like a cow."

"You don't look like a cow." He rubbed his nose against mine. "When you waddle, it gets me so hard. Seeing you pregnant with my kid... Nothing is a bigger turn-on."

"Even so, this is the last one. But we can pretend we're trying to get pregnant."

"Not the same." Crow went from being hesitant to have kids to needing as many as possible. He gave up his former job in a heartbeat when I got pregnant with Vanessa, and there was nowhere else he'd rather be than at home with me and the kids.

I chuckled when I realized just how different he was. His innate darkness had faded, and the light that shone in his eyes was bright whenever he looked at his kids.

Crow caught the reaction. "What?"

"Nothing."

He didn't shove himself inside me even though he was desperate to. "What?" He gripped both of my wrists and pinned them over my head, dominating me the second he didn't get his way.

"I just think it's amusing how different you are. You're nothing like the man I met all those years ago."

Slowly, the hardness of his eyes and jaw faded.

"It's like you're a different person."

He relaxed his hold on my wrists and continued to stare at me. "I am a different man."

"In a very good way." I ran my hands down his chest before I pulled his hips to me, wanting him deep inside me.

He kept his hips straight and didn't move. "When you came to my home, you said I saved you. I saved you from that ruthless man whose name I'll never say again. You claim I put you back together and fixed you."

My eyes never left his.

"But you saved me, Button. I wouldn't have everything I didn't know I wanted without you." His hand cupped my cheek, and he rubbed his nose against mine, giving me the delicate touches I'd come to expect every morning and every night.

"We saved each other."

Penelope Sky

Thanks so much for reading *Buttons and Pain*. I loved writing this story so much, and Crow and Pearl are very close to my heart. If you loved it too, it would mean the WORLD if you could leave a short review. It's the best kind of support you can give an author.

Hugs,

Pene

Penelope Sky

Buttons and Pain

Some Scotch?

Check out my new book, *The Scotch King*

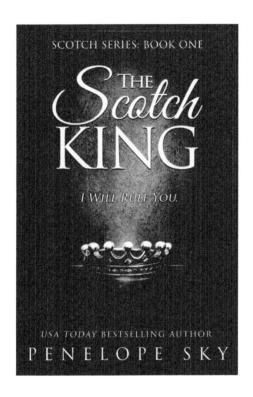

ORDER NOW

Penelope Sky

Keep in touch with Penelope

Subscribe to my newsletter for updates on new releases and giveaways.

Sign up today.

www.PenelopeSky.com

LIKE Penelope's Facebook page for updates on new releases and giveaways.

Penelope's Facebook

https://www.facebook.com/PenelopeSkyAuthor

CPSIA information can be obtained
at www.ICGtesting.com
Printed in the USA
BVOW06s0222030717
488383BV00017B/209/P